Mystery
PARKER
Kate

Parker, Kate

The killing at
Kaldaire House

Also by Kate Parker

The Victorian Bookshop Mysteries
The Vanishing Thief
The Counterfeit Lady
The Royal Assassin
The Conspiring Woman
The Detecting Duchess

The Deadly Series
Deadly Scandal
Deadly Wedding
Deadly Fashion

The Milliner Mysteries
The Killing at Kaldaire House

THE KILLING AT KALDAIRE HOUSE

KATE PARKER

JDP PRESS

The Killing at Kaldaire House copyright ©2018 by Kate Parker

ISBN: 978-0-9976637-0-9 [e-book]
ISBN: 978-0-9976637-1-6 [print]

Published by JDP Press
Cover design by Kim Killion of The Killion Group, Inc.

Dedication

To Ken, in exchange for your practical advice early in my career, I'm giving you a family that will make you smile.

To Corey, Adrienne, and Jen, for turning out normal despite your mother's fascination with murder. Your Dad and I are blessed.

London in the reign of King Edward VII

CHAPTER ONE

If I hadn't been desperate, I wouldn't have been creeping around the ground floor of Kaldaire House late at night. My heart pounded harder when I saw a light on in the room I planned to burgle, leaving me with two unpalatable choices—leave without the *Lady in Blue* or risk being captured. Curiosity, always lurking on my shoulder, pushed me forward. Respectability, and my longing for it, held me back.

I tiptoed up to the doorway, luckily avoiding any squeaking boards, and opened the door ever so slightly. The light, after all the darkness in the house, made me blink. All I could see was a sliver of the room. Dark, well-polished paneling, a red Oriental carpet just inside the entrance, and a corner of a messy desk. Lord Kaldaire had people to clean up after him. Why would he keep his desk in such disarray?

Chancing my luck, I pushed the door open a little further. Now I could see that papers had slid off the desktop and a book lay on the edge of the carpet. I couldn't believe Lady Kaldaire would allow this in her otherwise well-ordered house.

When I'd been here in the daylight I'd found my route to the study and the painting. It had taken me less than half a minute to find my way in complete silence to

Lord Kaldaire's study. But now I was wasting precious time lingering outside the door, raising my chances of being caught.

Getting caught would mean my ruin. The end of everything. My business. My reputation. My dreams.

I should have crept out the way I came. Instead, I nudged the door a little more and rubbed my nose to keep from sneezing at the smell of pipe tobacco.

Wait. Lord Kaldaire didn't smoke a pipe. He was a cigar man.

Looking to the right, I could see a thin plume of smoke rising from an ashtray, but there was no pipe there. He must have had a guest earlier and left a single light on when he showed the man out.

I straightened. That would mean someone, his lordship or a servant, was coming back.

I needed to move fast. Matthew's future depended on my taking the *Lady in Blue* hostage. Supposedly, the risqué painting of his great-grandmother was the careless Lord Kaldaire's favorite possession. How else, after numerous dunning notices and personal pleas, would I convince him to pay the huge millinery bill Lady Kaldaire had run up?

I slipped into the room and glanced around. No one else was there. I let out a sigh unimpeded by a corset and was reminded once more of why I preferred to do my housebreaking, or bill collection, in boys' clothes.

One would think in 1905, with King Edward replacing his mother on the throne and motorized carriages running wild on London streets, times were modern enough I could wear trousers and forgo a corset. But I couldn't. Some things still caused a scandal.

And although ten years my junior, at fourteen Matthew was nearly as tall as I was. For tonight's efforts, I was forced to wear his clothes.

As I made my way to the far side of the room, I kept my distance from the desk for fear of triggering a landslide of papers. The entire house seemed to hold its breath with me as I maneuvered toward my target. The painting was hung in a recess, invisible from the door but not from Lord Kaldaire's chair.

Once around the desk, I froze. Lord Kaldaire lay facedown on the floor behind his leather chair, spilling blood on the blue patterned carpet. The back of his head had been smashed in with the equally bloody, ornate marble bust of Sophocles on the floor next to him.

I stood there for a moment, blinking in shock and trying not to gag on the metallic smell of blood. All the colors around me started to swirl together. I bent over, breathing hard through my mouth with my hands propped on my knees.

I'd only met him a few times, but I couldn't help thinking, *Poor old sod*.

I had two choices. Thinking he was dead and not wanting to hang, I moved toward the recess where the *Lady in Blue* hung, planning to grab it and go. Maybe I could sell the painting to recoup at least some of what Lady Kaldaire owed.

But then Lord Kaldaire groaned.

He was alive. I gave up the idea of running away with the painting. Feeling a weight settle on my shoulders, I walked over and pulled on the bell rope.

It took a half-dozen pulls and two minutes before a sleepy-eyed servant, his hair standing on end, walked in. He stared at me and the paper-strewn desk in confusion as I gestured him over. I realized that was a mistake as the man looked down and gagged.

I shoved him back toward the doorway. "Get a

doctor and the police. There's been an attack on your master."

He stumbled away, shouting.

The household quickly came awake in confusion, with running footsteps and groggy voices. Then I heard the clear tones of Lady Kaldaire and knew her husband would be in capable hands.

Relieved, I headed toward the door.

And came face-to-face with Lady Kaldaire.

She walked into the room, her hair in a long gray-and-brown braid, her face slack with sleep, and the rest of her wrapped in a thick housecoat of pink wool. "Emily? What is happening and why are you here?"

I doubted this would end well for me, but I knew honesty was the best policy with Lady Kaldaire. "I came tonight hoping to borrow the *Lady in Blue* to convince your husband to pay your bills. Instead, I found your husband attacked."

Her eyebrows went skyward as she strode forward. She gave a small gasp as she rounded the desk and saw her husband for the first time. "Is he alive?"

"He groaned. I sent the first man to answer the bell to get a doctor and the police."

"Oh, Emily. Don't be so squeamish." She bent down and felt his wrist, keeping her housecoat out of the blood. "Poor man. He's still alive. Gregson!"

An older man hurried into the room.

"Has someone gone to fetch the doctor?"

"Yes, my lady."

"Get him in here as soon as he comes. And where are the police?"

"Here, my lady. Another's gone for reinforcements."

The bobby, a young, blond-haired man, took off his helmet as he moved hesitantly into the room and gave her a quick bow. "Sir," he said to me as he glanced my way before heading toward Lady Kaldaire. "What's happened?"

I gestured to him to come over to us, not wanting my voice to give away my gender. His eyes grew big as he looked down and saw the injured man. "Have you called for a doctor?" he said, swallowing hard.

"Yes," Lady Kaldaire said.

"Who found him like this?"

Blast. I couldn't avoid speaking. "I did."

He gave me a startled look and then gazed at me from head to toe. "Why are you dressed like that, miss?"

"It's a long story," Lady Kaldaire said.

I gave her a grateful smile. I wasn't sure if the police would arrest me solely for wearing trousers, but my clothing might lead them to consider me a violent thief. If they found out who I was, they'd lock me up and throw away the key.

The bobby pulled out his notebook and pencil as the doctor entered the room carrying his bag. He called for hot water, linen bandaging, and two strong footmen before throwing us out.

Lady Kaldaire called for tea and led the way to her morning room while the bobby remained outside the study door. A maid lit a single light, bright in an otherwise dark, sleepy world. The glare made me squint at all the yellow on the walls and sofa cushions.

Once the lady was settled, she looked up at me and said, "Do you mean that Horace hasn't been paying you for my hats?"

Under the circumstances, I decided not to wait for an invitation to sit. I shifted to a more comfortable stance. "No, my lady."

"For how long?"

"Eight months."

"Good heavens. It's not that we don't have the money. Or that I don't. And what is this about the *Lady in Blue?*"

I took a deep breath. "I planned to hold her hostage until he paid me what I'm owed."

"That won't work with me. I can't stand that painting."

"He's the one who is supposed to pay me. He kept putting me off. I'm afraid I got impatient." I stood with my hands clasped in front of me, unwilling to go into my reasons.

"And so you hit him."

I looked at her, horrified, shaking my head as my eyes widened. "No! I found him on the floor like you saw him. And before you ask, I didn't run into anyone in your house or in your gardens."

"For some reason, I believe you." She stared at me, her face hard. "You'd better not be lying to me."

"Everything I've told you is the truth, my lady." I just hadn't told her everything.

Her tea came in. For the next few minutes, the only sounds in the room were clinks of silver and china. I'd have loved to have been offered a cup. Now that the shock had worn off, I kept blinking to keep my eyes open.

Elsewhere in the house, I could hear heavy footsteps and men's voices. "How did you plan to steal the painting? You can't just walk down the street with it," she asked.

"I have a boy waiting with a horse cart around the corner." *Dear Lord. Matthew.* How could I get a note to him to tell him to go home? As long as the police didn't find him, he'd be safe.

"Well, you've certainly been thorough in your plans to collect on your bill. Are you always this ruthless?"

"I have to be, my lady. No one waits on a tradesman's bills as long as they do those of the aristocracy. I have need of my money."

"I'm sure you do. Horace used to be so reliable. What has happened?"

I decided there was no answer for that.

"And you, Emily, dressed up like a boy." She shook her head. "Why did you ring for the servants? Why not just run?"

"Because he was hurt, my lady. All I wanted was my money from him. I couldn't leave him injured, unaided and alone." He was a human being, never mind that he was an aristocrat.

She considered my words for a moment, staring hard at me. When I stared back, unshrinking, she said, "For that you should be rewarded. Bring me your bill in the morning, and I will write you a bank draft myself."

"Thank you."

"You understand I'll back up whatever ridiculous story you tell the police as long as you remain completely honest with me." After a pause, she added, "And aid me in a little investigation of my own."

Her last words struck me full in the face, making me jump. What did she have in mind? "What little—? How would I—?"

"Oh, you'll manage very well, or I shall have to go to the police with the truth about your uninvited presence here tonight."

Blast.

There was a loud knock on the door before a footman admitted a bobby, followed by a man in a baggy brown suit with a matching vest. His collar looked tired and his trouser legs were mud-splattered. As he came close to me, the light caught the look of fatigue in his gray eyes.

He barely glanced at me before facing the seated woman. "Lady Kaldaire, I'm Detective Inspector Russell. What can you tell me about events here this evening?"

"Has my husband regained consciousness?" she demanded.

He shook his head.

Lady Kaldaire sat still for a moment, I guessed to pull her thoughts together. I needed to do the same, but when I did I pictured the back of Lord Kaldaire's skull and had to breathe deeply.

"My husband said he had no plans for the evening. I retired early and was awakened by a commotion. My maid said my husband was injured and to come downstairs."

"And you?" he asked, turning those gray eyes on me. They no longer appeared weary. They were sharp, intelligent, cunning.

"I'm Emily Gates. Lady Kaldaire's milliner."

"Do you always make house calls in the middle of the night, dressed as a boy? As a boy in all-dark clothing?"

As soon as he said those words, I knew the copper guessed why I was here, and I was in trouble.

Before I could make a mess of things, Lady Kaldaire spoke up. "She had an appointment with my husband. She came in to find things as you saw them and roused the household."

"And the nature of this appointment?"

"Is none of your business," I told him in my most scandalized tone. I'd learned a lot from my clients.

He grinned at me. "Decline to answer, do you?"

What he thought Lord Kaldaire and I had planned was clear in his expression.

I glared at him. I hadn't needed my clients to teach me how to scowl at an insulting man.

"Perhaps you could remove that ridiculously large cap and let me see you properly." He'd gentled his voice, but I could hear the steel in it. He expected to be obeyed.

I pulled out the hatpin and removed the shapeless black cap. Unfortunately, my reddish curls came loose and tumbled onto my shoulders and down my back. I must have been a disheveled sight with my hair wantonly loose and wearing men's clothes. My cheeks felt like they would burst into flame.

He stared at me for a moment in surprise before he held out his hand. I gave him my hat and hatpin. Then he looked down and with almost a laugh said, "Thank goodness. No blood."

"Why would there be?" Lady Kaldaire asked.

"No reason. Just another puzzle in a night full of them." His eyes and voice, so expressive before, shut away all emotion. "Perhaps you can tell me what you found when you came in."

I quickly pulled all my hairpins free, set them down, and began to put up my hair. I could only hope a modest hair style would lend me the dignity my outfit didn't. "I noticed at once the desk was a mess. Papers scattered everywhere and fallen onto the floor."

"When I walked around the desk, I found Lord Kaldaire," I said with a swallow, "as the bobby and the doctor saw him. When he groaned, I used the bell to summon help. I don't know the name of the servant who answered my call, but I sent him for a doctor and the police."

"How did you get in?"

"Get in?"

"To the house. Did Lord Kaldaire let you in?"

I looked at him, wide-eyed. "No. He couldn't have, could he?"

"Then how did you get in?" His eyes, showing me a light into a mind that appeared calm, bright, and nonjudgmental, drew the answer out of me.

I glanced at Lady Kaldaire. "The French doors to the breakfast room don't lock properly."

Lady Kaldaire made a small *humpf.*

"How did you get here? You'd have stood out on the streets like that, a fine-looking woman dressed as a boy."

"Fine-looking" shocked me for a moment. No one ever noticed me. Only my hat designs.

I felt heat on my cheeks at his unexpected words. I knew he'd seen my blush when he smiled and said, "So, how did you get here unnoticed?"

"I rode over on a horse cart."

I immediately realized my mistake when he nodded to the bobby, who left the room.

"He'd be gone by now. He wouldn't know anything. He can't help you!" The last thing I wanted was to involve Matthew in this mess.

"Your protestations tell me he can. I see you wear gloves. Is that to hide fingerprints? Did you know we can identify you by your fingerprints now?"

I looked down at my smooth leather gloves, so handy for the heavy work of steam-pressing ribbon and hat brims and now dyed black. I drew myself up to my middling height. "No. I'm not trying to hide my fingerprints. I'm not a criminal. And no, the cart boy can't help you."

"Well, we'll soon find out."

I prayed Matthew had given up on me and returned home when he first saw the police. He was so young. Would he know instinctively to run at the sight of bobbies?

The inspector sounded cold and impersonal, and I knew he'd learned all he wanted from me. "If you both could come with me, I won't have to delay you much longer."

I nodded and walked out of the room. The trousers and shirt that had felt so liberating earlier were now overly warm and scratchy. I stopped in front of the study where I could see the front door and wondered how long it would be until I was released.

Inspector Russell and Lady Kaldaire came up behind me. As if he could read my thoughts, Russell leaned over my shoulder and said, "I don't think it'll be much longer now, do you?"

To my puzzled gaze, he merely smiled.

"What do you want to show us, Inspector?" Lady Kaldaire asked. "I would like to see how my husband is faring."

"In here." He led us into the study. "I wondered why one of the paintings hanging on the wall has been disturbed but not the other."

I shrugged.

"As you've already discovered," the lady said, "there is a safe behind the painting that was moved. The other is merely an example of poor taste executed with wasted talent."

The detective walked around the mess of papers that had cascaded onto the floor and moved the painting. We could see the door to the safe behind it was ajar.

"And the contents?" Lady Kaldaire asked.

He swung the door wide. Empty. "What was in there?"

"I don't know. Very little, I suspect. My jewelry is in my room. Stock certificates and deeds are there also or in the bank."

"In your room? Out where anyone can take them?" the detective asked.

"Better protected than whatever was in this safe," she replied drily. "None of the things in my room have been taken."

"You don't know what was in this safe?"

"I already told you, Inspector. I don't."

I was certain she did know. I couldn't imagine Lord Kaldaire having many secrets from a wife who kept the stocks and deeds in her possession.

"Is there anything else, Inspector?" She sounded weary of dealing with him.

Without waiting for a reply, she turned and walked into the hall. I followed her, the detective on my heels. At that moment there was a ruckus at the front door. We all turned that way to see two burly policemen dragging one skinny boy into the house.

Matthew.

He was mewling like a frightened kitten and struggling until he saw me. He stopped and, with a heartbreaking sob, managed "Em."

"Let him go, Inspector," I demanded, moving in front of the man and staring into his eyes. I was glad to see they weren't laughing now.

"He wouldn't tell us nothing, sir," one of the bobbies said. "We found him a block away on a horse cart. When he wouldn't say anything, we brought him back here. Struggled all the way he did, for being a slip of a boy."

"Let him go," I cried out. "And if my horse and cart

are stolen—"

"No one's stealing anything," Russell snapped back at me. "Constable, are the horse and cart safe?"

"Yes. One of the lads is bringing them here now."

"Good. Now suppose you tell me exactly what is going on. And who is this lad?" The inspector's tone told me he expected the truth.

"He's my brother Matthew."

"Well, tell Matthew to answer our questions." He sounded annoyed.

All my frustration and anguish from the events of this night came out as I blinked back tears. "How can he? Matthew is deaf."

CHAPTER TWO

"So that's why..." Lady Kaldaire started and then broke off.

"Why what?" Detective Inspector Russell asked with a sharp look.

The older woman ignored him as she pinned me in place with her gaze. "It's none of your concern, Inspector."

I walked over to Matthew and put a hand on his shoulder. His clothes were rumpled and one sleeve was ripped, but I didn't see any bruises. I kept a protective hand on him, knowing he watched me as I faced the detective. "May Matthew go home, please? He has nothing to do with this. He's never met Lord Kaldaire nor been in this house before."

"Does he live with you?"

"Yes. He's only a child. Please?" I was begging and didn't care if they all knew it. He was my little brother.

Something flashed in those gray eyes of the detective inspector. "Tell him to go straight home and take care of the beast."

I turned and led Matthew to the door.

"No. You stay here."

"I have to show him what I want him to do. I can't tell him." I loosed an exasperated sigh. Did he think this was easy? "I'll be back inside in a minute."

He must have quickly discounted the risk of my

fleeing, because he nodded.

Matthew and I walked out to the cart, followed by an older constable. I patted the horse, then pointed to Matthew and mimed grooming. When he nodded, I pointed to him again and put my head on my hands like a pillow. He nodded again and I hugged him.

He pointed to me and then pointed to the cart. I wished I could leave, but it would be safer for him if I stayed. I shook my head and gave him a smile. Then I waved good-bye and walked toward the house, swallowing my fear for myself. Matthew was safe.

When I heard the cart wheels and the hooves clatter on the paving stones, I turned to watch Matthew drive away. He didn't look back. At least none of the constables hindered him.

When I entered the house, I found Lady Kaldaire missing and Detective Inspector Russell waiting with his arms crossed over his chest. "Where is—?"

"Seeing to Lord Kaldaire. Now, come with me, and answer some questions."

He led me back to the morning room, where one light still burned, and told me to have a seat. He sat across from me while an older constable took a seat a little way from us and pulled out his notebook. "I believe you said your name is Emily Gates. And your brother is Matthew Gates?"

"Yes."

"Your address?"

I gave it to him.

"Is that your hat shop or your residence?"

"Both. We live over the shop."

"And your parents?"

"My mother's dead."

"And your father?"

"I haven't seen him in a while." That was true. I avoided him and my uncles and cousins like they carried the plague.

The damage they could do to my reputation would be worse than any plague. If I tried to utilize their techniques on occasion to convince my aristocratic customers to pay their bills, that was my own fault and had nothing to do with them.

I hoped he wouldn't make the connection between my father's disreputable family and me. If he did, my only hope was for Lord Kaldaire to recover and name his attacker. Otherwise, I'd go to prison.

Prison. The hell my father threatened me with when I misbehaved as a child. A cold shiver of apprehension ran down my spine.

"Tell me again what you saw when you came into the study tonight."

I told him, swallowing hard when I came to the part about finding the master of the house in his study, sprawled out on the floor. I shuddered as I pictured the hair and blood and brains...

"And your reason for being here dressed like a boy, Miss Gates? It is Miss Gates?"

"Yes, it is. Lord Kaldaire and I were playing a game..."

"One involving grievous bodily harm?"

"No!" How was I going to answer this detective without telling him my plan? It seemed so stupid now.

"What does this game consist of?"

"His wife owes me for some hats I've designed for her. Lord Kaldaire makes a game out of paying me. I suppose if you have everything, life must get dull."

"I wouldn't know," he admitted.

"I do. I have a very posh clientele. Wealthy or

aristocratic. Sometimes both. Anything they want, they just have someone create it for them. Including excitement if life gets boring." That much was true. Now I'd find out how much I could slide past this man.

"What kind of excitement did you create for Lord Kaldaire?" His eyes looked cold as steel.

"I was to pretend to break in and demand money from him. Each time I would have to choose a different hour and a different disguise. As you can imagine, this is embarrassing." As was lying, but if it kept me out of jail...

"Does Lady Kaldaire know about this?"

"I'm not sure. She's his wife. He may play games with her, too."

The detective winced at that.

Good. Now maybe he'd drop his line of questioning.

"How often have you two played this game?"

"This is the first time. I doubt it will be the last." I let my distaste for everything, my story, begging for payment, the police, the expense of a school for Matthew, leak out in my voice.

"Why do you let your clients treat you like that?" His voice held an answering dismay.

"I need the money."

"Not that badly."

His scorn angered me. "You don't know anything about me."

"Tell me. What sends a respectable young woman like you out in the middle of the night playing at burglary to collect the price of a few hats?"

I must have been tired to ever admit anything to him, but he'd met Matthew. He'd understand. He had to. "Do you know how much a place at the Doncaster School for the Deaf costs?"

He shook his head, never taking his eyes off me.

"My hats are some of the most admired in society. They cost quite a lot. But it takes selling a great number of hats to send one boy to the School for the Deaf, and pay for his travel, his books, his lodging, his food, and his school clothes."

"Must be like attending university."

"I wouldn't know." Then I looked at his face and saw that he did know. "Did you finish your course of study?"

He shook his head. "I could only afford one year and never managed to go back. Do they have scholarships to the School for the Deaf?"

"Very few, and the need is huge." I hid my yawn behind my hand. "Is there anything else?"

"Did you see anyone in the area when you arrived here? Anyone in the house before you awakened the servants?"

"No one. The place was like a graveyard."

"Do you know a man called Jeremiah Pruitt?"

The change in topic surprised me. "No. Who is he?"

"No one." He spoke in an offhanded tone, but I doubted he did anything without a good reason. I would remember the name.

He asked me a few more questions about my business and Matthew, and finally let me go.

When I arrived back at our flat above the shop, I found Matthew asleep and Noah, my mother's cousin and our business partner, waiting up for me. His gray hair was disheveled and he'd wrapped a blanket around himself against the night chill. "The boy said you were in trouble, but he couldn't tell me anything else."

"Going after the *Lady in Blue* was a mistake." I dropped into a chair.

He sat across from me. "I told you using your

father's family's techniques would blow up on you. You were caught."

"No. I had to summon the household. I found the master in his study with his head bashed in."

"You should have left him for someone else to find," he lectured in his sleep-graveled voice.

"He was alive. Hopefully he still is."

"Oh. That is different." He rose and began to pace. "What did you tell them?"

"As little as possible. And if the police question you, you know nothing about my comings and goings."

"I helped raise you," he grumbled. "It's a little late to act like I'm only your hatmaker."

"The police don't know that." I hoped for his own safety he would lie.

"What about her ladyship?"

"Told me to come back in the morning to get a bank draft from her. She had no idea why her husband wasn't paying the bills." I rose stiffly. "Go to bed, Noah, and don't worry. I'm innocent. They can't hang an innocent woman."

At least I prayed they couldn't.

He snorted. "You've listened to your father's family too often."

Fear of the consequences of this mad night made me shiver. "If—if they're wrong, and the police take the easy way out and decide I struck Lord Kaldaire for the money he owes me, promise me you'll see that Matthew and Annie are taken care of."

Noah stopped in front of me. "Come here." He wrapped his arms around me. "Don't fret, Emily. We'll find a way to send Matthew to Doncaster. You two are my family. I've known you both since you slept in the workshop in a basket as babes. I've always tried to do the best for your mother and you. And we'll turn Annie into the best milliner of her time."

His embrace made me feel secure. I looked down at the lopsided fabric flowers Annie had been practicing on earlier, remembering going through the same steps under my mother's guidance. "I'm not sure Annie will ever be a milliner. Let's hope we can at least help her conquer her fears. Has she given you any hint about her life before we found her?"

"Nothing. You?"

I shook my head. She had told us nothing beyond her first name.

* * *

The next morning, I headed to Kaldaire House before the people of their class would have read their morning paper. The omnibus was full of office clerks, typists, and sales assistants. I was dressed a shade better than the rest of the riders, in a brown walking suit with matching gloves. I wore a high, mannish collar with a small purple bow that was repeated on my wide hat brim. I had topped the hat off with a few purple feathers, dyed and curled to look rarer than the domestic duck they had come from.

Since I had to walk the last few blocks through Mayfair to Kaldaire House, I was glad the overcast sky didn't open up, drenching me. I didn't slow down when I saw the bobby on the stoop; I merely nodded to him and went up to ring the bell.

The butler opened the door and said, "I'm sorry, but..."

"Lady Kaldaire asked me to stop by this morning."

She came down the stairs at that moment, flanked by Detective Inspector Russell and the doctor I'd seen for a moment last night.

"How is he?" Their grim faces turned my voice into little more than a whisper.

"He died a few minutes ago without ever gaining consciousness." I was surprised by how little emotion Lady Kaldaire put into that statement.

"I am so sorry." Those bare words did little to describe the feelings running through me. I was shocked by Lord Kaldaire's death, even if he'd never thought of me as important enough to pay. I was sad for Lady Kaldaire, who was more decent than most of her class. But mostly I was frightened for myself, since any hope of Kaldaire saying who really attacked him was gone.

"Thank you, my dear." Lady Kaldaire turned toward her morning room.

"I need to talk to you, Miss Gates," the inspector said.

I took an involuntary half step back, wishing I'd waited to come here until after the police had left. I tried to swallow away the feel of the noose around my neck.

"I will also be present," the new widow said, turning back to us.

"I don't think that's a good idea." Inspector Russell clamped onto my wrist with a strong grip.

I didn't mind Lady Kaldaire listening in, and even if I did, I couldn't see a polite way to dissuade her.

"I will not have an unchaperoned woman questioned by a man, alone, in my house."

"Sergeant Dawson will be there also."

"Two men with a young, unmarried lady? Scandalous."

Russell pressed his lips together for an instant as he tamped down the humor in his eyes. Then he stared directly at me. "You may not want your customers to hear what we are going to discuss."

My father's family. My heart tipped over and sank into my stomach before I could release a breath. "I don't want Lady Kaldaire to hear our discussion," I sneered out the last word, "but she has lost more than anyone. I suspect she wants to hear everything that is said, and I think she deserves to have all of her questions answered. No matter how embarrassing it is to me." Or how ruinous.

I hoped she'd keep my secret. Oh, she had to stay silent. Already my face was burning.

"Quite wise, Emily." Her no-nonsense tone told me she wanted nothing less than the truth. Her husband was dead. I'm sure she felt she deserved to know all.

She ordered the butler to have the staff hang black crepe at every door, window, and mirror before she led us into her morning room, where we each took a seat near the warming fire. I took off my gloves and made myself as comfortable as I could for the grilling that was to come.

Before the police could begin their questions, I hurried to speak first. "Lady Kaldaire, I was playing a game with your husband to get him to pay my bill for your hats because my brother, Matthew, is deaf. I want to send him to the School for the Deaf. It's in Doncaster, a residential school, and a very good place. It's also very dear. Hence my need for every penny I'm due."

"Has he been deaf long, Emily?" she asked.

"When Matthew was eight, he and my mother both fell ill. Mother died of the fever, and Matthew lost his ability to hear. Then he gave up speaking and can't be persuaded to try. I took over her millinery business and raising Matthew." I gave a sound that was half-chuckle, half-sob. "It's a good thing I have a talent for making hats, because I have none at all for raising young boys."

She nodded and gave me a small smile. "They can be difficult. You've raised him on your own?"

"My mother's cousin, Noah, runs the workshop and keeps Matthew out of trouble when I'm in the shop."

"But he wasn't watching your brother last night," Inspector Russell said.

"No. Not last night."

"Whose horse and cart was it?"

"The workshop's. Cousin Noah's." I held up my hands. "He's run the workshop since before I was born. I don't know what's his and what's mine anymore."

"Is the workshop near your shop?"

"Just across the alley, facing out on a side street. It's very convenient."

"I'll bet it is," Russell muttered.

I gave him a level stare. I guessed he thought he could be rude because of my father's family, but I'd try to prevent that if I could.

The look he returned appeared innocent. Then he said, "Where does your father's family fit into this cozy arrangement?"

"It doesn't." The fury in my eyes should have knocked him to the floor.

It didn't seem to bother him in the least, as he gave me a cold smile. "Does Lady Kaldaire know your father is part of the notorious Gates gang—robbers, burglars, gamblers, confidence tricksters, and thieves?"

"I've never heard of this Gates gang," Lady Kaldaire said with a note of disdain.

"They're suspected of the Grand Metropolitan Hotel robbery and the Covington Art Exhibit robbery. The list goes on and on."

I heard her gasp as I glared at him. How dare he? How dare he expose my most painful secret to my client? My hands curled into fists as I snapped, "I don't know why she would. I have nothing to do with them."

"I don't believe you." He displayed no emotion at all.

"Believe what you like, Inspector Russell. You're wrong about me."

"I looked you up in the records room at Scotland Yard after I left here last night. You're Henry Gates's daughter, and my, but he has an impressive file."

It was a good thing I was seated, because I felt as if the floor had dropped out from under my chair. I couldn't catch my breath or move my limbs. He had destroyed my business.

In the silence that followed, Lady Kaldaire said, "I believe her, Inspector."

"With all due respect, ma'am—"

"If you'd use your brain, you'd know she wouldn't have had to deal so extravagantly with my husband if she had criminals to force him to pay her, or if they were paying for the boy's schooling out of their illicit gains." She raised her graying brows and looked at him with her lips pursed together.

"We searched her shop—"

"You did what?" I was incensed. Had they put their dirty paws on my hats? Or rooted around the till or examined my books? And then my anger slid into fear. What had they found?

He gave me a satisfied smirk. "We searched your shop storeroom and found items from a recent burglary. Specifically, jewelry."

Blast. I'd taken that jewelry to force Lady Eddington to pay my bill rather than her gambling debts. Her response was to tell me to sell the jewelry. And then she had the nerve to report the worthless paste stolen as real jewelry. *Witch.*

"Whose is it, Emily?" Lady Kaldaire asked.

I looked at her, wide-eyed.

"It's obvious from the look on your face you know about the jewelry. No prevaricating." Her look was stern.

I lowered my head. "It's Lady Eddington's." *Evil, rotten...*

"I'm not surprised," the older woman told me. "Julia has never been particularly timely in paying her bills. Was this another of your little games to get the upper class to pay what they owe you?"

"Yes, ma'am." What else could I say?

"Does the value of the jewelry cover her bills?"

"No, ma'am, it does not." Which made me even angrier. At Lady Eddington, not Lady Kaldaire.

"I think you should tell Inspector Russell the truth about the jewelry."

I looked into her eyes and saw she knew. And that she found the whole situation amusing.

"What truth about the jewelry?" the detective asked.

"Have you had it appraised?" she asked him.

To Russell's credit, he immediately understood. "No, we haven't. And when we do, I gather we'll discover they aren't worth enough to charge you with a serious crime." He looked from me to Lady Kaldaire. "But how did you know they're fake?"

"I guessed. Knowing Lady Eddington, it's the only possible conclusion," Lady Kaldaire said.

"And you?" Russell asked, eyeing me closely. If he hoped to discover I'd asked a member of my father's family, he'd be sadly disappointed.

"I was taught how to tell real from fake by studying the stones." I didn't want to tell him it was a game I had played as a child with my grandfather.

"Then why take them at all?"

"It takes close examination in good light. Not something I could do while removing them from Eddington House."

"Why keep them if they're worthless?" Inspector Russell appeared genuinely curious.

"It's a game, Inspector. I have something she wants returned before her friends and my fellow tradesmen discover she's as phony as her jewels. I don't care about her reputation. What I want is for Lady Eddington to pay me for the hats I made for her."

He shook his head at my revelation. "Nevertheless, you admit to breaking into Eddington House and into here. I have to charge you for that. And I doubt your customers will like doing business with a criminal. The daughter of a criminal."

"You do realize, don't you, Inspector, that I will testify under oath that Emily didn't break in here." Lady Kaldaire gave me a tiny smile. "And Lady Eddington doesn't dare press charges. She'd have to admit the fakes you collected are hers." She gave the inspector what I thought of as the aristocratic stare.

Bless Lady Kaldaire. She defended me to the police about the attack on her husband and now over the break-ins I'd committed. She was doing her best to protect me.

I glanced over at the gray-haired sergeant. He was studying his notebook, pencil poised, with a face as devoid of expression as Lady Kaldaire's. It was a technique I needed to learn.

When I looked at Inspector Russell, he was examining me with calculation in his eyes. He had something else planned for me. I wished I knew what.

"I suppose you have us stymied for now, Miss Gates,

but don't think this is finished. We still have a murder to solve," Inspector Russell said as he rose from his chair.

The sergeant was immediately on his feet.

"I want you to solve the murder, Inspector. I don't want anyone thinking I would do such a thing. Even my notorious relatives wouldn't kill a man." I knew he couldn't deny that. They'd never been suspected of murder. Why did I have to be the first in the family?

I walked with Lady Kaldaire to the front hall and she made certain there were no other policemen in the house before the butler showed them out. "Now, Emily, let's return to my morning room. We need to talk."

I could feel my business, my income, my life falling apart. Matthew would never get to go to the School for the Deaf. I could feel the weight of this murder, with police investigating and people suspecting me, pressing me down. I felt myself shrink and my feet turn to lead.

"We'll need tea," she told her butler.

Tea? She wouldn't be terminating my services over a shared cup of tea. My body was suddenly lighter.

When we were both seated with the door shut, Lady Kaldaire said, "You are obviously a young woman with some unique talents, and you have a commendable goal in sending your brother to school. I need you to do something for me. I need you to retrieve the contents of the safe. In return I will pay you handsomely, which you can put toward your brother's education. And I will keep your secret about your relatives."

Surprised, I said, "After I admitted to planning to steal the *Lady in Blue* from you?"

"That is a ridiculous and scandalous pose for a great-grandmother to take."

"She wasn't a great-grandmother when the painting was done." I suspected the scantily dressed woman in the painting had been twenty when she posed for it.

She dismissed it with, "She knew she would be one day. I don't care if I ever see the painting again. It is the contents of the safe that are dangerous."

CHAPTER THREE

Dangerous? My breath caught. Being suspected of murder was quite enough danger for me. What was I getting myself into? "What exactly was in the safe?"

"A letter."

"Yours or Lord Kaldaire's?"

"He had obtained it. I would never be so indiscreet as to keep anything of this nature."

I believed her. "What's in the letter?"

"That's none of your business."

"Then how will I know who stole the letter or whether I have the right one?" She was being difficult, which made no sense if she wanted my help. And what had her husband been doing to receive an embarrassing letter?

The tea arrived at that moment, forestalling conversation until the maid was gone, the door shut, and the tea poured. We both took a great deal of sugar in our cups. Once Lady Kaldaire had a fortifying sip, she set her cup back in its saucer and said, "I suppose you'll need to know. Horace heard rumors about a royal who was not as royal as that person claimed."

"You mean a bastard?"

I received a dirty look for my language before she continued. "He began an investigation into the allegations, quite discreetly. He purchased the letter that started the rumors and put it in the safe.

Apparently, his investigation wasn't as discreet as he'd hoped."

"If it's the royal family who had that safe opened, I stand no chance of getting that letter back. It'd be burned by now."

"I don't believe the royal family has anything to do with this. I suspect the perpetrator was an enemy of our royal family or our nation."

A knot of apprehension formed in my stomach. Being hanged for murder seemed at that moment to be a more peaceful way to die. "Aren't they the same thing?"

"Not at all. There are foreign governments who are against British interests, but who wish our rulers no harm. Then there are those who plot against our royal family because…"

When she fell silent drinking her tea, I said, "Why would anyone plot against our entire royal family? Or is it just one? There are quite a lot of them."

"There is a faction that wants to replace our current line of succession with another. Or if not replace it, embarrass our sovereign."

I couldn't help it. I laughed. "So who is supposed to be illegitimate? King Edward? Queen Alexandra? Prince George? His young sons?"

"Victoria."

I fumbled my teacup and nearly dropped it, splashing tea in the saucer. "You're going to try to tell me that Queen Victoria's parents weren't married? I'm sure someone would have known before now if that were true."

"No. The letter purports that Victoria's mother had a lover who was Victoria's true father. That the Duke of Kent was impotent. That Victoria didn't have a drop of royal blood."

What a foolish thing to worry about all these years later. No one would know for certain or care. "Who would gain by raking up that muck now?"

"The King of Hanover, who is also the Duke of Cumberland, and his heirs. The original Duke of Cumberland was next in line of succession of George III's sons after Victoria's father. Can't you picture the donnybrook that would cause, with competing claims and Parliament trying to sort everything out?" The smile slid off her face. "It would be a national disaster."

"Who would really benefit by declaring Victoria illegitimate?" Not that I could imagine it. She'd reigned for over sixty years when she died. Entire generations knew her as queen. No one would believe this.

"Ernest Augustus, Crown Prince of Hanover, a kingdom that no longer exists, as well as titled the third Duke of Cumberland. And his brother, Prince Maximilian of Hanover, who is a good friend of the kaiser. And Kaiser Wilhelm, although a descendant of Victoria's, derives his royal title from his father's side of the family. What Wilhelm and Maximilian would both like is for King Edward to be embarrassed."

"Why?"

"They can't stand him." She spoke with such simplicity that I nearly giggled at the image of rulers acting like small boys.

That sounded like a stupid reason to break into a safe to steal a letter about a birth almost one hundred years before. The letter was nonsense, ludicrous, absurd.

"Prince Maximilian's the one you need to investigate, Emily. And to watch out for."

"Well, if he's in Germany—"

"He's not. He's here in London. He has a house nearby in Mayfair. He always appears to be in mourning, even when he's not. Of course, he could have tried to steal the letter and become my husband's killer by accident." She lifted one hand and wiggled her fingers, as if she were calling someone. Which was odd, since we were the only two in the room.

"This reminds me; I need to get someone in to make up some mourning clothes for me. Will you do two hats to begin with? One with a medium, curved-down brim and lots of long net to hide my face during church services and trips to the cemetery after the funeral. I hate people peering at me, trying to guess if I'm truly sorrowful. The other hat should be similar to the style I like, only in black, and with a veil."

"But what about your widow's veil? It's worn with a cap."

"Do you really think I could wear a widow's cap while not knowing who murdered my husband and put me in mourning clothes? Never. First, we'll find his killer. Only then can I wear crepe ribbons." She paused and sighed before saying, "You do understand, Emily?"

"Of course, my lady." I'd never forgiven my father and his family for their role in my mother's death. That meant I had never been able to properly grieve.

What I wasn't expecting was the fit of sobs that burst out of Lady Kaldaire. She had been stoic until that moment. Now I found myself awkwardly patting her shoulder and murmuring as I would to a child who'd lost a toy.

After she dried her tears and blew her nose, she said, "He was such a fool, but he was my fool. We were never a love match. We married for all the usual reasons anyone in our set makes these alliances. And when I failed to give him an heir, my one and only duty, he never blamed me. He was more optimistic about our chances than I was whenever it was mentioned. And then he simply said, 'Oh, the title will pass to Laurence's oldest' without a word of recrimination. He could be a kind man. Oh, Emily, I've just discovered I miss him."

She cried softly for so long that I felt it necessary to hand her my clean handkerchief. I'd never seen any show of emotion from any of my customers before. I realized she was the first customer I actually liked, because she thought me worthy to see her as human.

"Thank you, Emily. You're very kind." She dried her eyes and said, "Don't tell anyone what I told you about the contents of the safe. But think about it. How will we get that letter back?"

"Why do we want to get back something that is just so much malicious gossip?"

"Because," Lady Kaldaire said in a tone to be used on a peasant, "Lord Kaldaire's killer thought it was worth stealing."

"And once we get it back?" I suspected her "we" meant I was to do all the dangerous, illegal acts.

"Burn it, of course. I don't know why Horace didn't. Probably expected an honor for returning it or some silliness like that. And now look at the mess. We must get it back and burn it for the good of the country."

"Shouldn't the government do that?"

"You think a bunch of men can accomplish something that needs a delicate touch?"

I stared at her. She was probably right, but that didn't mean I had to like sticking my neck out for the royal family. They wouldn't save me if anything went wrong. "That inspector will be watching me. If I do anything illegal, he'll put me in jail."

"Emily." Lady Kaldaire put years of practice at issuing orders into her voice. "I will keep your unsavory relatives a secret. Your secret is safe with me, no matter what. In exchange, I hope you will help me retrieve that letter."

My mother had kept her connection to my father's family hidden her entire married life, and I had done the same since her death. This was the first time our secret had been discovered, and it was my fault.

I felt obligated to retrieve the old letter from a possible killer. It was the only way out of this mess, sweetened with money for Matthew's school. *Gee. What could be easier?* I folded my arms across my chest. "I'll do it. I have no choice."

"All right, Emily. No need to be dramatic," she tsked. "I need your help. I don't know anyone else I can call on, and you are such a competent young woman. Help me. Please."

That was the first "please" I'd ever heard from an aristocratic customer. I nodded.

"I'll need the hats by the day after tomorrow." She rose and walked over to her desk, pulling out her checkbook.

I knew I'd been dismissed, but at least I was being paid.

* * *

It had been a very long night. Now it promised to be an equally long day. When I'd left Kaldaire House, I'd gone to Lady Kaldaire's bank to get my money. I'd only returned to my shop half an hour before Noah came out from the back room. My saleswoman, Jane, who was helping me set a finished hat to its best advantage on an American industrialist's wife's head, saw him first and took over with a nod.

By the time I reached Noah, Inspector Russell had joined him.

"Come with me, gentlemen." I led them through the storeroom behind the shop where we made minor adjustments to hats. Each creation rested in one of our easily identifiable boxes, stored on a shelf ready to be picked up by a customer.

When we reached the alley, I was glad to see it wasn't raining. This was the only good I could find now that these irritating policemen had invaded my business during the day. Then I stopped and shivered, wondering what they wanted now. With as brave a voice as I could find, I said, "Can this wait? We're busy at the moment."

"No. It can't." The Scotland Yard detective gestured for me to precede him into the workshop.

I walked in to find our employees and Matthew standing in a tight group watching the bobbies search everywhere in the building. Annie, my apprentice, had backed herself into a corner and stood there, clutching a broom as tall as she was in defense. The older sergeant I'd seen before with Inspector Russell was now standing guard in front of the door to the little room where we stored our hatmaking materials.

I couldn't afford production to stop. Glowering at Matthew and the employees, I bellowed, "Get back to work."

Russell held up his hand, palm out, toward them and said, "No."

I turned on the detective, fury in my voice. "Why not?"

"First we need to discuss what we found in your storeroom."

They'd searched my shop and now they'd returned to search the workshop. The storeroom held felt, feathers, netting, ribbon, and straw. Nothing that could interest Scotland Yard. I gave Noah a puzzled glance.

He shrugged. "I don't know either."

We walked over to the sergeant, who opened the door and turned on the electric light in the ceiling. Everything looked to be in place until I looked at one corner. "Noah?"

We both began to move forward, but were stopped immediately by the inspector and the sergeant.

I pointed to the corner. "Why are there paintings in my storeroom?"

"We hoped you'd tell us that, Miss Gates," Inspector Russell said.

Matthew walked up to stand shoulder to shoulder with Noah and me. He couldn't understand a word of our rapid conversation, but he wanted to demonstrate his faith in us.

I put an arm around him, but he shook me off with an embarrassed sigh. Noah punched him in the arm and the two exchanged man-to-man nods. My little brother was growing up faster than I realized.

I turned my attention back to the paintings. "Noah?" He ran the workshop. He must know. Otherwise, I saw my future spent in prison.

"They weren't there when I closed up last night."

"And this morning when you opened up?"

He sighed, looked at the concrete floor, looked away, and then studied the ceiling. "I planned to tell you, but you left for Lady Kaldaire's so early, and then you've been busy in the shop after this lot kept you up half the night..."

I had the general idea. "But you don't know how they got there?" We exchanged a look.

His expression said he was as puzzled as I was.

"No."

I turned back to the inspector. "And neither do I. You're welcome to them. Where did they come from?"

"They were stolen from a private collection last night." Those smiling gray eyes of his looked hard as steel now.

"You know where I was, and it wasn't stealing paintings."

"Then how do you explain the appearance of these paintings in your storeroom?"

"I can't, Inspector. Why did you decide to look for them here?"

"We got an anonymous tip." I could see he found it amusing. I suspected he also found it suspicious.

I certainly did. "And who was supposed to have taken these paintings and put them in my storeroom last night?"

"I know it couldn't have been you or your brother. You two were busy elsewhere. But your foreman or employees could be involved."

I crossed my arms. "I don't believe it."

"I don't believe so, either. But there is the Gates gang. Do any of your relatives have a key?"

Blast my father and his family. They'd done nothing but cause trouble for me all my adult life. Steam came out of my ears whenever they were mentioned. Everyone who knew me knew I refused to have anything to do with them and blamed their criminal activity for my mother's early death. "Yes. My cousin Noah and my brother. Neither of whom could have had anything to do with this. If you think the Gates gang did it, then they must have broken in."

"We see no sign of a break-in."

How could he sound so calm and dispassionate

when talking about my father's terrible family? "If they could break in and steal," I said, pointing across the crowded space, "a half- dozen valuable paintings without leaving you any clues, they could certainly break in here without any difficulty. We have little security."

"How often have they hidden their loot here before?" the detective asked.

"Never that I know of. And I don't know why they did last night. Did you interrupt their thieving?"

Inspector Russell looked away and said, "This couldn't have been the first time."

A verbal sleight of hand. I'd learned to recognize that as a child. My temper flared at a policeman who would think the offspring of con artists wouldn't notice. "You did interrupt them. Why didn't you stop them instead of letting them break in here?"

He looked into my eyes and said in a level tone, "We wanted to see where they hid their loot."

"Which member of my father's illustrious family was it?"

"That hid the paintings here? It was Petey."

I was almost too angry to speak coherently. "He's a moron. And that's his idea of a joke. Noah, keep an eye on everything. I'll be back shortly." I turned around and marched out of the workshop.

Inspector Russell was on my heels. "You can't—"

"Just watch me."

He grabbed my arm and swung me around in the alley. Fortunately, no one saw us, because we ended standing too close for the rules of etiquette. "You'll get to face him, just not yet."

I studied his face. His nose was slightly bent where it had been broken, probably more than once. His lips were a little thin, but that might have been because he was being obstinate at that moment. His jawline was square, adding to that stubborn look. His bowler hat hid most of his short brown hair that appeared to be a rich, warm shade. But it was his eyes that arrested me.

The gray was flecked with blue, silver, and a shade that was almost black. At the moment, his eyes flashed anger and a heat that built an answering tremor in my chest. I had no idea what he thought as he studied my face. "What do you have in mind?"

"I'd like to use you as an informant on the Gates gang."

I laughed. "They'll never trust me."

"You'll have to make them trust you. Otherwise, you're the one receiving stolen property."

I saw where this was going, and it brought tears of anger and frustration and fear to my eyes. "If you arrest me, you'll ruin my business. A business I've spent years building. I'll spend so much time trying to save it I won't have time to help you."

"Maybe I should just arrest Noah."

"Noah? Why?" I felt like a rock struck me in the stomach. The detective was using everything in his arsenal, and with every attempt to intimidate me, I became more irritated as well as frightened. He was a peeler. He could make a judge believe whatever he wanted and ruin my life. Destroy all my plans for Matthew. Put me in prison.

"He has a key. He locked up last night and opened this morning. Maybe he didn't lock up so Peter Gates could just walk in."

"You're not going to arrest Noah. You can't. He's worked here as long as I can remember. He was my mother's business partner. I rely on him." Now I was begging. And I could see it wasn't doing me any good. I made my final argument. "He's not a Gates."

All through my childhood and my first years as a hat designer, my mother and Noah had worked together, patiently, tirelessly, showing me the best ways to carry out our trade. To allow him to arrest Noah was almost like defiling my mother's memory.

He looked at a spot over my head. "By rights I should arrest you for the murder of Lord Kaldaire."

I sucked in my breath and felt the hangman's rope burn my neck. I bit my lip to fight off my tears. "I didn't do it."

"You were wearing gloves. His killer didn't leave fingerprints. You had broken in wearing boys' clothing. You had a vehicle waiting for you down the street. You easily could have bludgeoned him."

"But I didn't. Would I have called for help if I'd attacked Lord Kaldaire? Better to sneak away before anyone knew I was there."

"I don't know. Would you?" He gave me a half-smile.

I studied him for a moment. He believed me innocent in Lord Kaldaire's death, but he saw a benefit in keeping me on the list of suspects. "You have a plan. And I'm the bait."

CHAPTER FOUR

Inspector Russell looked like a fox that had been handed the key to the henhouse. "No. You're only going to work for me. Unofficially, of course."

"I don't think so." I could think of a dozen reasons why this wouldn't work.

"Either you go to work for me, or I'll have to arrest you for the murder of Lord Kaldaire. That will destroy your business."

I must have looked like I was ready to cry or murder him, because he added, "I don't want to. It would be much better for you to work with me than to sit in a cold cell with a group of prostitutes."

"You'll ruin my reputation." That sounded like one of the most unpleasant possibilities facing me. There was no way for me to come out unscathed and no way to avoid working for the inspector. "And once I help you bring down my father's relatives, then you'll throw me in jail."

"No. Not unless you killed his lordship."

"I didn't." The inspector was difficult. Dreadful. Horrible. But he certainly knew how to manipulate me. Just like Lady Kaldaire. I was frustrated, trapped, and worst of all, it was my own fault. I put myself in this position when I broke into Kaldaire House.

"If you work for me, you and Noah and Matthew can go on as before, safe from the Gates gang and murder charges."

He was a bobby. I couldn't trust him. And that lack of trust filled my voice. "Can I have that in writing?"

He grinned. "You know I can't do that."

I knew he wouldn't. He was the enemy as much as my father's family was. And that thought made me worry about another thing he'd said. "Why did you look for blood on my hatpin last night?"

"You've heard of the Central Line killer?"

"Yes. It's been in all the papers." Over the past year, three men had died close to Central Line stations under mysterious circumstances. Men now looked over their shoulders when using the Underground at night.

"A fourth victim was struck down last evening near the Bond Street station. Near where you were. His name was Jeremiah Pruitt."

"And you suspect me?" What little was left of my temper frayed. As I stepped toward Inspector Russell, my index finger ready to poke him in the chest, I saw Noah and the sergeant peek out into the alley and then slip back inside the workshop. Cowards.

"I must be a one-woman crime wave. I killed a man by an Underground stop, then ran over to Lord Kaldaire's to murder him, broke into a safe, called for help and then stole several other paintings from another location that showed up in my millinery workshop. You must find me amazing." Sarcasm wasn't much of a weapon, but at the moment, it was all I had. That, and the poking.

Russell must have tired of being poked, because he grabbed my wrist. "Yes, you are amazing. Do you know how hard it is to be suspected of several unrelated crimes in one night?"

"Well, I didn't do any of them." I realized I'd shouted

at him and snapped my mouth shut.

"Then don't be so difficult. The Gates gang trusts you more than they do the police. You have a unique opportunity to do some good for society. Help me put criminals in jail."

He held my hand against his jacket where I couldn't avoid feeling the rough wool fabric and the strong muscles underneath. I could smell coal fires, soap, and the essence of a man who wouldn't take no for an answer.

"You want me to betray my family to the police."

"No, Miss Gates. I know you won't do that. But there are ways you can help protect the law-abiding residents of London. Ways to do good."

I stared into his eyes for a minute before I said, "You really believe that."

"Yes."

Wow. Having lived among my Gates relatives and worked with the rich and aristocratic, all of whom shared the same code of *Whatever benefits me is right*, I was astonished. "It's been a long time since I met anyone who believed so completely in the power of right and good."

"And the majesty of the law."

"You're serious?" Oh, my. I'd never met a man like him before.

"Yes. Help me, Miss Gates. You have ways to talk to these people that I can never accomplish. Otherwise, my bosses at Scotland Yard will want an arrest. Any arrest. And you're our prime suspect."

My mouth opened in shock. "All that nonsense about the majesty of the law and believing in right and wrong. I almost fell for it."

He grinned at my fury. "I believe in it, Miss Gates. I

never said my bosses do."

"So I have two choices. Do as you ask or go to jail." I hated being used, and Inspector Russell appeared to be a master at using people. I wanted to lash out, run, hide. Anything but stand here and listen to this wickedly clever man manipulate me.

Much the same way Lady Kaldaire could, but she offered to pay me. Inspector Russell threatened to arrest me.

Two people were pulling me in different directions, and I didn't want to go in either. Especially since the inspector wanted to imprison my relatives for theft and breaking in, and Lady Kaldaire wanted me to risk jail time to carry out her dangerous fancies. Was there no solution?

He looked hopeful. "You won't find a better boss than me."

"I've worked for myself since my mother died."

"Not any longer. Not if you're smart."

The sergeant came over and Inspector Russell dropped my wrist like a hot coal. "Sir, there's something else you should see. We found it behind the paintings."

Russell walked back into my factory. I followed, noticing with frustration that my employees still stood idle, waiting for the police to finish. Their work sat unfinished at their places along the two long tables, ribbons half folded, needles stuck in edges, fabric cut halfway through.

Those hats wouldn't make or trim themselves.

We went into the storeroom where the paintings had been moved and stacked near the door. In the corner was a burlap sack, a bobby standing guard over it.

The sergeant went over and picked the bag up to

bring it to the inspector. "Looks like the Gates gang hid more than just paintings in here. These match the description of some jewelry taken in a heist three nights ago." He held out his hand and poured the contents into it.

Russell picked up a jeweled necklace that had to be worth a fortune and held it up near my face. "You've been hiding a lot of goods for them. What'll it be, Miss Gates?"

Matthew stepped next to me and put an arm around my shoulder. I held my fist up, our sign for "Thank you." He was trying to protect me, while I was trying to do the same for him.

Words of my grandfather's came to mind: *Unspecific verbal agreements carry no weight. And it's always permissible to lie.* "All right. I'll do it."

I never said what "it" was.

And as maddening as Inspector Russell was, I wouldn't have minded seeing him again. There was something about that man...

It took some doing, but I finally got rid of the police and nagged the workshop back into production by reminding my employees that none of us would get paid until the work was finished. I told Noah about the hats Lady Kaldaire had asked for and worked up some designs. From those, using the measurements we had for her ladyship, Noah made the frames.

At the end of the day, I still had plenty to do, but first I needed to pay a call.

My grandfather claimed to run a livery stable. However, that was too honest a profession to interest him. He left the stable business under my grandmother's fierce gaze and spent his days watching the rich and famous for telltale signs of goods purchased and the means of access to those goods.

He dressed for these excursions as an elderly man of leisure, the kind who looks familiar but for whom you can't quite put a name to the face. His white mustache and eyebrows drooped like those of so many men of his age. His top hat and frock coat were of an older style but immaculate, as if he had a very good valet. He carried a silver-headed walking stick pinched in a burglary long before I was born.

I went to the lodgings down the alley behind the stable, knowing I'd find him there at this time of day.

"Emily, how's my little angel? It's been far too long since you visited your poor old grandfather." He gathered me in a hug as he ushered me into the dining area that served as his conference room. "Ma, look who's here."

My grandmother came in from the kitchen, looked me over with suspicion and said, "What does *she* want?"

I'd never get anything past her. She and my mother had detested each other, and she now aimed her animosity for my mother at Matthew and me. I decided to attempt to be civil. "It's good to see you, Grandmother."

"See? She can't even call me 'Gran.' And what do you want?"

"To talk business with Grandpapa."

"Bah." She stomped from the room.

"Tea, Aggie," my grandfather called after her. "Here, have a seat. Have you been to see your father?"

We sat on hard chairs on either side of a corner of the long dining table. "No. I need to discuss this with you."

He scowled. "You in some kind of trouble, pet?"

"Thanks to Petey. He hid loot from two different

jobs in the stockroom of my hat workshop. The police followed him and saw what he did, and they searched my premises. They took it all and threatened to throw me in jail."

He shook his head. "Petey. I might have guessed. All the planning that goes into a burglary, and then he just throws the loot away. Who's the investigating officer?"

"Detective Inspector Russell."

Grandfather looked heavenward. "Oh, bother. Not him again."

"You know him?"

"Since he was a bobby on patrol. I tried to slip him a backhander and he punched me in the nose. I managed to get out of jail after a week for that one, and he's been after us ever since."

My stern, sharp-angled grandmother marched in with the tea on a tray, banged it on the well-scrubbed table, and left with another "Bah."

"Does he know you're one of us?" Grandfather said as he poured tea.

"Yes."

"And how did that happen? The shop's in your mother's family's name."

The hat business originally belonged to Noah Duquesne, my mother's cousin, and my mother. Angry with my father, she had agreed to name the shop Duquesne's Millinery.

There was no hope for it. I'd have to tell him. "There was a bit of trouble at the home of a customer last night."

He handed me a cup of tea. "Well, don't keep your grandfather guessing. What happened? And why were you at a customer's late at night?"

I told him a shortened version of the truth. He was

too sharp for anything else.

"And Inspector Russell was the detective on the scene?"

"Yes."

"Bad luck, that." And then he laughed. "That showed real initiative, pet. Is this the first time you've tried to get what's owed you this way?"

"The second." I told him about the debacle with Lady Eddington.

His loud laughter brought my grandmother into the room. "She's got a real flair for this, Aggie. Terrible luck, but a real flair. She's one of us."

"Bah." Grandmother marched out again.

"But you called for help rather than leave that man to his fate." Grandfather nodded and then took a sip of tea. "That shows decency in you. Of course, if it was left to the widow, you still wouldn't get paid."

"She paid me because I risked everything to call for help."

"In real cash?" I don't think he trusted anyone outside the family.

"I cashed the bank draft this morning. It was good." I had a sip of tea and added, "Have you heard of a Jeremiah Pruitt?"

"He was all over the newspapers for being stabbed to death with a hatpin near the Bond Street station last evening. Here. Read it for yourself."

He reached over to take a daily newspaper off the sideboard and handed it to me. Jeremiah Pruitt was in his late twenties and from an old, respected family. He'd apparently been going out for the evening when he was approached on his way to the station and stabbed to death. "That would have to be a tougher, sharper hatpin than my customers use. More like a thin dagger. Had you ever heard of him before?"

"Yes. Bit of a wastrel. A dandy. Not the sort you want your granddaughter to know. Why are you asking?"

"Inspector Russell is checking to make sure I didn't kill him as well as Lord Kaldaire. The two murders happened close to each other." I drank more of my tea before I said, "Please ask Petey not to store anything else in my shop."

"I will. Now, are you going to say hello to your father?"

"No." Emotions I'd held in check for years seeped out. "Why didn't he come when Mama was dying? She called for him, over and over, and he didn't come. She died wanting one thing. To see him."

"He didn't know, pet."

"Noah came for him. He wouldn't see her. Said he was too busy. And he was the one person she asked for. Not Matthew. Not me. She wanted Henry, and he couldn't be bothered. Now I don't want to know him." I rose, not wanting to cry in front of this man, this link between my father and me. "Please tell Petey what I said. Thanks for the tea."

I rushed away, not even saying good-bye.

I spent the walk home remembering how my mother took care of us and kept food on the table with her hatmaking skills during my father's frequent absences. I was nine or ten before I realized his "visits to friends in Newcastle" meant he was in jail.

And all that time, she made me practice folding strips of cloth, curling feathers, and drawing designs until I knew instinctively what looked good on a hat and how to make it. She constantly reminded me that a woman needed to be prepared to make her own way in the world.

Nothing rattled her. She never raised her voice or bemoaned her lack of jewels or finery. I never lacked for food or love. I never heard her cry until she was dying and Noah had to tell her Henry wouldn't come. I never forgave my father for those heart-wrenching sobs of utter despair that came from her room.

I never lost the feeling she died of a broken heart, not a fever. And I wanted vengeance against the man who killed her.

CHAPTER FIVE

Still lost in memories, I reached home and unlocked the door to the stairs leading to our flat. In the next second, I gasped when a large male hand appeared on the door at eye level.

"Miss Gates."

Blast. Inspector Russell. "Have you been following me, Inspector?"

"Yes."

"Well, I made it home safely. You can go now."

He didn't move. He just leaned on the door in silence.

"I'm not inviting you in."

"I don't expect you to."

I turned to look him in the eye. Curiosity made me ask, "What do you want?"

"I want to know how you do it." He looked serious, puzzled, and worn out. His bowler hat sat at a correct angle, not the jaunty one I expected to see from a peeler following me.

"Do what?"

"You have this entire criminal empire behind you, and yet you run your business on your own without your customers knowing how fragile your façade is. How unacceptable your background. And how powerless you are without the Gateses backing you." His face was mere inches from mine. I should have felt threatened with him looming in the twilight next to me.

Yet I didn't feel threatened. Perhaps I was just too angry. But I realized there was something in the line of his jaw, the intelligence in his eyes, and the ironic curve of his lips that spoke to me. I knew not replying would be my best choice. "Good night, Inspector."

Clattering footsteps in the stairwell made us both step back from the door. A moment later, Matthew appeared, all long-limbed clumsiness from his growth spurt, smiling at me. Then the smile slid from his face as he recognized the inspector.

I put a hand on my brother's shoulder and gave him my most reassuring expression. "It's all right, Matthew."

He jerked his head toward Inspector Russell.

Russell put out his hand. "How do you do, Matthew?"

Matthew looked at me in surprise and then warily shook the inspector's hand.

"He's a loyal brother to you. Tell him I mean you no harm." The inspector smiled at me. "Good night." Then he walked away whistling.

* * *

I spent the evening in our flat with a dummy head and some scrap muslin material trying to figure out the best way to fill Lady Kaldaire's request. Matthew and Noah both read, and Annie, our little apprentice, attempted dressing her doll in scraps of fabric, leaving me alone to mutter as I pinned lengths of light fabric over the mushroom-shaped, buckram and wire form that represented her favorite style of hat.

"Noah, do we have any soft black crepe in the stockroom? I'm thinking of doing a braid on the brim of Lady Kaldaire's long-veiled hat."

He set down his newspaper. "Yes. Going for a

French style of mourning hat for the lady?"

"Yes. She doesn't seem to think our standard English style suits since her husband was murdered."

"I don't think English styles meet with her approval at any time." He turned his attention back to his paper and I considered how I would create a hat in Lady Kaldaire's usual style that wouldn't flout convention too badly.

I finally decided on a plaited crepe fan to fall down her back with a separate light veil over the front brim she could put up or down, depending on the situation. Or her companions.

I had both hats ready for Lady Kaldaire early the following afternoon. Since I knew she couldn't leave the house, the rules of society strictly dictating a women's behavior before a funeral, I took the hats to her.

We were in the middle of the spring and summer season for fashions. I had a few more weeks of supplying hats for this season, so I stopped at a feather supplier and a ribbon supplier with a list of supplies we had run short of in the workshop. Then with Matthew driving the horse cart, I directed him to take me to Lady Kaldaire's with her two new hats. When I climbed down and waved him home, he gave me a grateful smile and took off before the policemen of his memory could grab him.

I rang the bell at the black crepe draped doorway. The butler answered and said, "Her ladyship is in her boudoir. Follow me." Leading me upstairs, he opened the door for me and then quickly shut it as soon as I slipped inside.

Lady Kaldaire stood in the middle of the room in her corset and black shoes with black stockings, being fitted into a black skirt by a woman from the mourning store. A second woman sat on a chair stitching an adjustment to the high collar of a blouse. The widow's lady's maid was busy making adjustments to alter old mourning garb into the latest styles, her needle flashing as she sewed.

"Oh, good, Emily. Thank you for bringing those so quickly. What do you think?"

The two women from the mourning store shot me sideways glances. They were fellow women's fashion tradesmen and we would work together again. I came over and examined the material and the seams. "The quality and the cut are quite good. Black will never be your color, but at these sad times, you have no choice in color."

Both women seemed to relax and ignore me after that.

"Show me the hats."

I opened the first box and lifted out a medium-crowned, curled-down, wide-brimmed hat dyed black with black ribbon. Crepe spilled down the back in a fashionable cascade, and I demonstrated how to raise and lower the separate face veil. This was the style she liked, minus the veil, and she nodded approvingly at the ease of changing from formality to visiting with close friends.

I set that one back in its box and opened the other. I wasn't sure I'd captured what she wanted for this hat. This one had a slightly higher crown with a wide brim covered in layers of black net and a crepe braid on the base of the crown. It looked a bit like a beekeeper's helmet. I lifted it up to show her, and the two modistes ooohed.

"That is exactly what Mrs. Henderson wanted," one of them said.

"Well, please don't tell her about it until after I can wear mine," Lady Kaldaire said. "I'd hate to run into my hat the first time I attend church after the funeral."

She stared straight at me.

I knew an order when I heard it. I looked at the funeral modistes and said, "Perhaps your future customers might be interested."

They nodded and went back to their tasks.

"If you're pleased with the hats, I'll leave them here." I knew when I should leave.

"I'll try them on later. Could you come back to get your payment at five when I'll be at home?"

It was an odd request. No doubt family and close friends would be making condolence calls at five when she would be at home and receiving visitors. This must have something to do with Lord Kaldaire's murder. Did she think his killer would be calling on her today?

There was no way to find out except to return at five, dressed for the occasion. "Of course, my lady."

I went back by omnibus to the shop. After I'd seen to my customers and done sketches and measurements for two of them, I checked to see how things were in the workshop.

Our employees were hard at work under the electric lights, sunlight from the high windows on the street side also shining on their sewing and braiding and edging. Matthew was studying a mathematics text and drawing a pattern for a hat frame. Noah looked up from the hat he was putting the last stitches in and said, "We're nearly caught up from yesterday."

I remembered the conversation I had with my grandfather when he denied my father knew my mother was dying. Truly, I could think of little else. I shouldn't have pursued the issue, but I couldn't leave it alone.

"Noah, come outside in the alley for a moment. The rest of you, continue on your work. Annie, that includes you."

Annie, perhaps nine but appearing younger, clung to the broom she'd been leaning on and put on her most innocent face. As if I'd believe her.

Once we were outside, I said, "I spoke to my grandfather yesterday. He said my father didn't know my mother was dying. That you never spoke to him."

Noah's lips thinned. "This is a conversation you need to have with your father. Not with me."

"You found him? You told him?"

"You need to talk to your father. And that's all I'm going to say on the matter. Leave the past in the past, Em. I need to get back to work and so do you." He marched back into the workshop, slamming the door as he went.

I went back into the hat shop and spent the next several hours dealing with customers and accounts, but my nerves were on edge. My attention kept drifting from the task at hand, and I found I wanted to pace.

I wanted things the way they had been before Lord Kaldaire's murderer, Scotland Yard, and my father's family collided to turn my life upside down. I doubted it would ever be the same again.

Most of all, I was angry. It wasn't fair. Life wasn't fair.

And then I had to smile at myself. I spent too much time around the wealthy, watching their actions, to be surprised when my middle-class life wasn't fair. I shook off my mood and went back to work.

At four o'clock, I left Jane in charge of the shop and went upstairs to get cleaned up and dressed. I needed to look as if I belonged at a visit to a grieving widow who happened to be miles above me on the social ladder.

I chose a dark blue gown with ivory lace at the high neck and the sleeves. The hat that went with it was blue straw with a darker blue ribbon around the brim and flowers around the crown made from the same color ribbon.

I'd gained more than a few customers from wearing that hat. It made the months that I'd spent as a child practicing on ruined ribbon until I could make perfect violets, roses, daisies, and dahlias worthwhile. My mother had made me start again on some pretty good practice flowers. She told me they had to be much better than "pretty good."

As a result, I was an artist with ribbon before I was in my teens. Annie could barely sew a straight line. I kept hoping she'd develop some skills, but I feared we'd have to find another trade for her.

I met Matthew at the bottom of the stairs. He mimicked handling a horse's reins, but I shook my head. He gave me a puzzled frown. I signaled that I'd return for dinner and left to take an omnibus to Mayfair.

I reached the Kaldaire house a few minutes before five. When I arrived, the butler took me directly to the large formal parlor.

Lady Kaldaire came toward me when I walked in, her hands outstretched. "You look very sophisticated."

"You mean, not like a milliner."

"No, I mean very charming. Very attractive. That may be useful. No one will realize just how bright you are."

Lady Kaldaire was being so gracious that I immediately knew either something was amiss or society had turned upside down. "What happened?"

She slipped a piece of good notepaper out of her pocket and handed it to me. I unfolded it and read:

DON'T GET INVOLVED IN YOUR HUSBAND'S AFFAIRS OR YOU WILL PAY THE PRICE. I'LL BE WATCHING. The note was written in block capitals and unsigned.

"How did you receive this?"

"I found it among a flood of condolence notes. I suspect whoever sent this will be at the visitation."

She looked very pale. "Are you all right?" I asked, touching her arm.

She drew in a breath. "I feel so vulnerable. Someone wishes me harm. I don't know who it is and I'm frightened."

At that moment, the butler announced the first arrivals, an older couple who couldn't possibly have had anything to do with a midnight burglary.

"Keep an eye out," Lady Kaldaire whispered. "And stay."

She'd promised to pay me for two expensive hats that evening. I was staying.

Because of my red hair, a full, thick head in a gorgeous deep shade if I must say so myself, and my slender shape, I tended to cut a memorable figure in my stylish larger-brimmed hats. I made it through the first hour in Lady Kaldaire's parlor without being recognized. Or if I was recognized, no one said anything.

None of those who came to give Lady Kaldaire their sympathies appeared likely to have broken into this house in the middle of the night and opened a safe. Few of them stayed for any length of time.

Shortly after six o'clock, Lord and Lady Eddington entered, and I knew she was one person who'd say something as soon as she saw me.

I tried to stay out of her line of sight, but as soon as she gazed around the room, she spotted me. "Emily, what are you doing here? Not looking for trade, I hope."

The crowded room grew quiet.

I walked over to her, trying my best to copy the manner and attitude of the grande dames I designed for. "It's so nice to see you, Lady Eddington."

Meanwhile, my mind was churning. What probable excuse could I give for being here dressed as a guest?

"I asked her to come," Lady Kaldaire said from behind me.

I nearly sighed in relief.

"I've never heard of a milliner being invited to a home to receive condolence calls before." Lady Eddington pitched her voice to be heard in the corners of the room.

"She needs to see how this room functions with a large number of people moving about in it before she can make any suggestions on how to improve it in my new house."

What?

Lady Eddington moved her gaze from Lady Kaldaire to me. "You're a decorator now as well as a milliner?"

Before I could make a coherent sound, Lady Kaldaire said, "I like her style, Julia. And her designs would certainly be a breath of fresh air after some of the interiors I've seen recently." She kept a pleasant expression on her face as she spoke, but Lady Eddington looked skeptical.

It was all I could do not to look surprised. I knew Lady Kaldaire had a rich imagination, but I had no idea what she had planned. Whatever it was, I suspected it would take up too much of my time or be risky. Or both.

It didn't matter whether I wanted to be involved. The price Lady Kaldaire charged for keeping my secret was rising. I felt trapped.

More people entered the parlor. The two ladies and Lord Eddington continued their conversation on neutral topics, and I backed away to avoid Lady Eddington's glare.

"Lady Kaldaire must trust your taste implicitly. She's always relied on her own sense of style in the past," a man said behind me.

I turned and forced a smile. "She finds I have a different approach." I was good at sketching and at mixing and matching colors, since a lady needed a hat for every outfit and my business required me to be both tasteful and original. But an interior designer? I hoped this would be an excuse Lady Kaldaire would quickly drop.

The man standing in front of me was good-looking, with a lean face and a sharp nose that went with his angled cheekbones and thin lips. He had a full head of black and silver hair. Despite being obviously past fifty, he had a trim body that looked elegant in his black and white evening clothes. I guessed he was a fencer from the thin scar on his cheek. He stood before me with the military bearing of someone accustomed to being in charge. "Ah, the joys of youth. The creative spark has not been extinguished yet."

"Then our hostess must be young, because she is very creative." Just listen to the wild tales she told people.

I watched his pale blue eyes as I spoke. They were a lovely shade. They made a chilly accent shade in an otherwise overheated room. But right now, the expression in them frightened me. They looked as if he were choosing a spot in the woods to bury my body.

"You're obviously fond of Lady Kaldaire." His voice was an attractive baritone, but the coolness in his tone was almost as fearsome as his expression.

"I admire her very much. She's a very perceptive woman."

"She would have to be to think to use a milliner as a decorator."

So he'd heard Lady Eddington's announcement. I hadn't noticed him before she entered, and I thought I'd have noticed this man. "The two skills are not dissimilar. Both require a sense of color and balance. Of proportion and texture."

Good heavens. I was becoming as glib as Lady Kaldaire.

"The senses of an artist."

"An artist? Thank you, but I think that is more flattery than my talents deserve." I didn't really, but modesty was a woman's most valuable asset, particularly when dealing with rich and powerful men.

His smile was sardonic. "I didn't think you'd be so bourgeois as to downplay your talents. Your hat alone speaks highly of your skills."

"Thank you."

"Don't thank me for speaking the truth." Making no effort to converse with our hostess, he continued to stand behind me, making me face away from the center of the room.

"Then I will take it as a genuine compliment, Mr.-?"

"Emily," Lady Kaldaire said from behind me.

I swung around and said, "Yes, my lady?"

Her face was rigid with disapproval. "I doubt you've been introduced to this gentleman. Miss Gates, may I present Prince Maximilian of Hanover?"

CHAPTER SIX

Prince Maximilian. The man supposedly most likely to want the letter that had been in the safe in Lord Kaldaire's study.

I paused a moment to gather my wits and let my heartbeat steady. Then I held Lady Kaldaire's gaze for a second and gave the smallest nod. Turning to him, I said as I curtsied, "I'm pleased to make your acquaintance, Your Highness."

"And I yours, Miss Gates." He then turned his attention to Lady Kaldaire and I was able to step back, listening in without being part of the conversation.

The next man to walk into the room immediately caught my attention. He appeared to expect fanfare with his arrival. He posed like a statue a few feet inside the parlor, drawing my eyes to his beefy face and egg-shaped body. From his thinning hair to his fleshy lips, he looked like Lord Kaldaire come back to life.

Lady Kaldaire came forward. "Laurence, I'm so very glad to see you at this sad time."

"It's Lord Kaldaire now. I came ahead, but Cecily won't be arriving until midday tomorrow at the earliest. I'll take my brother's room, shall I?"

"Of course. Let me see to it." Her head held high as she ignored the snub from her husband's brother, Lady Kaldaire walked past him to speak in a low voice to the butler. Then she returned to receiving condolences while the new Lord Kaldaire spoke in an overly loud voice to others present.

He was even worse than his brother. I wanted to tell him to lower his voice in a house in mourning.

I was so busy watching the new Lord Kaldaire that I didn't notice Lady Eddington sidling up to me until she said, "You may have fooled Lady Kaldaire, but you haven't fooled me. You'll do anything to get ahead, won't you?"

Fortunately, she kept her voice lowered. I faced her and said, "I don't know what you mean."

"Have you used this death to steal some of *her* jewelry?"

"Of course not. *She* doesn't owe me any money," I said with a wide smile.

"Don't be cheeky. I'll find out your secrets." With a huff, she walked away, leaving me more shaken than I wanted to admit. If she found out about my father's family, she wouldn't keep quiet like Lady Kaldaire. She frightened me.

I spent another three-quarters of an hour being pleasantly vague or acting like part of the wallpaper while I listened for a clue to fall from someone's lips. Slowly, the room emptied as the guests departed. Prince Maximilian was one of the last. On his way out, he stopped and gave me a militarily precise bow.

Surprised, I gave him a deep curtsy.

Finally, only the two titled Kaldaires and I remained. "And who are you?" the new Lord Kaldaire snapped.

"Miss Gates has been assisting me. Now we have some business to see to, and I'm sure you're tired from your travels, Laurence. Dinner will be served at eight."

Lady Kaldaire's tone left a layer of frost over the room.

Even a newly christened lord knew a dismissal when he heard one. He gave his brother's wife a small bow and stomped out of the room without acknowledging me. "Have someone pick up my bags from Claridge's Hotel," he tossed over his shoulder.

Once the door closed behind him, Lady Kaldaire raised her eyebrows. "That was the new Lord Kaldaire. Much worse than the old one, I'm afraid. And his wife! Don't expect to be paid for any hats you design for her."

"Thanks for the warning." I needed to avoid aristocratic customers who didn't pay their bills. One or two deadbeats could mean the difference between sending or failing to send Matthew to a very expensive school.

"Let's go to the morning room."

I knew her checkbook was there. I also knew Lady Kaldaire felt most at home in that room, where she wouldn't be overheard by servants or newly minted lords. We took the hallway to the back of the house.

Once I shut the door, she went over to her desk and gave me pound notes for the two new hats. As she handed them to me, she said, "Laurence has forced my hand. He'll waste no time in throwing me out of here—"

"He can't do that." Lady Kaldaire had been decent to me when faced with police questions concerning the attack on her husband. I was ready to do battle on her behalf.

"Oh, my dear, he can. This is his inheritance. This property is entailed, along with the estate up north where he and his family were living, waiting for Laurence's chance to snatch the title and take over."

I felt guilty taking her money. "Surely he'll make some provision for you. Or your husband did."

She smiled. "Don't worry about me. I'll be glad to get out of this mausoleum. And the stocks, bonds, and deeds to the other properties are all in my name, not Horace's. Laurence will discover his title is an empty boast."

I was both relieved and surprised. "You'll be all right."

"Absolutely. And since I'll have to decorate a new home in Mayfair, we'll put it around that you're doing the decorating. It will give you reason to meet with me and to investigate Prince Maximilian."

I was shocked that her idea, mentioned as an excuse for my presence to Lady Eddington, wasn't discarded as quickly as a soggy hat. "Me? A decorator?"

"Just do a few sketches of the interior, decorated and furnished however you imagine. I'll hire someone else to do the actual work."

"But—"

I wasn't quick enough. "Emily, I've seen your sketches. They're wonderful. And you have an amazing eye for color. That's one of the things that makes your hats so special. Each one is the perfect shade for the outfit it's worn with."

"But that doesn't—" I was going to say, *have anything to do with sketching. That's a matter of matching ribbon to fabric to dyes.* Lady Kaldaire had some strange ideas about what milliners could accomplish.

She didn't let me finish. "Don't argue with me, Emily. I need a reason for you to come to my new house. A reason for you to drop in to see me at odd hours." Then she gave me a hard gaze. "Can you think of a better excuse for you to spend time with me while we investigate what happened to the letter and who killed my husband? And you may not realize it, but Julia

Eddington is curious about why we're spending time together. And no one likes to spread gossip more than Julia. I'm trying to protect your secret."

"Thank you." She was the only aristocrat I knew who'd try to prevent her social equals from learning a milliner's guilty secret. Being obligated to do some sketches of Lady Kaldaire's new home was not too high a price to pay.

And until the new widow found another outlet for her energies, I was stuck helping her. "All right. But how will we investigate a great-grandson of King George III?" I wasn't convinced I wanted to focus my attention on him. Maybe I just wasn't sure it was safe to investigate him. The look in his eyes had been frightening.

She gave me a conspiratorial smile. "I own the house next door to Prince Maximilian. And it's currently vacant."

"Good grief." Lady Kaldaire was full of surprises. All of them aimed at getting us both into trouble.

She continued as if I hadn't spoken. "They share a communal back garden with some other houses. Using my house as a base, you'll be able to enter and search his house."

"Next door? Is that wise?"

"I wanted to make our task as simple as possible."

She made it sound so easy. I knew better. "This will require a great deal of planning and surveillance. There are the schedules of the servants to consider."

"Oh, Emily, you're so good at everything. You'll figure it out."

I took a calming breath and attempted to reason with her. "Lady Kaldaire, I know you want the answers to your husband's death as quickly as possible, but this will take time. And patience."

"Of course. I'm a very patient woman."

From her tone of voice, I knew she wasn't joking. "You want me to draw possible interiors of your new home while I find out if Prince Maximilian was responsible for your husband's death and retrieve that ridiculous letter about Queen Victoria from him, but I have a business to run. I have customers to wait on, hats to design and their construction to oversee, supplies to buy, billing and accounts to work on—"

She waved a hand at me. "I take your point. I'm willing to help with the investigation. And you'll only need to do a few sketches to make the story plausible."

Giving me an amused smile, she continued, "Did you think your family of highwaymen are the only ones who tell stories? This is an excuse for you to be in my company. The sooner we find the letter, and Horace's killer, the sooner you'll be able to get back to your business."

That was as good as I could hope for from Lady Kaldaire that evening. "There is something you can do to help. Find out from Inspector Russell what they've learned about your husband's murder. Perhaps they found a clue that means nothing to them, but that you can link to the prince. Or someone else."

"I'll go down to Scotland Yard tomorrow and ask him."

Oh, dear. That would make Inspector Russell suspicious of her. "I think you have to wait until he comes to you. Aristocrats don't go to the police. They expect the police, like servants, to come to them."

"Nonsense. That might take ages. I don't have a bell pull to summon him. By the time he calls on me, we'll have solved this murder."

"Lady Kaldaire—"

"All those years I was married to Horace, I had to behave like a respectable matron. A wife. Well, I'm now a widow. I will immediately be thought of as elderly, expected to wear shawls, and use a cane. I can be as batty as I want, and no one will think anything of it."

Leave it to Lady Kaldaire to use the newest slang. I tried to hide my smile, but it didn't quite work. "You're enjoying this, aren't you?"

"I didn't want Horace to die. That was mean-spirited of someone. But we must make the best we can of the situation." She looked around. "This is the only room in the entire house that I'll miss."

"Do you want the new house to look like this room?" I took in the yellow walls and white lace curtains, white mantel and baseboards, yellow and pink and blue upholstery. "Bright and sunny?"

"Exactly. Now, did anyone here today seem suspicious?"

"Is the new Lord Kaldaire always like that?"

"Yes."

"Then, no. Most of your callers couldn't have broken in or bested Lord Kaldaire in a struggle. Did he have any enemies?"

"He must have, mustn't he?" The lady gave me a dry look.

"Besides me, did he owe anyone money?"

"I've discovered he hadn't paid any of our tradesmen in months. I don't know what he was doing with the money I gave him for the household bills."

"You gave him?" I was getting a surprising view of the Kaldaire marriage.

"Of course. I told you. He had the title and this house. I had the money. And the common sense."

I nodded. It sounded unusual, but it fit what I'd seen

of Lady Kaldaire. I gave up any more dissent to her plan as futile. At least until either we solved the mystery or I found a way to wiggle out.

"Who did Lord Kaldaire owe money to? Who owed him money? And what was he doing with the money you were giving him to pay me?"

"How can we find out who he owed money to?" Lady Kaldaire tapped her lips with a fingernail.

"Go through his private papers."

As soon as the words were out of my mouth, I could have kicked myself. My curiosity was getting me in deeper. Following clues in letters and bills was a sort of puzzle, a game I'd played with my grandfather when I still had parents. I'd done well with deciphering correspondence under my grandfather's guidance. But I needed to learn to guard my tongue around Lady Kaldaire.

She didn't notice my change in mood. "Laurence will probably go through them soon."

I'd made the suggestion. I couldn't take it back now, much as I'd like to. Perhaps I could stop what I saw coming. "Would he have thrown anything out?"

"No. That would be foolish. He doesn't know what's important and what's not." She smiled like the cat that had cornered a mouse. "At least not yet. Will you be available for an evening in the near future?"

I thought of all the work I had to do. Why had I opened my mouth? "Why?"

"If he and Cecily go to the opera, we'll have the evening to go through the papers. Cecily is very fond of opera."

"Won't one of the servants tell them?"

"And what will Laurence do? We'll have found what we need and have it hidden away by the time they return."

It might be the fastest way to solve this mystery. Which would be the quickest way to get my life back. And that would be heavenly. "Do you have someone to send to my shop with a message when you know they'll be gone?"

"Yes. Someone who won't go telling tales to the new Lord Kaldaire." She looked very satisfied.

She and my grandfather would make a dangerous team.

"Here is the address to my new house, so we can begin planning our investigation there when we're ready." Lady Kaldaire handed me a piece of paper. "Prince Maximilian's is the residence to the right as you look at it from the street. You can look for weaknesses in his defense at the same time."

We weren't laying siege to a castle, we were planning a break-in. I very much doubted Lady Kaldaire would ever develop the right outlook for burglary, but she was generous and she treated everyone as they deserved to be treated. She lacked aristocratic snobbery. That was more than enough to make me appreciate her.

I headed home in the twilight, the pound notes for the hats buried deep in my purse. I needed every penny for Matthew, so I was particularly wary when I heard someone following me as I walked down the alley to check on the workshop.

As the footsteps closed in on me, I grabbed the lid on the ashcan and swung around, clipping my assailant on the ear.

"Ow, Emmy, that's not nice." Petey Gates stood before me, holding the side of his head and looking more surprised than angry. His grimy derby was on the ground.

"You idiot. You should know better than to sneak up on a lady."

"You? A lady? Well, la-dee-da. I thought you was family." He bent over to pick up his hat, displaying no fear of me.

"Family doesn't hide stolen goods on one another's property without a warning. So what happened? You didn't warn me and the police took your haul from two jobs. It's your own fault."

"Three jobs." He sounded miserable. Once more, I was reminded he was not the brightest of Grandfather's descendants.

"Petey, why are you here?"

"Grandfather said I needed to apologize to you about using your factory without permission." He looked down and dragged the toe of his right boot along the paving stones. A sure sign he was mouthing the words without thinking about them.

"I forgive you, Petey, but don't ever do that again. You could have had us both locked up, and I can't afford it."

"I don't want to go inside neither."

The fabric of my patience had already been worn thin, and now Petey seemed determined to tear a hole in it. "What are you doing with your life? Nothing, while I'm running a business and trying to provide an education for Matthew."

"Why would you try to educate Matt? He's deaf." I could hear the laughter in his tone.

Furious, I said, "There are lots of things he'll be able to do if he gets an education. Besides, he's family. Don't talk about him like that. Go on. You said your piece. Now go."

"Gran said you'd be mean to me." Petey slunk off, looking as if I'd given him a thrashing. A sure way to win Gran's sympathy. Nobody messed with her grandsons. Not even me, her only granddaughter.

"Interesting family you have there."

The man's voice set all my nerves on edge and robbed me of breath. I'd thought I was alone. I gasped as I twirled, the ashcan lid in my hand ready to swing again. I had to protect the money in my purse.

CHAPTER SEVEN

Inspector Russell took a step back, his arms up to block my blow.

How had both Petey and I missed seeing or hearing Inspector Russell?

I prepared an argumentative tone since my body was going limp in relief. And tingly. Odd how he caused a funny response every time I saw him, far beyond the anger and fear from being startled. "He was only here because I spoke to Grandfather. And that wouldn't have happened if you hadn't insisted that I do so."

"Miss Gates, we had two murders in the vicinity of where you were the other night. If you're not our murderer—"

"I'm not." I snapped out the words.

"Then you might have witnessed something. If the murderer thinks that, you could be the next victim." He sounded somber and weary.

I shivered despite my intention not to show any emotion. That was the unsavory side effect of investigating a murder. The murderer would try to stop the investigation. Lady Kaldaire should be hearing this lecture, not me. "You should be home by your fireside eating dinner, not spending your off-duty hours hanging around here."

He gave me a rogue's smile. "But the most interesting things happen here. With the best-dressed lady in town."

My cheeks felt so hot they must have flamed at his compliment. "There's nothing here to interest you now. Go home, Inspector."

He held up a hand to stop me before I walked away. "I didn't follow my instincts once and people died. I don't want to make the same mistake again. Especially not with you."

I felt warmth inside me. People rarely worried about my well-being. "I have to go in and warm up what our neighbor left us tonight for our dinner. I won't go out again." I spoke quietly.

His voice was even softer when he said, "At least you have Matthew and Noah and Annie to share it with."

I doubt he meant for me to hear it, but I heard his words and the sound of emptiness inside them. "You don't have anyone?"

"If I did, do you think I'd be hanging around your alley?" He sounded both amused and hurt.

I spoke before I thought. "Would you care to join us? Mrs. McCauley always leaves us more than enough."

"No, I can't just drop in to dinner…"

My hands went to my hips. "With the grandchildren of crazy-like-a-fox Zachariah Gates?"

He held up his hands in surrender. "I didn't say that, Miss Gates."

I fought down the pout that sprang up every time I remembered my criminal relatives. "You didn't have to."

His face went hard and expressionless. "Because you said it for me. I thought there was more to you than that." He tipped his bowler to me and sauntered off.

He was playing with me, and I didn't like it. After I was certain Petey hadn't been in the workshop again, I stomped upstairs to find Noah, Matthew, and Annie waiting. I quickly changed into a work dress, plain muslin with marks and stains from cooking and hatmaking, and went into the kitchen. "It's roast chicken, bread, and vegetables," I called out to Noah as I worked. "It'll be hot in a few minutes."

"Good. We're hungry."

"Have you seen to the horse?"

"Yes. Matthew took care of him while I locked up the workshop. Jane locked up the shop."

I didn't have anything more to ask while I readied dinner and set it on the table. Noah and Matthew came out and devoured the food as if they hadn't been fed in the past week, and I thought scrawny Annie might have eaten her weight in food. I nibbled, trying to puzzle out my surprise visit from the Scotland Yard inspector.

It didn't make sense. Petey waiting for me I could understand. Grandfather wouldn't have been happy if anyone in the family didn't do as he said. Had Inspector Russell followed him? Or did he believe I knew something more than I'd told him?

I wished I'd seen more, so I could tell him who killed Lord Kaldaire. Then I wouldn't have to worry about who might be following me around London besides Inspector Russell.

He could follow me all he wanted.

Noah finally tired of the silence and asked why I was so quiet.

While I brought in more tea, I told him about Lady Kaldaire's "request" for me to sketch the interior of her new home and Petey's apology.

Noah poured a cup, took a sip, and then said, "I know you're not concerned about anything Petey says, because he's probably forgotten it already. But designing an interior? Do you have enough time to run the shop, design hats, and take on this commission for Lady Kaldaire?"

"She only wants me to do some sketches for her, not take on the project. She'll have someone else do the work. One of my other customers is getting very nosy about why I was at Kaldaire House. Lady Kaldaire dreamed this up so I had a reason to be there. So no one else finds out about the Gates gang."

He looked at me over the rim of his cup. "I understand why you're going along with this. Your mother was just as secretive about her connection with the Gateses."

"It won't take me away from the shop for long, or often. And she is going to pay me for the sketches. Money for Matthew's schooling."

At least, I hoped she would.

"I don't like this, Emily. She just has to snap her fingers, and you come running. We'll get the money another way if we have to." He scowled at me. "What happened over there the other night?"

"I told a lie to the police, and she backed me up. I owe her."

"She *owns* you. I would have thought your grandfather would have taught you better than that." Noah leaned back in his chair and lit his pipe, scowling at me the entire time.

"I like her. I can't explain it. She's not our class, but she's not like the rest of my customers. She has a zest for life. She appears to be following all of the upper class's customs, but then you realize she's only going so far to meet their expectations. Far enough to get along, but she's not behaving the way society thinks or expects of a lady." I put more sugar in my tea. I needed it.

"Well, she has you doing what she wants."

"So far, Noah, it's what I want, too." I wondered how long that would last.

We fell silent, staring at each other. Matthew watched us for a while, no doubt aware of the tension between us, and then walked away to read a book.

Our apprentice Annie, who had entered our lives when we found her sharing a stall with our horse in the dead of winter, apparently alone in the world, was always afraid of disagreements. She had long since left the table. I suspected she'd already disappeared into some dark corner.

"I think we frightened Annie," I said.

"She is terribly timid," Noah replied. "How old do you think she is? She was only working at a six-year-old level at the local school when we enrolled her."

During the school term, she could only work as our apprentice after school and on weekends. I wanted her to get an education, but at that rate, she wouldn't pay us back or learn any part of the trade for several years. "She says nine, and I think I believe her. Have you had any better luck finding out where she came from or what happened to her before she moved into the stable?"

"I've learned nothing from the people in the area of the stables," Noah said, rising from the table and taking his cup and saucer into the kitchen.

"No one in our neighborhood seems to know anything about her, either. And Annie won't tell me a thing." I did want to know. Why did Annie cling to me whenever I asked her about her past?

CHAPTER EIGHT

Over the next few days, Lord Kaldaire's funeral was attended by the great and the good men of London and covered by all the newspapers. Also mentioned was that the new Lord and Lady Kaldaire had taken up residence in Kaldaire House.

Except for a glance at the newspapers and an occasional sick feeling in my stomach when I pictured poor Lord Kaldaire collapsed on the floor, I pushed all thoughts of the Kaldaires from my mind. I had plenty to do in my shop.

After dinner one night, I was working hard on designing newly ordered hats. A tap on the shop door didn't catch my attention, but Noah, who'd been working with me, heard it and answered the door. He returned within moments with a note that had my name on the outside.

Tearing it open, I wasn't surprised to find the message was from Lady Kaldaire and she wanted my assistance immediately. Then she said to make sure the new Lord and Lady Kaldaire had left for the opera before I showed myself. I should come in by the French doors in the breakfast room.

She was enjoying this too much. "I have to go out for a while."

"Lady Kaldaire?" Noah asked.

I nodded.

"Emily, do you think this is wise?"

"It's the best of a large selection of bad choices." I gave him what I hoped passed for a smile. "I'll be back as soon as I can. Don't wait up."

"Of course I'm going to wait up. I should go with you."

"Better you don't." I finished the task I was working on and went to my room to change. Matthew glanced up from the book he was reading with a puzzled expression. I waved and he returned to the story. I looked in on Annie and found her in bed curled up in a ball. The same way she had slept in the straw meant for the horse when we found her in the cold.

"I have my key," I told Noah and left our building.

Once again I entered Kaldaire House by the French doors and found my way through the dimly lit house to the study. At least this time I was properly dressed for a social call.

When I knocked, I heard Lady Kaldaire's voice say, "Enter." I found her bathed in light behind the desk going through piles of papers. "They've been picked up but not organized," she told me.

I pulled up a chair and began to look through one of the piles. It quickly became apparent the late Lord Kaldaire hadn't been paying his bills.

"What had he been doing with the money?" I asked. "Any clue yet?"

"That's why you're here. To help me find out," her ladyship said, a pair of pince-nez glasses perched on her nose. "By the way, I like the hat. I've not seen that one before."

"Something I whipped up for clerks and shop girls to look elegant while riding the omnibus," I replied. "Had you seen any of these letters requesting payment from," I flipped through a stack of correspondence, "every tradesman in the area?"

"No. Whenever I asked him about a complaint, he said he'd taken care of the problem."

A letter caught my attention. "Who is Edward, Viscount Taylor?"

"A friend of Horace's. A bit younger than he was and terribly earnest. Why?"

"In this letter, he threatens to kill Lord Kaldaire. Over a young lady." I looked up to see Lady Kaldaire's eyes widen.

"Horace wasn't one to get seriously involved with a lady. Or any woman, for that matter. He was more passionate about his position in society and betting at his club than about any woman. Including me."

I gazed at her over the letter. "Then who is 'my darling Amanda'?"

Lady Kaldaire raised an eyebrow. "I don't know."

We both searched for more correspondence from Edward, Viscount Taylor, without success. I did, however, find an unsigned letter saying: *You need to desist, or the Secretary of the Club will learn of your behavior.*

The handwriting matched that of the viscount.

"Is Viscount Taylor a member of Lord Kaldaire's club?"

"Yes. The Imperial. Full of upstanding gentlemen, many of them titled. Dreadfully dull."

"Who is the secretary?"

"I have no idea. It would have to be someone who is both dreadfully dull and full of himself."

I suppressed a smile. Lady Kaldaire was becoming more outspoken by the moment. "Who would know of an Amanda in Viscount Taylor's life?"

After thinking for a moment, she spoke with glee. "Marjorie Whitaker. Dowager Marchioness of Linchester. She knows the Taylors well."

"You need to contact her as soon as possible and find out about Amanda." I didn't need to be involved.

"We need to visit her together." There was more than a hint of steel in her voice.

"I need to do up those drawings for you and run my millinery shop. Besides, she'll speak more freely if it's only you."

"I suppose you're right. We are old friends." She flipped through more papers. "What was he doing with my money? Clearly it wasn't paying the tradesmen."

"You said your husband liked to gamble."

"Not that much."

I thought of *my darling Amanda* and hesitated to bring up my next idea. "Could he have been blackmailed?"

My words brought peals of laughter from Lady Kaldaire. After she caught her breath and dried her eyes, she said, "He would have to be in possession of a secret or a vice or a passion. My husband had none of those. He was as stuffy as they come." She stopped for a moment and thought. "Poor Horace. That sounds so sad. As if he missed out on his life."

Her words silenced us both of a minute. Then I said, "Pretend you didn't know him and search through these papers for some evidence of a reason why someone would blackmail him. Sometimes people surprise us. And it would explain what he did with the money."

I began with the stack of papers in front of me. Nothing but dunning notices. "How much more time do we have?"

"At least an hour."

I started on another stack while Lady Kaldaire perused letters at her leisure. As much as I wanted to tell her to hurry up, I knew I'd be wasting my breath. The lady hadn't had timing drummed into her by a larcenous family.

"Interesting. Here's a letter from Laurence asking Horace for money. Told him not to tell Cecily or me. Now there is a man who would have secrets." She tapped the letter with one finger.

And get himself blackmailed, I said to myself. Aloud I asked, "Is it possible someone attacked the wrong brother?"

"Really, Emily. They don't look alike."

"I thought they looked a great deal alike. Of course, I didn't know either man well…"

We both froze as the bell, footsteps, and voices could be heard in the front hall. "Cecily has a headache," a male voice reached us. "Where is Roberta?"

"I'm not certain, my lord. I believe she has retired."

"Good old Gregson," Lady Kaldaire said with a smile.

"Then why is there light coming from under the study door?"

As footsteps approached the study door, I darted behind the draperies. In the style of well-to-do houses everywhere, the draperies were hung a foot or two into the room. The space between the window panes and the draperies allowed for air to be trapped, separating the frozen drafts of winter slipping in through the cracks in window sashes from the heated air of the room.

"Roberta. What on earth are you doing in here?"

"These papers were knocked onto the floor when Horace was attacked." I heard Lady Kaldaire's voice getting closer to me. "I was looking for a clue to the identity of his murderer."

"Oh, please. Leave the detecting to the police."

"I'm going to bed," a bored female voice said at a distance. That had to be the new Lady Kaldaire.

"You're home early from the opera. Is Cecily unwell?" Lady Kaldaire said.

"Headache. I think it was the singing."

"Well, it's time for me to go to bed, too. Good night, Laurence. Sleep well."

I heard her cross the carpet and then give a little gasp. I glanced through the gap to see the new Lord Kaldaire gripping her wrist.

"Don't be vulgar," she said with a sneer in her voice.

"We'll talk tomorrow. And whatever Horace allowed, this is my study now. Remember that."

"Don't you want his killer found?"

"Let the men who are paid to do it find his murderer." He let go of her wrist with a little toss. "Good night, Roberta."

"Don't be peevish, Laurence. Good night."

"It's Lord Kaldaire, now." I couldn't see his face, but I knew from the sound of his voice he was furious. And closer to my hiding place. Lady Kaldaire could certainly goad him, but was that wise?

The draperies were pulled back and I found myself face-to-face with the new Lord Kaldaire. "Who are you and what are you doing in my study?" he demanded.

From the look on his face, I knew I was in trouble, and like the stories I heard about so many of his class, I suspected he could be violent.

"I'm Miss Gates. Lady Kaldaire asked for my assistance in going through her husband's correspondence." I made a good show of acting as if I should be there, but my knees were ready to give way beneath me. At least my voice hadn't failed me yet.

"You won't find any correspondence behind the draperies," he said with a sneer. "Gregson! Gregson!" he shouted.

"Yes, my lord?"

"Ring Scotland Yard. We have a burglar."

"Nonsense, Laurence," Lady Kaldaire said. "She is here because I invited her."

"You don't invite anyone into my study. Stay right there," he added when I tried to move around him into the room.

I still planned to walk into the room. Apparently, I had to wait until he decided to move before I could do so. Despite the seriousness of my situation, I was too angry at this brand-new boorish lord and his lack of reasonableness to consider how the night was going to end.

He finally walked over to Lady Kaldaire and I stepped into the room.

"Did I give you permission to move?"

I only stared at him, thinking that was the best reply I could make.

He strode back and glared at me, shoving his face toward mine. He wasn't the first aristocrat to try to bully me. Close up, I could see wrinkles beginning to form in his pudgy face. He was clean-shaven and well groomed, but his breath smelled of brandy and rotten meat. I put a hand in front of my nose and mouth and turned away, making a face.

He grabbed my wrist, dragged me forward, and gave me a hard shove into a chair. At my first move, he raised his hand to me. "Stay there, you—tart."

CHAPTER NINE

"Laurence." Lady Kaldaire strode over to him. "You simply misunderstand. There is no cause for being rude."

"She was Horace's dollymop, wasn't she?"

I rose, furious at his allegation. "I certainly was not."

"It would explain a few things," he said, smirking as he walked away.

"Only if you have a fevered imagination and no taste," Lady Kaldaire said, holding me back when I moved to go after him.

She was right. He was trying to goad me. And he was doing a good job. I relaxed my fists and dropped back into the chair. Lady Kaldaire sat in another nearby.

Then, after an interminable wait, Detective Inspector Russell walked in with his sergeant. From the expression on his face, all I could think was everything was over. Matthew would never get to school and my business, along with my reputation, was destroyed.

I tried giving him a smile, but the muscles in my face quickly sagged at the sight of his glare.

Lord Kaldaire went through a lengthy explanation of how I'd entered his study, in fact his house, without his permission and was a burglar. He sounded affronted, annoyed, and foolish, especially when he called me a dollymop to the inspector, whose face lost all expression.

When he finally wound down, Lady Kaldaire refuted his claims in the tones of an empress.

Finally, Inspector Russell walked over to me. I stood and faced him. "Since Lady Kaldaire vouches for you, there's no reason for me to take you into custody."

"I demand you arrest her. This is my house, and I don't want her in it," Lord Kaldaire said, glowering at the inspector.

The inspector turned his glare from Lord Kaldaire to me. "But if I get called to this house a third time because of you, I will take you in front of a magistrate and charge you with every crime I can think of. Is that clear?"

"Yes, sir."

"Good night, Miss Gates."

I curtsied to him and to Lady Kaldaire and left the house.

* * *

I spent the next morning putting the finishing touches on hats I'd promised to two members of the Ascot set as well as several I kept in stock for impulse buyers. Leaving Jane to take care of the shop on her own, I spent time in the workshop checking on the repairs to a favorite hat of an elderly customer. This gave me an opportunity to show Annie and the women who helped as trimmers techniques on how to renew fabric using steam, mild soap, alcohol, and gasoline, and which materials needed which method.

I had Annie pull out the board to dry the lace after it had been cleaned and showed her how to pin the fabric to the heavily padded side of the board.

Lady Kaldaire sent me a note in the early afternoon to visit at her new residence. On my way out with my sketchbook, I reminded Jane of which customers should be coming into the shop and who needed to pay a deposit or be reminded of their bill.

Approaching Lady Kaldaire's new home, I saw the building was in the middle of the block on a quiet street of residences with black wrought-iron railings, black shutters, and dark bricks. At least they wouldn't show the worst effects of the millions of coal fires burning in London daily.

The house on the right, the one that Lady Kaldaire said belonged to Prince Maximilian, looked closed up. Lace curtains in every window partially hid the draperies pulled behind them. As I walked along the sidewalk, I looked into the kitchen area down the cement stairwell to the tradesmen's entrance. There were no curtains in those windows, but I didn't see any light or signs of life, either.

If I was going to successfully break into Prince Maximilian's home, I needed to know how many servants he kept and what their schedules were.

And then I wondered if I was going to be foolish enough to break into the house of someone who didn't owe me money.

Curiosity won out over sensibility. I walked up the stairs to Prince Maximilian's front door and rang the bell. A tall, thin, rather scary-looking man with a mouthful of prominent teeth and a beak-like nose opened the door. "This isn't Lady Kaldaire's, is it?" I asked.

"No." The door shut in my face.

I stood there for a moment, staring at the door. As I turned to leave, the man opened it again and said, "Come in."

I wasn't certain I wanted to. Then Prince Maximilian appeared next to his man. "Please, Miss Gates. Come in."

"That's very kind of you, but I'm looking for Lady Kaldaire's new residence. I have an appointment with her." I held up my sketchbook as a sort of explanation.

"More hats?" He sounded amused.

"No. She's asked me to work up some sketches of the interior of her new home."

"Ah, yes, I recall. A lady of many talents," he murmured. "Lady Kaldaire has taken the house next door." He pointed. "May I escort you over there?"

"It's really not necessary, Your Highness."

"Please. A simple 'Prince' will do. And I enjoy watching a talent at work. You'd be giving me a treat, Miss Gates."

I gave him a smile, wondering what he was up to. "Then of course. Please join us, Prince."

He picked up his hat, gloves, and cane from the table inside the door and joined me on the steps. He gave me his arm and we climbed down one set, walked a short distance, and went up the corresponding steps next door.

At our ring, a maid answered the door. "In here, Emily," Lady Kaldaire's voice rang out.

"I have Prince Maximilian with me," I replied as I walked toward the open double doors to my left.

Lady Kaldaire came to the doorway. "Prince, it's so nice to see you again. To what do I owe this unexpected pleasure?"

"I'm afraid Miss Gates came to my door by accident. I thought I'd come watch her process for sketching interiors of your new home." Maximilian sounded as if he found this whole charade amusing.

As if he recognized it for what it was.

"Please come in. You're certainly welcome. I can't even offer you a cup of tea, though," Lady Kaldaire said as she bustled over to give him both her hands.

"I don't need tea, my dear lady. Only the company of two women as lovely and clever as yourselves." The prince dropped her hands and faced me. "Now, Miss Gates, let's see what ideas you come up with for this house."

I took a deep breath and walked into the bare dining room. At least I hoped it was a dining room. There was a crystal chandelier in the center of the ceiling and a chair rail around the room. "What basic color would you like in a dining room?"

"Blue. No, gold," Lady Kaldaire said. "No, blue."

"I can combine them," I told her.

"Good. Now I think across the hall—"

"Let's finish in here first. Do you already have furniture you plan to use in this room?"

"No. I need to get some, except for the morning room. Most of the furniture in Kaldaire House belongs to the house. Belongs to Laurence now," she said.

"What style do you plan to buy? Art Nouveau? Arts and Crafts? Queen Anne? Chippendale?"

She looked around, appearing a little overwhelmed. "I don't know. I've never had the opportunity to choose before."

I wasn't surprised. The aristocracy kept everything as it was, generation after generation. "Let me pace off the room and do a quick sketch of the floor plan and then we can go across the hall." I gave her a smile, then set down my sketchpad and paced off the distance from the window to the door, then from the fireplace to the far wall.

"You have talent," the prince said. He sounded amazed.

I glanced over and saw he was looking at the sketch

I'd made of the *Lady in Blue.*

"I seldom get a chance to practice my drawing skills. I had a chance to do a pencil copy of the painting, and you see the results."

Prince Maximilian raised his brows. Did they all learn that skeptical expression in the aristocratic nursery? "You included the dimensions of the painting."

Oh, dear. I should have erased that. "It gives me a feel for the proportions. I don't often get sizes right. That's the reason I need to measure these rooms. I don't know how I'm going to get the height of the walls, though."

"This floor and the two above it have ten-foot ceilings," the prince told me. When I looked at him, surprised, he added, "This house is exactly like the one next door where I live. Who knows? When you get done, I may find I have a commission for you, too."

Even if this weren't a ruse, I wouldn't want to take any employment from him. I'd again caught him looking at me as if he were measuring me for a coffin, a thin smile playing on his lips. I paced across the room in silence.

"I think perhaps a mahogany, triple-pedestal, claw-and-ball foot table in here. With Queen Anne style chairs," Lady Kaldaire said.

I jumped, still aware of the prince's gaze on me. "Perhaps pastel blue seat cushions to go with pastel blue and gold draperies. Do you have any artwork you want displayed in this room?"

"The *Lady in Blue*?" Prince Maximilian asked, barely concealing his smirk.

"I wouldn't have it in my house. As it happens, it belongs to Laurence." Lady Kaldaire strode across the room, tapping her parasol on the bare floor.

"Carpets?" I asked.

"I'm sure we'll find something."

I was surprised the prince stayed with us for the entire session, while I asked questions and Lady Kaldaire gave vague answers. If he would have left, I'd have been free to depart for my shop.

Instead, I remained as I discovered she liked inlaid designs in furniture, comfortable seating, and lots of space in her rooms. "Kaldaire House was always so crowded, with dark, heavy furniture sitting everywhere. I want some light in this house."

"Then I doubt you'd like my home, Lady Kaldaire. Lots of heavy, dark furniture. You'd find it oppressive," the prince said.

"Nonsense. I'm sure it suits you."

"Then perhaps both of you ladies would like to have tea with me today."

"Oh, I'm sure you—" I began, thinking how much work waited for me at the shop.

"We'd love to, wouldn't we, Emily?" Lady Kaldaire said over my protest.

Maneuvered once again into doing something I didn't want to do involving Prince Maximilian, I managed a polite, "Yes, my lady."

We'd hit the principal rooms: the dining room, the morning room, the parlor, what Lady Kaldaire called the music room, and her suite of rooms on the second floor. I doubted she needed me for anything else.

"So come along. We're done here for the day." She sent the maid back to Kaldaire House, gave the prince her arm, and the three of us walked next door.

As soon as I saw the parlor, the word "Teutonic" jumped into my head. An eagle motif was carved into the mantelpiece and a massive cabinet. All the wood was dark. All the upholstered chairs and sofas were large and solid, with dark patterned fabrics. A suit of armor in one corner and a coat of arms over the mantel completed the look.

Prince Maximilian might be the brother of an English duke, but he'd always be German in my mind. And quite possibly in his own.

However, the tea his skeletal manservant brought in, a silver service with delicate china cups and saucers and thin sugar biscuits on a small tray, was pure English. Lady Kaldaire served the three of us.

We went through the usual topics of weather, relatives and other aristocrats, and the arts. When we ground to a halt, Prince Maximilian rose and walked over to the cabinet. "This is a very old piece. Built by a master carpenter to provide several hiding places during periods of religious and political warfare."

"You can hide people in that?" I asked in surprise.

"No, my dear Miss Gates. It is designed to hide papers, letters, documents. Things that might incriminate the author." He gave me an amused smile. "But you knew that already."

I would have if I'd been thinking about something besides work. "Then I'm sure in times past it helped your ancestors avoid embarrassing questions." And raised a new one. Why was he showing me this?

The cabinet was the logical place to hide the letter stolen from Lord Kaldaire. Was the prince daring me to break in and find it? But then, how would he know I was searching for it? Who had Lady Kaldaire talked to about the missing letter?

I set down my teacup and walked over to him. I didn't have to fake the eagerness I put in my voice when I said, "Show me."

CHAPTER TEN

"But how can I be sure you're not a burglar?" I was almost certain Prince Maximilian was laughing at me. His expression and tone made clear he knew what Lady Kaldaire and I were up to.

"You have documents hidden in there that would start a war?" I tried hard to sound scandalized.

He did laugh then. "Nothing that would start a war in this day and age, but a man chooses which secrets to keep. This is a good place to keep them."

"I'm sure it is." I ran my hand over wood that had been polished to smoothness over the years. The top part opened with two doors, the bottom into four large drawers, and all had handles of metal shaped like eagle shields on rings. "May I open the doors and look in?"

"Of course."

I pulled the doors open and looked inside. There were dozens of pigeonholes, some with papers and envelopes inside, and dozens more little drawers. I didn't see any blank spaces that could hide a secret panel. This would take time to check out.

Time I didn't expect to be given. Prince Maximilian was looking at me as if he were sizing me up for a hangman's noose.

"What a lovely and unique piece of furniture. I congratulate you on your good fortune to inherit this from your family." It sounded like something these aristocrats would say.

"Please, Miss Gates, I expected less stuffiness from you."

I gave him a smile. "I think it is incomparable. You are a very lucky man."

Lady Kaldaire looked at the abundance of cubbyholes and tiny drawers and said, "I'd have to have directions written down to remember where any of the hiding places were. Otherwise, I'd hide something and forget how to find it again."

"I'm sure you don't give yourself enough credit," the prince said.

"I'm sure I do if it's deserved. I have no talent for anything mechanical. Show me how you open one. One that's empty, unless you have a fabulous jewel tucked away to admire." Lady Kaldaire gave him an eager smile.

Too eager. I could see right away he wouldn't honor her request. "No, but I might be persuaded to let Miss Gates try to find one."

"Oh, do, Emily. You're so clever, I imagine you could do it."

Wonderful. Lady Kaldaire was showing her enthusiasm too clearly, and the prince wore a smile that said he was waiting for me to break in and try to open all the compartments that master carpenters had hidden away centuries ago.

"I doubt I can, but I'd love to try. How many hidden places are there in this cabinet?"

"Four, for the four gospels. You may try for a minute if you'd like, Miss Gates." The challenge in his eyes was unmistakable.

"You don't mind? Although I doubt I could find anything in a minute." I put some innocent eagerness in my voice. I'd heard it frequently in my shop from debutantes attempting to get another hat out of the tight purse strings of an aunt or guardian, and I enjoyed mimicking my customers.

He stepped back and made a sweeping gesture toward the cabinet.

I stepped forward and ran my hand over surfaces, feeling for a spot that was worn from being touched many times. Nothing. I spread out the area I touched and felt for joints that were slightly off as well as worn. The cabinet felt like what it was: a magnificently crafted piece of furniture.

I was aware of the prince moving and Lady Kaldaire putting out a hand to stop him, but, open or closed, my eyes weren't seeing. I'd shut off my sight and worked strictly by touch. I began to feel the grain of the wood under centuries of polish.

That eventually led me to a tiny nick at the bottom of a drawer. I pushed and slid my fingers over the spot. My eyes sprang wide as a piece of wood dropped open into my hand. "Oh, dear. Have I broken it?"

"No. See? There's a small hiding place under this drawer," the prince said as he studied me.

Uncomfortable under his gaze, I bent over and peered into the gap. It was empty. And it was too small to fit more than a couple of short notes.

I straightened up and gave Lady Kaldaire a sigh. "It's empty. None of Prince Maximilian's secrets are hidden there."

My overacting was enough to gain a smile from both of them.

"We've taken up too much of your time, Prince. I have to return to deal with my newly arrived sister-in-law, and I'm sure Emily wants to draw up some designs." Lady Kaldaire slipped her gloves back on and I followed her example.

"You're certain I've not damaged the cabinet?" I asked.

He put the piece back in place. I couldn't see where it had come off. "Not at all. I'm amazed you could find the release. My congratulations." He took my hand and stared into my eyes. "I must remember never to underestimate you."

I shrugged. "I'm not important enough to concern you. I thank you for allowing me to poke around in your cabinet. It was great fun." I hoped he bought my act. I knew there were three hidden spots in the cabinet I'd not found, and I was willing to bet the letter Lady Kaldaire wanted me to find was in one of them.

"Come along, Emily. I want you to walk me back to Kaldaire House." She had her parasol and was headed toward the door.

I grinned at the prince. "Thank you, Your Highness. It's been a lovely afternoon, but I must be on my way."

He glanced at Lady Kaldaire's back and then nodded, his expression showing he was reconsidering my abilities. "It's been a pleasure to discover your talents."

His manservant silently appeared and held the door open for us. After our formal good-byes, I followed Lady Kaldaire out and walked down the pavement with her.

After a minute, she said, "One down. Three to go. That was brilliant, Emily. You obviously know what you're doing."

"My grandfather taught me to open puzzle boxes. They were always fun." As was everything I did with my father's family before my mother died. "You do realize he knows we're after the letter."

"Nonsense. Why would you think that?"

"I could see it in his eyes. He was taunting us with that cabinet."

"Well, we'll just have to be cleverer than he is."

"How many people have you told about the letter?"

"No one." She looked aghast. "Discussing the legitimacy of our royal family would be social suicide."

"Then how many people have you asked about a letter missing from the safe the night your husband died?"

"I may have—hinted that a very old letter disappeared at the time of Horace's murder and asked if anyone had heard of someone having such a thing for sale."

Lady Kaldaire's hints were more like orders. "And Prince Maximilian has heard about your questions and knows you are hunting for the letter."

"Nonsense. I doubt he listens to gossip."

"I'm sure he does if it concerns him."

She looked at me with that "the servants are getting above themselves" stare and shook her head. "Foolish Horace, keeping that letter. If he weren't dead, I'd—"

"You don't have to rescue the letter, my lady."

She stopped and looked straight into my eyes. "Yes, I do. I need to finish the tasks Horace couldn't finish. Please help me. I could tell the police about the night my husband died, but I won't. I'd rather have you as my ally."

I could go to jail if I were caught breaking into the prince's home. I could hang if I were convicted of murder.

It was odd that Lady Kaldaire and I were willing to work together and that she would say "please" to me. We had nothing in common. Not social status nor age nor wealth. Perhaps it was because she was never sneaky. I always knew what she wanted of me. And she paid on time.

Lady Kaldaire smiled complacently as she tapped her parasol on the pavement. "Shall we proceed? I'm looking forward to seeing your sketches, Emily."

As we walked along, I said, "Hypothetically speaking, who else would gain from your husband's death besides someone who wanted that letter? Was there anything else in the safe?"

"I don't think so."

"But it's possible that there was something else in there. Documents someone else would kill to get their hands on."

"I suppose." Then Lady Kaldaire's tone changed from thoughtful to certain. "Horace wasn't clever enough to stumble over the evidence in two scandals."

"Would his brother kill to gain the title?"

"Yes. And will he be surprised when he realizes he's getting a valueless title." The lady gave a tiny chuckle.

"So we have to consider the new Lord Kaldaire for our villain. Who else?"

"We have two choices. I doubt there is anyone else."

I glanced at her. "If the police are willing to suspect me simply because I was present, then I suspect there are one or two more people who should be looked into."

She walked in silence for a minute. "How would we find these other candidates?"

I admitted I had no idea.

* * *

The next day, I was able to carry out my business without being interrupted by the police, my father's family, or Lady Kaldaire until three in the afternoon. Then Lady Eddington showed up at my shop.

"I'm looking for something in green to go with this

fabric," she said as she examined the hats on display, sighing in dismissal.

She was always a hard-to-please customer. Today she seemed to be more difficult than ever, but I was always up for a challenge where millinery designs were concerned. And I'd learned never to deliver a hat into her hands until I was paid if I could possibly manage it. I examined the sample of lawn, a brilliant white with green stripes of different widths. "How will you be wearing this fabric?"

"Afternoon garden parties."

"What sort of parasol will you be carrying? What sort of jewelry will you use to accent the gown?"

She frowned at what she must consider my impertinence. "Why would you want to know that?"

"To determine how best to dress up the hat. Would you prefer a white hat with green detail or a green hat with white detail?"

"Oh, I think a white hat. Green ribbon and feathers to match this." She pointed to the swatch. "And silver details. How are you coming with your designs for Lady Kaldaire's new house?"

"Slowly, I'm afraid." I tried to drag her attention back to her order. "A high crown or a low one?"

"Oh, somewhere in the middle. No, a high crown. Will she be taking a lot of furniture from Kaldaire House?"

"Not a lot, I wouldn't think. And the brim. Wide and flat, since you'll wear it out of doors to garden parties?"

"Yes. Roberta seems terribly cut up by Horace's death," Lady Eddington said in an offhand manner. Then she looked me in the eye. "Murder. Really. Who do you think did it, Miss Gates?"

"I couldn't guess. None of my customers, surely." I

made a great show of writing down all of Lady Eddington's directions in my order book. "High crown, wide, flat brim…"

"I've heard Horace, the former Lord Kaldaire, was involved in scandal. Poor Roberta. How she'll be able to hold her head up after this is anybody's guess." Her tone was calculating. I wondered if Lady Kaldaire had her true measure.

My first reaction was to say something scathing, but that wouldn't help me find out what scandal Lady Eddington was referring to. And wouldn't help me keep customers, even customers who didn't pay on time. "Lord Kaldaire involved in a scandal? I find that hard to credit."

"He was. It was over some shady business involved in theft or a swindle and a lady of low repute. I wouldn't be surprised to learn Roberta bumped him off herself, or whatever the slang is these days."

Two of us could play this game. "Lady Kaldaire would be sorry to learn she was sharing her husband's affections. Any woman would. Who is this lady of questionable reputation? Not a customer of mine, I hope."

Lady Eddington looked at me through widened eyes and gave a sniff. "I'm not one to spread gossip. You'll have to ask elsewhere."

No, I decided, Lady Eddington wasn't one to provide gossip to a mere tradesman. However, she didn't appear to be above trying to pry it out of me. I stared back and asked, "Let me get our card with your measurements. How much do you plan to spend on this hat?"

* * *

That evening, I was sketching interiors for Lady Kaldaire's new house while Matthew read, Annie drew, and Noah snored. A crash that sounded like it came from the shop downstairs sent me to my feet while Noah awoke and sat up. He gave me a puzzled look.

"I'd better go check," I said and headed down our interior staircase to the shop.

Movement frequently alerted Matthew, and he bounded down the steps with youthful enthusiasm before Noah joined me. At the bottom of the stairs, I flipped on the overhead light before I poked my head through the doorway.

I saw immediately that the glass in the street door was broken. "Noah, we'll need to—" I began before I saw the rock wrapped in paper with a string around it.

I walked over to the rock as Noah looked past me and said, "We've got boards in the workshop that'll cover the hole until morning." He headed out to the alley and the workshop beyond.

Unwrapping the rock, I read the note. In block capitals, it read, *STAY AWAY FROM KALDAIRE HOUSE.*

CHAPTER ELEVEN

The sounds of a scuffle came from the back of the shop. Running toward the thuds and groans, I found Noah collapsed on the dirty bricks of the alley and a dark figure running away. I knelt next to him and dabbed at the blood coming from a cut above his left eye with my handkerchief. "Are you all right?"

"He jumped me as I came out the door." With Matthew's help, Noah rose and propped himself up on the outside wall.

"Can you make it upstairs? Matthew and I will cover the broken glass." I shoved the note and the string in my pocket. Those words would only confirm Noah's worries concerning Lady Kaldaire.

He shook off our hands. "I'm not such an old man I can't take a few blows. I don't think he meant to hurt me as much as scare me."

"Well, he scared me. Go sit down inside. Matthew and I will get the boards." I signaled Matthew and we unlocked the workshop and collected a couple of boards, a hammer, and nails.

When we locked up the workshop again and crossed the alley, I shoved the note and the string in an ashcan. I saw no reason to upset Noah. I felt bad enough that his blows were probably meant for me.

* * *

In the second post the next day, a summons

appeared requesting my drawings at Kaldaire House at four that afternoon.

After I'd seen Noah's bruises that morning, Kaldaire House was the last place I wanted to go. However, I wanted to protect my livelihood more than I wanted to admit to being frightened.

And I wanted to find the culprit and stop him so I could keep Noah safe from more attacks.

Leaving the shop in Jane's hands, I took the drawings over at the appointed time. I was surprised to be joined on the front step as I rang for the butler.

I was especially surprised to glance at my fellow visitor and discover the man reminded me of a huge rat in an expensive suit with a brand-new collar. His cuff links were diamonds. Large, expensive diamonds. He looked me over as if I were posing for a dirty postcard. I shuddered and studied the doorbell, wishing someone would quickly answer.

As the door opened, the new Lord Kaldaire hurried up behind Gregson in the doorway. My lord gave me a look of disdain and said, "Come with me," to the man, taking his arm and hustling him toward the study.

Gregson faced me. "This way, Miss Gates."

I followed the butler to the door of the parlor, where I found three other ladies with Lady Kaldaire. They all turned to look at me with expressions that said I should not be here.

"I'm sorry, my lady. You have company. I'll leave the sketches with you and call again another time." I started to curtsy my way out of the room.

"Nonsense, Emily, bring them here. I can't wait to see them." She glanced at her guests and said, "You don't mind, do you? You might advise me on her designs for my new house."

To various murmurs, I came forward and handed Lady Kaldaire my sketchbook opened to the drawing of the morning room. She set down her teacup and studied it for about fifteen seconds. Then her mouth curled into a smile. "Excellent, Emily. This is exactly what I was looking for."

The other ladies craned their necks to see.

"How soon until you move out, Roberta?" a thin blonde with a pinched face asked.

"It's going to take me awhile, Cecily. Servants to hire, furnishings to move or to buy, all the details of decorating. You're so lucky this has all been done for you by Laurence's mother."

I knew Lady Kaldaire didn't care for the furnishings in this house. From her answer to Cecily, I guessed she didn't care for Laurence's wife, either.

An older woman whose hair and skin had faded to gray said, "This must be a difficult time for you, Roberta. Don't rush your decisions."

"I won't, Marjorie. You taught me well. But didn't you have the added burden of caring for a young relative at the time of the marquess's passing?" Lady Kaldaire flipped over a page in my sketchbook and appeared to pay close attention to my drawing of the dining room.

"Caroline. Yes. Such a silly girl. She and Amanda used to spend every waking hour giggling."

She must be Marjorie, Dowager Marchioness of Linchester, I decided. The woman Lady Kaldaire said she would speak to about the mysterious Amanda and the Taylors. I thought I made it clear to Lady Kaldaire that she should speak to the woman on her own. Apparently, she wasn't as good at taking advice as she was at giving it.

"Oh, how tiresome. Particularly when you're grieving," the fourth woman said. I shifted slightly to see her face. Oh, bother. It was Lady Eddington. "Amanda is usually more sensible."

"I don't think we need to worry about grieving where Roberta is concerned," Cecily said, her nose in the air.

In the silence, you could have heard a pin hit the flowered carpet.

"Is Amanda a relative, too?" Lady Kaldaire asked after a pause to let Cecily's nasty faux pas register.

"Oh, no," Lady Linchester said. "She's Viscountess Taylor now. They married just last year. Before that, she was the widow of Commander Dennison. Now, there's a story."

I inwardly cheered. We knew who Amanda was. Viscount Taylor's wife.

In the silence that followed, Lady Kaldaire said, "Now, Marjorie, you can't just leave us all hanging like that. Do tell."

"Amanda was a beautiful woman. Still is. And from the way she giggles, you'd think there isn't a brain in her head. But there must be, mustn't there, because of the way she can keep a secret and never let men realize she knows all their private business."

"Wasn't Commander Dennison mixed up in that railroad stock scandal several years ago?" Cecily asked.

"He was in it up to his neck," Lady Eddington said with some scorn. "And he was the only man who came out ahead."

"I'd forgotten, Julia, that your family was also swindled by Dennison," Roberta, Lady Kaldaire, said. "I am sorry."

"As was the Prince of Wales," Lady Eddington said

with a sniff, "although he could afford it."

"Dennison died two years later," the new Lady Kaldaire said, "and supposedly no one knows what happened to the money. However, I'd bet the former Mrs. Dennison knows what happened to all that beautiful DMLR railway money."

"If she knows, she's never told a soul. She's very discreet." Marjorie took a sip of her tea.

"Perhaps that is how she became a viscountess. Many women, both debutantes and widows, aspired to that title for a year after the first viscountess died. And Lord Taylor is a healthy specimen." Cecily raised her eyebrows and smirked.

Now even I was staring at Cecily. Didn't that woman ever know when to be discreet? *Healthy specimen* was a euphemism that brought a blush to the dowager marchioness's cheeks. It would have to mine, too, if my upbringing had been more ordinary.

"Amanda Hemmings, Lady Linchester's niece Caroline Whitaker, and I were presented during the same season. Amanda loved Commander Dennison very much. Just as she now loves Viscount Taylor. She's a sweet but misguided woman, as well as beautiful," Lady Eddington said with heat.

"Lord Taylor is like all of our husbands. Scrupulously honest, at least toward one of us. If he discovered she had the missing money from the DMLR Railroad Company, he'd make her return anything she had left to the other investors," Lady Linchester said, presumably in an effort to support Julia Eddington and her friend. "To do otherwise would be like cheating at cards. It's not done."

Balderdash. I'd learned from my father's family that the wealthy would cheat their friends as fast as they would any other class. And they were as easy to swindle. That was how all of the Gates earned their money, except for Matthew and me.

What had happened to that railway money, and did Amanda, Lady Taylor know? I bet my grandfather would have some ideas.

I was drawn away from my musings when Lady Kaldaire said, "I think I want more pink in the drawing room."

I made a show of penciling in a note on the sketch.

"Where is Caroline these days?" Lady Eddington shook her head at the offer of a biscuit.

"In New York. She married an American." Marjorie helped herself to another tiny sandwich. "She even manages to giggle in her letters."

"How extraordinary," Cecily said.

The other women gazed at her in silence for a long moment, until Lady Kaldaire said, "Would anyone care for more tea?"

I made my escape soon after that and headed straight to my grandfather's house. In his part of London, narrow streets and dead-end alleys were the rule, making it easier for someone familiar with the area to escape anyone following them—the police, perhaps, or an angry gang of thugs. I found Grandpapa in front of the stables, studying a contraption with my uncle Thomas.

"Pet," my grandfather called out as soon as he saw me, "look at what your uncle has."

"What is it?" As if I didn't know. It had wheels and seats and shone in the sunlight. What it didn't have was a place to hitch the horses.

"A horseless carriage. Can you imagine London streets filled with these things?" Grandpapa's voice held a note of wonder.

"Won't they scare the horses?" I hoped they wouldn't turn it on or expect me to ride in it. Uncle Thomas was a daredevil with anything that moved.

"Soon, they'll replace the horse," Uncle Thomas said. "These are all the rage with young toffs. And a lot of the omnibuses are motorized nowadays."

I'd ridden on motorized buses and considered them safe, although liable to break down. But the buses weren't driven by Uncle Thomas.

"And you bought this?" my grandmother said, coming out from the stables and looking askance at the three of us.

I held up my hands and took a step back as I shook my head.

"Want to go for a ride, Ma?" my uncle asked.

"I should think not. How much did you pay for it?" My grandmother now had her hands on her hips. Uncle Thomas was reckless, so much so he often worried my grandmother.

"Pay for it?" my uncle asked innocently. "We just have it on trial while we study on an idea."

I knew what that meant, and I didn't want to hear his *idea.* I was sure the vehicle was stolen and they'd use it for something illegal. "Grandpapa, I'd like to pick your brains when you're free."

"No time like the present. Tom, put that away before somebody sees it. And Aggie, put the kettle on for tea, please. Our granddaughter wants to talk."

Grandpapa and I went inside to sit at the dinner table, where all family talks took place. Uncle Thomas stayed outside admiring "his" motorcar, and Grandmother went into the kitchen, shaking her head and muttering.

"Now, pet, what do you want to discuss?"

"What do you know about the DMLR railway?"

"That wasn't any of us," he said, holding up one hand.

"I'm sure of that. I need to know how the trick worked and who the players were."

"Why? That was years ago."

"It may have to do with Lord Kaldaire's murder."

Grandpapa changed from scoffing to deadly serious. "Pet, you'd better tell me why you're interested in Lord Kaldaire's murder. You're not in any trouble, are you?"

"I found him. He wasn't dead yet, and I called for help. Lady Kaldaire, who's a force to be reckoned with, won't tell the police I broke into her house if I help her find out who killed him. And Lord Kaldaire was an investor in the DMLR railway and was somehow mixed up with Commander Dennison's widow."

My grandmother walked in, set down the tea things, and gave me a puzzled glance. Then she walked out in silence.

Grandpapa poured the tea and then settled in to tell me the story. "It wasn't a con. It was pure bad luck."

"You're certain?"

"Absolutely. We study these things, you know, so we can improve our business by learning from others' mistakes." He stopped and took a sip of tea.

"They had to bridge a river." He made a gesture with his long, aristocratic hands. Fingers adept at lock picking and sleight of hand. "Not usually a problem, but they were in the wilds and it turned out there was quicksand all over the area. Equipment, supplies, men, all sucked in no matter where they tried to build. Eventually, they gave up. Out of money. Out of luck."

"And declared bankruptcy?"

"Yes. A lot of swells lost money in the venture. But no one made money. It all ended up in the quicksand." Grandpapa chuckled. "And it didn't appear that anyone figured out how this venture was going to end. No one sold out early."

"Are you certain of all this?"

He frowned at me. "No. I'm not. It just seems to be the logical result from what is known. Is it important?"

"It's believed Commander Dennison made money on this company. When he died, they believe his wife ended up with this bounty. She later married Viscount Taylor, who was one of the investors."

"Interesting." He steepled his hands. "Who is 'they'?"

"It's only gossip among people who lost money on the deal. Could Commander Dennison have made money on the DMLR railway through fancy bookkeeping or out-and-out theft?"

"It's possible, but I don't know how." He scowled, studying the ceiling as he thought. "Do you want me to look into this further?"

"Yes, please. Could you?"

"Yes, on one condition. That you find a way to distance yourself from Lady Kaldaire and this murder."

I wished I could. He had no idea how relentless Lady Kaldaire could be. "I'm trying, but she has me designing the public rooms for her new house."

"I hope she's paying you." When I gave him a nod, he continued. "Try harder to distance yourself from her, no matter how much work she gives you. You've forgotten the first rule when dealing with murder."

"What's that?"

"Once murderers strike, there's no reason for them not to kill again to save their necks."

CHAPTER TWELVE

I looked at my grandfather in alarm. "You think Lord Kaldaire's killer will strike again?"

"If you can prove who did it, or even come too close to finding out, he'll kill you. He'll already swing for the first murder. They can't hang him twice."

His words made me shiver. I took a sip of tea, but found it had cooled too much to warm my insides. Or maybe it was the warning that chilled everything.

"What do you think I should do? Lady Kaldaire can get me in a lot of trouble with Scotland Yard. Trouble the shop can't afford. Trouble I can't afford."

"Can you keep stalling her until she gets over her grief or finds another interest?"

I shook my head. "It's not grief. It's more a desire to see the murderer punished for killing her husband. She's very determined that the right thing be done for Lord Kaldaire."

He nodded. "Vengeance can be a strong motivation, particularly if she feels guilty."

"Oh, Grandpapa, she didn't kill him. I'm sure of it."

"Not guilty of striking the blow, pet. Guilt of putting him in a position where someone else felt obligated to bludgeon him. Or not caring that someone else struck him down."

An interesting thought, but I didn't see where it would help with my problem. "What do I do?"

"Do enough to keep Lady Kaldaire satisfied. And if you feel you're in danger, tell me. Tell one of your uncles. Tell your father. We'll help you."

I sat back and folded my arms. "No. Not my father."

"He wants to help you."

"Not. My. Father." I'd wanted nothing to do with him since my mother died and I didn't want to forgive him.

He nodded. "All right. If you feel you're in danger from this investigation, come and see me. We'll think of something."

"There's another problem."

"Another one? Pet, you surprise me. I thought you were the sensible one of my grandchildren."

I'd thought I was the sensible one, too. How did I get trapped between Lady Kaldaire's plans and spying for Inspector Russell? "Ever since Lord Kaldaire was murdered and Petey hid his loot in my hat factory, Inspector Russell has been after me to work for him and to let him know what you and the family are planning. He's certain I'm guilty of something, so he's having me followed twenty-four hours a day."

My grandfather smiled. "That'll make it harder for milord's murderer to attack you, with a bobby dogging your steps."

"It's not funny."

His voice turned soothing. "I know it's not, pet. I've known Inspector Russell has had you followed since the first time you came over here, but I'm glad you told me."

"You knew?" I felt like a fool.

"Yes, and if he asks what we're up to, tell him you have no idea."

"That's the truth." I gave him a rueful smile.

"I'm not going to let you be cornered. Family doesn't do that to family."

"You mustn't be related to the Kaldaires." When Grandpapa gave me a puzzled look, I told him about my late-night capture behind the curtains in Lord Kaldaire's study.

When he stopped laughing, Grandpapa said, "Poor Inspector Russell. He seems to be the one caught in the middle. That could be to your advantage."

I couldn't imagine how. Inspector Russell suspected me of burglary, theft, and murder. He was certainly keeping an eye on me. Not that I would have minded if it were for some other reason than my supposed criminal skills.

* * *

For the next two days, I revamped my drawings for Lady Kaldaire's new house while designing several hats that had been requested for summer weddings and trousseaus, balancing accounts, and keeping my employees busy. Annie was getting better at curling feathers and pressing hat brims, but I despaired of her ever learning to make ribbon flowers.

Then Jane came to tell me I was summoned to Kaldaire House and to hurry. When I arrived, I was shown into the morning room when Lady Kaldaire finished speaking to one of the maids.

As soon as the door shut, Lady Kaldaire said, "Ah, Emily, what a relief to see you. You're sensible. There's nothing more tiresome than having to interview servants you already employ for positions in a smaller house. Everyone is wondering who is going to be chosen and what the wages and duties will be. And Cecily is beside herself because I'm taking some of her staff, which means she'll have to hire new."

"Will you take all of your staff from here?"

"I would if I could. Gregson hasn't given me an

answer, and the cook refuses to work in a widow's establishment." She gave a theatrical sigh.

"While you've been talking to the staff, have you asked them if they saw anything unusual the night Lord Kaldaire was struck down?" It seemed a likely line of inquiry. Then I wondered if that thought came from spending too much time with Inspector Russell or with my grandfather.

"They should have all been downstairs in the servants' hall or upstairs in the attic in their rooms."

"But were they?" If I had been where I was supposed to be, I wouldn't be involved in this murder.

"You think I should assume none of my servants were where they were supposed to be and question them all?" She gave me a sideways glance as she shook her head.

"I think you should question them all in the hopes that one of them wasn't where he or she should have been and can tell us something useful."

"I hope this will be worthwhile." Lady Kaldaire used the bell pull and a maid answered her summons. "Please have Gregson come here."

The maid curtsied and left the room, shutting the door behind her.

"Why Gregson?" I asked.

"He's the butler. The last person to bed at night. He makes sure all the doors and windows are bolted and he keeps a general watch over the ground and basement floors. He answers the door and the bell after dinner. If anyone knows what happened in here the night Horace was murdered, it would be Gregson." Lady Kaldaire sipped tea and watched the door.

Gregson arrived almost immediately from wherever he'd been in this huge house, but he walked in, neither out of breath nor ruffled. "You wanted me, my lady?"

"Tell me what happened the evening my husband died."

"I've already been through this with the police."

She fixed him with a steely glare.

He glanced toward me and said, "In front of the young lady?"

"Yes. Emily is helping me discover what happened to my husband."

"If I may say so, my lady, the young lady found his lordship. And the police are not satisfied with her innocence." He acknowledged me then with half a bow.

"If Emily were an innocent, she'd be no help at all." I winced, but Lady Kaldaire continued, unaware of the double meaning in her words. "I'm certain she had nothing to do with Horace's death. Now, please answer me."

"I would imagine that the time your ladyship is interested in is after you went upstairs to your room?"

"Of course, Gregson. Why are you acting as if I were going to attach you to the rack with thumbscrews?"

He blinked. "I don't believe it works that way, my lady. You see, thumbscrews—"

"Never mind that, Gregson," Lady Kaldaire snapped in exasperation.

"I merely wanted to ascertain exactly what you wanted to know." The man was beginning to look a little red in the face.

"Are you clear on this now?" Lady Kaldaire's tone was acidic.

"Yes, my lady. May I proceed?"

Lady Kaldaire nodded wearily. I recognized someone bartering for time while trying to find a way to be economical with the truth. I suspected the butler's code didn't allow for lying to his employer, but Gregson had no plans to be honest about something.

"Viscount Taylor arrived shortly after ten. He stayed in the study with his lordship for perhaps half an hour. I heard footsteps and a door shut. By the time I arrived in the front hall, no one was about. Apparently, his lordship had shown him out."

"Did you speak to my husband then?"

"Yes, my lady."

"How was he?" Lady Kaldaire asked, a modicum of curiosity in her voice.

"He seemed to be in good spirits. I asked if there was anything else. He said no and wished me a good night. He said he was going upstairs shortly, and that I could finish locking up. At that moment the front doorbell rang."

After a pause, Lady Kaldaire said, "Who was it?"

"Prince Maximilian. He walked into the hall as if this were his home, assured me he needed to see his lordship that evening, and then he followed me into the study so I could announce him. I left them, and after making certain the rest of the ground floor was secure, waited for a summons in the servants' hall.

"Not ten minutes later, the bell rang from the study. I went upstairs in time to show Prince Maximilian out. Then I went into the study to find his lordship alone. He said, 'This night is interminable,' and told me he would go to bed in a few minutes and he'd take care of turning off the lights."

"And then, Gregson?" Her voice was hard.

"Well, I wasn't summoned again. When the clock struck eleven, I went back up to find the house quiet and the lights extinguished. I checked to make certain the front door was locked. Then I went downstairs since it was time to lock up the servants' entrance."

"And did you?" Lady Kaldaire sounded as if she were running out of patience.

"Finish my rounds? Yes, my lady. I was satisfied all was secure and my duties were finished for the day."

"So you went to bed," Lady Kaldaire said.

"Yes, and that is the last I heard from anyone until this young lady rang the bell from the study."

"How far did you walk into the room the last time you entered the study?" I asked.

"Just to the doorway. His lordship appeared to be alone. I took his wishes to be that he didn't want to be disturbed further."

This didn't sound like the Lord Kaldaire I'd dealt with. "Was this typical of his behavior?"

"Was what typical?" I could tell Gregson was trying to gain time to think of a prevarication.

"To go up to bed without ringing you to lock up. To leave lights burning. To walk off with his desk in a shambles."

"He could be abrupt. And he knew he could count on the staff to correct any deficiency in the state of the study."

"So one of the maids would pick up the papers on the floor and put them on top of the desk without regard to organizing them?" Could Lord Kaldaire's money problems be connected to his sloppy recordkeeping?

"Of course. His lordship would organize them at some point."

Then it was a good thing Lady Kaldaire kept an eye on her own business affairs. "And at eleven you didn't check to see if the light was off in the study or that the window was latched?"

"There was no light showing underneath the study

door, and I knew the window had been latched earlier at his lordship's request."

All of this made his actions plausible. But if he was telling the truth, who turned the light back on? "Was he being abrupt when you last saw him, or was he preoccupied? Angry? Frightened?"

The butler frowned. "Annoyed, perhaps. He'd had an uninvited guest at a surprisingly late hour."

"Prince Maximilian." Lady Kaldaire gave a ladylike snort.

"I was certain that as soon as he finished whatever he was doing, he'd go upstairs," Gregson continued.

"What did you see when you showed the prince out? Did you hear footsteps? Voices? Anything?" This time period had to be critical to Lord Kaldaire's death.

"I heard Prince Maximilian say good night before I shut the door. I didn't see anyone else in the area."

"And you told all this to the police?"

"Oh, yes, miss." He was very quick with that answer. It made me wonder what he had failed to tell us. Had he also failed to tell whatever he was holding back to the police as well?

"Did anything odd happen before Lady Kaldaire retired for the night?" I continued.

"Odd, miss?"

"Yes, odd, Gregson." Lady Kaldaire sounded annoyed.

"No, I don't believe so, my lady."

"Very well, Gregson. Thank you."

He bowed to her ladyship and left the room, silently shutting the door behind him.

"I wonder what really happened," I said, studying Lady Kaldaire.

"You don't think Gregson told us the truth?"

"Some of the truth. He hesitated too much before he told us anything. That's a sure sign he was trying to decide how much to hide from you without actually lying."

"How do you know so much about human behavior, Emily?"

I thought of my father. "It comes from observation."

"Well, I know Gregson. He doesn't lie often enough to become good at it. He considers what he told us was a lie, but it might be only that he left something out. I wonder what it was." She was frowning now.

I glanced at the door Gregson had left through. "He said the light in the study was out, but it was definitely on and the door was open a little when I reached it. I wonder if he saw the killer?"

"I would hope if he had, he'd tell us."

"He wouldn't if he had more to gain by not telling us." Could Gregson be blackmailing someone? Or protecting a murderer out of love or duty?

CHAPTER THIRTEEN

"This makes me wonder how much I can trust any of my servants." Her ladyship's frown deepened.

That was not a problem I could relate to.

She interviewed several maids and the cook without learning anything. Unfortunately, they had all been where they were supposed to be, and with witnesses.

When she called in Newton, the first footman, I wasn't impressed with his character. He knew he was good-looking and thought everyone else noticed it, too. He had the measure of Lady Kaldaire and guessed the best response was an appearance of open, honest answers.

He readily admitted he'd not come back from the pub until later than he was supposed to return. "Beggin' your ladyship's pardon, but I got chatting with a mate, a footman for the Duke of Morehead, and forgot all about the time."

"What did Gregson say?"

"He said, 'It's too late to lecture you tonight. Now I can lock the door and go to sleep peacefully.'"

"Did he later speak to you about your tardiness?"

"With the death of his lordship, all other concerns were set aside. Don't worry, your ladyship, I have chastised myself."

I'll bet, I thought as Lady Kaldaire said, "What time

did you return?"

"The church clock tower was just chiming eleven."

"Did you see anyone around the outside of the house?"

"I saw a figure walking away from the house at a good pace. I thought maybe he'd just walked past our door, though, not come from our house."

Lady Kaldaire and I exchanged glances. "Could you describe him?" I asked.

He turned from me and spoke directly to his employer. "It was dark and he was in shadow, on account of those trees by the streetlamp. He was in evening clothes, wearing a top hat. More than that, I can't say."

Prince Maximilian leaving the house? Someone passing by? Or someone we hadn't considered yet?

"Can you be absolutely certain this man was walking down the street and not leaving Kaldaire House?" I asked.

It wasn't until Lady Kaldaire nodded to him that Newton answered, "No. He was there, but where he'd come from, this house or further down the street, I couldn't say."

He couldn't tell us anything else. The second footman, Rawlings, admitted that Newton had come in late that evening, agreed with the time Newton had given us, and then immediately assured us Newton had been sober. It was the first thing any of the servants had volunteered. I didn't believe him.

When Rawlings left, Lady Kaldaire said, "I wonder if Viscount Taylor waited outside. If he was dissatisfied with Horace's cavalier treatment of his wife's honor, he might do anything."

"Or it might have been Prince Maximilian leaving.

He would have left about that time. Remember, Gregson told Newton now that he was home, Gregson could lock up and go to bed. That must mean Newton saw this man about the same time your husband told Gregson to go to bed."

Lady Kaldaire looked at me with a piercing glance. "Then that would mean you killed my husband. You were the only person to come in after Gregson locked up."

I stared back, refusing to be intimidated. "I didn't. Someone else could have broken in that night, or someone walked in the front door before Gregson locked up."

"Surely they would have knocked or rung the bell and Gregson would have heard them."

In many ways, Lady Kaldaire was an innocent who needed to be protected. "Not if they'd come to murder your husband. Now, why did you ask me to call on you?"

"I didn't."

I stared at her, momentarily speechless. "You didn't send a young footman to the shop to ask me to call today?"

"No. Who said I did?"

"Jane, who's not familiar with your household." My heartbeat raced. "Excuse me, my lady. I'd better check to make certain things are all right at home."

I rushed back, cursing the heavy traffic under my breath, to find the shop was a shambles, but at least the newly repaired front door was intact.

Jane sat in a chair, blood seeping from a bloody nose. Hats and hatboxes were scattered across the floor of the shop and the storeroom next to it. One of the mirrors lay smashed on the floor. Noah and Matthew were picking up the stock while Annie held a damp rag against Jane's cheek. Nothing appeared badly crushed or stolen.

"Here. Let me see your face. Are you hurt anywhere else?"

As I bent over to look at Jane's face, she said, "Just shaken. When he came in, I was the only one in the shop. He picked me up and tossed me aside like a rag doll. Then he started knocking hatboxes off the shelves in the back room and throwing hats around on the floor."

She sniffed, nearly in tears, and said, "I screamed, and that's when he picked up a table and threw it against the mirror. The sound alerted Annie, who was coming across the alley. She ran back to Noah and he and Matthew came over armed with scissors and a broom."

"Your nose and cheek look puffy, as if he struck you. Let's send you home. Put cold cloths on your face, and lie down for a time. Can you make it home by yourself or do you want me to go with you?"

"He's long gone and I don't live far from here." She gave me a wobbly smile. "I can make it."

"What did he look like?"

"A big man, maybe thirty. Dark hair. Oh, and he has a long scar down his face. On the left side."

When Jane refused my company, I had Annie walk her home and then had the child come right back. While she was gone, Noah verified the description and added, "He was big, but when he saw us, he ran. One punch and we'd have been defeated, but he took off instead of fighting us. A robbery, do you think?"

"I don't know." I began helping to pick up the shop. On top of one of our hatboxes, I found another note in block capitals with the same message as the first.

STAY AWAY FROM KALDAIRE HOUSE.

Noah looked at the note and then folded his arms over his chest as he glowered.

First Noah was attacked in my place, and now Jane. If I could find a way to distance myself from Kaldaire House and everyone in it, I would. I didn't want to see my family or my employees hurt because my curiosity led me astray. It wasn't fair to them.

I'd have felt better if I'd been the one to be ambushed.

I slept badly that night. Whenever I dreamed, shadows followed me.

* * *

I was in the shop the next morning showing a customer some new designs in yellow when Detective Inspector Russell arrived, filling my feminine shop with the gruff, wrinkled presence of tweed and coal dust.

Both the lady and I must have look shocked because he doffed his hat to us and said, "Pardon me, ladies. I'll just wait for you in the alley, Miss Gates."

I recognized when misfortune was inevitable. "Of course."

"Who was that man?" the lady asked. "He looks like he spent the night in a coal bin. Still, he does look like he cleans up well." She gave a last, wistful look at the now-empty doorway and focused once more on hat brims.

Her maid continued to give the doorway a longing look.

Jane, recovered from the attack the previous day, returned carrying more yellow hat possibilities and took over waiting on the customer. When I reached the alley by our back door, I found Russell leaning against the sooty brick wall of our building, his eyes closed. "Is that how you got covered in coal dust?"

Without opening his eyes, he said, "I spent the night staking out a criminal gang. We arrested the lot of them at daybreak and confiscated their loot." He opened his eyes and focused his tired gaze on me. "It wasn't anyone you're related to."

I admit to hiding my great feelings of relief. Aloud, I asked, "Why are you here instead of in your bed catching up on your sleep?"

"I heard about the attack on your assistant."

"The attack was meant for me." I showed him the note.

He pocketed the note while he asked me for a description of the assailant. When I told him, he nodded.

"Do you know this man?"

"It sounds like someone neither you nor Lady Kaldaire should have anything to do with."

"But do you know who he is?" I was adamant. Knowing his name could be helpful.

With a shrug, Russell said, "I know you've been visiting your family. Have you learned anything?"

Part of the truth would probably be better than an outright lie. "Do you know the story of the DMLR railway?"

"Yes, but Kaldaire lost money in that venture. How could it lead to his death?"

"Lord Kaldaire had been communicating with Lady Taylor. She was the widow of the man in charge of the DMLR railway investment. And Lord Taylor, who also lost money on this, visited Lord Kaldaire the evening he died."

Russell's eyes narrowed. "Go on."

"I asked my grandfather to look into the venture to see if anyone could have made money out of it."

"A confidence trick." He nodded and then gave me a

smile. "I like the way you think about things."

"You don't mind me asking my grandfather for information?"

He shook his head and then rubbed his eyes with coal-stained hands. "No. Your grandfather is a decent enough man. When he breaks the law, I'm duty bound to try to catch him. But if I met him on the street, I think I'd like him."

Pushing himself off the wall, he said, "Share with me anything he figures out about that railroad business. This may turn out to be a useful idea."

As he walked away, I said to his back, "Where are you off to now?"

"A bath and my bed. Where did you think?"

I walked back into the shop, smiling. If nothing else, we agreed about my grandfather. Then I pictured him in his bed, and my smile grew.

* * *

The rest of the day and evening, I stayed close to the shop, designing, waiting on customers, trying to teach Annie to make ribbon flowers, struggling with accounts. A flyer for the Doncaster School for the Deaf sat next to me on my desk. How would I ever be able to pay for Matthew's schooling?

The next morning, I received a note from Lady Kaldaire requesting a look at the progress I'd made in her sketches. I wondered what she really wanted. Or if she was the one who sent it.

Jane said she wasn't afraid to work in the shop alone, but could Annie stay with her and learn the customer end of the business? Annie nodded gravely and I left.

Gregson opened the door to my ring. "Both Ladies Kaldaire are in the breakfast room. I believe you know the way."

A not-so-subtle reminder that I'd broken in that way the night Lord Kaldaire was murdered. I gave him what I thought of as the regal nod. "Yes, thank you."

He turned away as Lord Kaldaire came out of his study and said, "Gregson." I wasn't certain who the man was standing behind him, but it looked like the rat-faced man with the lecherous eyes.

I hurried away.

Both ladies were drinking coffee when I walked in with my sketchbook. The remains of toast and jam, eggs, tomatoes, and sausage littered the plates on the table. The smell made my stomach rumble.

"Will you have something, Emily?" Lady Kaldaire asked.

"Roberta, it's my house now, and I won't be feeding breakfast to tradesmen at my table." Cecily hissed without moving her lips, as if speaking this way meant I couldn't hear her.

"No, thank you, my lady. I received your message. I brought my sketchbook so we could get started."

"Just a moment. Cecily and I were discussing the ownership of the furniture in the morning room. Why don't you sit? I expect this to take more than a moment."

"No." Cecily sounded outraged.

"Yes," Lady Kaldaire said.

I chose to listen to Roberta, Lady Kaldaire. She was my employer, of sorts. I sat down, set the sketchbook on the table in front of me, and waited for an explosion rivaling Guy Fawkes Night.

"Roberta, this is exactly the type of thing I mean. You seem to think you can take whichever of the maids you choose, the cook threatens to put in her notice—"

"That has more to do with your complaints about

the food and your constant changes to the menu and the numbers to be fed than anything I've done. I'm not her employer. Mrs. Good has told me she won't go to a household without a master. Women don't eat enough to make cooking worth her time."

"I still won't have a milliner sit at my table." The new Lady Kaldaire spoke very clearly and very loudly. Apparently, she no longer cared if I heard what she said.

"It's not as though you invited her to eat anything." Roberta, Lady Kaldaire, stared across the table. "I brought the morning room furniture with me from my parents' estate when I married. Laurence should be able to remember the morning room before then. The furniture that had been in that room was moved into the attic."

Cecily huffed out an angry breath. "You can hardly think I want to dig around in the attic to furnish my morning room."

"You wouldn't, though, would you? The servants do that. Or you can have Laurence buy you new furnishings."

"You know he can't do that. What Horace did with all the money, I can't imagine, and neither can Laurence."

"Yes. It is puzzling." Roberta, Lady Kaldaire, rose and I immediately leaped to my feet. "The furniture is mine and I'm taking it, Cecily. What you do with the room afterward is totally at your discretion. Of course, you've been planning to take over my morning room since the moment Horace died."

Cecily's pale skin turned an angry red. "I didn't know Horace had died for hours afterward. And I was still at the country house. It was nearly two days later before I arrived here with my maid to take my rightful place as the mistress of Kaldaire House. So don't tell me I was planning to take over anything. And after all this time, you are still acting as if this were your house."

"Laurence was in such a hurry to get here he couldn't wait for you to pack? He couldn't wait until Horace's body was cold?" Lady Kaldaire appeared ready to do battle. Parasols at two paces, I decided.

"I had to hurry to meet up with him here, since you're more than a match for any man."

I heard glass break. I was facing the French doors leading from the breakfast room and glanced over in time to see something drop past the window panes. Something large and black and oddly shaped.

I ran around the table and threw open the French doors. Stepping outside, I crossed the narrow veranda and stood in the sunshine.

The figure, lying like a limp toy on the flagstones in the garden, had definitely been a man. And now was definitely dead.

CHAPTER FOURTEEN

I ran to where the black-clad figure had landed in the garden. Gregson. Blood seeped onto the flagstones beneath his head, and his body was sprawled and twisted like a rag doll. All around him lay glass and strips of wood.

Horrified by the sight, I looked away and breathed deeply to fight the roiling in my stomach. Shudders ran the length of my body.

While I fought for mastery of my stomach, I looked up at the back of Kaldaire House. One window was gaping empty and draperies were billowing out of the hole. One torn drapery panel flapped down the side of the house well below the window.

Both Ladies Kaldaire rushed out the French doors and stood on the veranda, staring at the crushed body. Various servants spilled out into the sunshine.

"It's Gregson, my lady. It looks as if he was thrown out a window," I told Roberta, Lady Kaldaire.

She walked toward me and then looked up at the broken window. "The green guestroom, I think. Emily, call the police." Her voice was firm. She didn't appear to have begun trembling as I had.

"No, Roberta. You can't. Think of the scandal." Cecily's voice rose an octave in a shriek.

"This is murder, Cecily."

"Maybe it was an accident."

As soon as I heard the current Lady Kaldaire say that, I hurried toward the French doors to telephone. I believed the new Lady Kaldaire would try to cover up this murder as an accident to avoid a scandal.

The whole window had been broken out of the frame. It would have taken a great deal of force to take out an entire third- story window and land so far away from the house.

"Death by defenestration? Hardly an accident," the elder Lady Kaldaire said. I glanced back to see her turning pale, her arms crossed over her stomach.

Avoiding a last look at Gregson, I went inside to the telephone in the hallway. Picking it up, I asked for the nearest police station in a quavering voice. After giving them all the particulars, I was certain the gears of the Metropolitan Police were turning.

The new Lord Kaldaire, Laurence, came in the front door as I hung up the telephone. "What are you doing on my telephone?" After the tiniest of pauses, he continued. "And where's Gregson? He's supposed to answer the door. I knocked for a full minute before I walked in. Anyone could have entered here without warning."

I hadn't heard him knock and I suspected he was exaggerating to voice his annoyance. I waited until he wore down. "Gregson is dead. He was thrown out of a window in the back of the house. I called the police."

"How dare you take it upon yourself to decide whether to call the police in my home." He strode toward me, his cane swinging toward my knees.

"Lady Kaldaire told me to telephone, my lord." I deliberately didn't say which one. Then I hurried toward the garden, Lord Kaldaire on my heels.

A semicircle of servants had formed around Gregson and the window glass shattered on the flagstones. A couple of the maids were openly weeping. Attempting to study the body without fainting, I could see what appeared to be a deep gash in Gregson's head on the side away from where his body met the ground. Blood still oozed from what looked like a knife wound.

"What's the meaning of this? Get back to work," Lord Kaldaire snapped at the servants and then turned to Roberta, Lady Kaldaire. "These things wouldn't happen if you'd move out and take your servants with you."

Lady Kaldaire pulled herself up to full argumentative battle stature and announced, "I assure you I had nothing to do with this death or the death of my husband."

"Oh, no, Roberta, do not tell me—"

As Lord Kaldaire rose to his loudest quarreling volume, I saw a bobby step through the French doors. I signaled him to come forward and gestured toward the body.

He walked closer to Gregson's corpse and after a good look, swallowed before he turned to face us. "If everyone could go inside, I'm to stand guard over the body until the inspector arrives."

Roberta, Lady Kaldaire nodded and gestured to me to precede her into the house while Lord Kaldaire began to argue. Once we were in the door, she said, "Emily, go up and guard the room. It's the green guestroom. No one is staying in it at the moment."

I rushed up flights of stairs, past the larger, better bedrooms to the smaller bedrooms and the nursery. The door to the green bedroom stood open, and I could feel a breeze cool my face.

Standing in the doorway catching my breath, I could see the opening for the window as well as most of the room. There was no glass on the polished floor or on the carpet that encircled the bed. There didn't seem to be any sign that the room had been recently occupied by the butler and his killer, so I walked in.

I could see the maids had been diligent in their dusting and polishing. I didn't see marks on any surface. Both the upper and lower sashes of the window had been broken out in their entirety and the frame was damaged. When I examined the draperies, I found they had been tangled around and partially pushed through the window with the body. I could see blood smears and pieces of glass on the fabric that remained in the room.

I heard men's voices in the garden below. Peering out, I saw two bobbies and Detective Inspector Russell. At that moment, Russell looked up. I jerked back, but I feared I was too late.

Crossing the room, I was in the doorway when I found a bobby in the hall. I glanced around. The only way out was past him.

Or falling forty feet like Gregson.

I was about to try to slip out when the bobby said, "Stay where you are until the inspector gets here, miss."

I didn't have long to wait, but it was long enough to examine my conscience and decide I had nothing to feel guilty about. Both Ladies Kaldaire could vouch for my movements before and after the murder. This time, Russell couldn't use my lack of an alibi to force me to spy on my father's family or to take on any other wretched assignment he dreamed up.

I watched him, looking tired and rumpled as usual, wearily climb the last half flight of stairs. "Miss Gates," he grumbled. "This the room?"

"Yes, and you'll notice blood stains and glass in the drapery fabric hanging inside the window. I think

Gregson was struck with a knife before someone threw him out."

He stared at me, slowly shaking his head, before he said, "I get called to a death by defenestration. At a house where there was recently a murder. Do you know how rarely people are thrown out of windows? And when I get there, who do I find staring down from the window from where the body fell? You. I've never seen a case like this. Nothing is normal when you're around." He grumbled as he glanced into the room.

"Don't be so irritable, Inspector. I don't like finding dead bodies when I go visiting." Now that the shock had passed, I was starting to feel weak. I'd respected Gregson. He was loyal to her ladyship and didn't block my way like some of my customers' butlers. This wasn't fair. This was wrong.

I must have turned a little pale, because he said, "Go downstairs with the ladies." I started to leave when he reached out and took hold of my arm. "You didn't find anything I should know about? Touch anything? Move anything?"

I shook my head. "I just looked."

He let go of me and I started down the stairs. About four steps down, I turned and found him watching me. "Inspector, find out who did this. Please."

"I intend to."

I walked down to the ground floor to find the widowed Lady Kaldaire with the current Kaldaires and a bobby in the parlor. "You have to stay here, miss, until you've been questioned," the constable said.

"Surely she can wait with the servants," Lord Kaldaire said.

"Oh, Laurence," Lady Kaldaire said in a weary tone. "We'll wait in the morning room."

"The inspector wanted me to keep an eye on all of you," the bobby said.

"We'll be in the morning room. We won't go anywhere," Lady Kaldaire said and walked past the constable. I followed her down the hall.

Once we entered the morning room and shut the door, she said, "I didn't think I could stand another minute with that odious man. Horace could be pompous and quite annoying, but he was never vicious. His brother is an evil creature. Do you know he's demanding that I move out by the end of the week? The house won't be ready by then. And he *thinks* I'm leaving the furniture in this room." She sat down on a couch and gave me an imperious look.

"I think I'd want to move out of a house where the butler was thrown from an upstairs window and the master was bludgeoned in the study." I wrapped my arms around myself, suddenly cold from my thoughts.

"These things didn't just happen, Emily. Someone is doing this and I want them caught." The knife edge in her tone matched the steel in her expression.

Unspoken was her insistence that I help her. I felt myself slipping deeper into her plans and nearly groaned in frustration. Still, I had to ask, "Why was Gregson up in that room?"

"Checking on the housekeeping. Making certain it was ready for a guest—"

"Is there anyone coming to stay in that room?"

"One of the children from Cecily's brood. The older two claim to be too old to stay in the nursery, so they'll have their own bedrooms on that floor."

"So someone could have known he'd be up there and waited for him, or someone could have followed him. Which doesn't exclude anyone, except you, me, and the new Lady Kaldaire. But why Gregson?" I started to pace across the room.

"Perhaps someone was angry because they thought he was going to leave here to be my butler? Someone who wanted a job with me?"

"Any particular reason why that would be a plum position?" I asked.

"None at all."

"He was loyal to you. And that could have made him dangerous for someone. But who? And why?"

"That's what you're going to find out, Emily."

Why me? I bit back any argument, knowing it to be futile, and put my mind to the problem. "I wonder if he knew something about the night your husband was murdered. Something he hadn't reported because he didn't realize how important it was. Or hadn't reported to protect someone."

I stopped in mid-stride. "Oh, bother. Unless he told someone, we'll never know what he knew. And we'll never find the killer."

And I'd never be free of Lady Kaldaire and her demands. Mentally, I shrieked in frustration.

CHAPTER FIFTEEN

"And I'll never know why he wasn't leaving to take a position at my house. Why he decided to stay on here as butler," Lady Kaldaire said.

I stared at her for a moment. That was an odd thing to think of right after the man's death. I shook my head. "When did he tell you that?"

"Yesterday afternoon." She brushed the importance of time away with one hand.

And was murdered the next morning. All I said was, "Why? Was it prestige? Money?"

"It couldn't be money. Laurence doesn't have any. But there would be a great deal more prestige in being the butler at Kaldaire House, as well as more benefits with this job, than in a widow's household. Maybe that was why he decided to stay."

"What kind of benefits?" This was a part of aristocratic life I'd never viewed.

"The butler maintains the wine cellar. There are ways to make money from that position in a socially well-connected house where the master isn't too observant. Laurence wouldn't be. And if he wanted to move to a grander house, this would be a good place to move from. Not from a widow's house. I'm sure Gregson negotiated a salary with Laurence that was at least as good as we were paying him."

"He wouldn't be in as good a position in your new

household?"

"Goodness, no. I expect to have very few dinner parties and even fewer houseguests."

"Could anyone be so angry he decided to stay that they would murder him?" I had no idea who would benefit from Gregson's death.

"The first footman, Newton, had already agreed to work at my new house. He would be the obvious choice, except he's already gained by my leaving and Gregson staying. The second footman, Rawlings, moves up accordingly," Lady Kaldaire told me.

"Gregson didn't have many relatives and probably didn't have much to leave them, so I can't see them creeping in and pushing him out a window." She frowned. "The usual people who would gain by a murder don't in this case."

I dropped into a chair uninvited. "Someone else has been murdered, and we're no farther forward in figuring out who killed Lord Kaldaire. And we haven't questioned Lady Taylor yet."

"I learned she's at their country house. Something about a horseless carriage race. Lord Taylor is said to be passionate about this new type of racing. I can't think of anything drearier."

A bobby came into the morning room. "Lady Kaldaire, the inspector would like a word with you now."

"I don't know what use I'll be, but I'll be glad to speak to him." She walked off with stately grace and a manner that said she'd soon straighten everything out.

I waited in the morning room for my turn. A few minutes later, the current Lady Kaldaire walked in and looked around. I could almost hear her valuing the furniture and knickknacks.

Rising out of politeness, I curtsied and greeted her.

"If you think you're going to be her favored pet forever, you're going to be in for a nasty shock." There was an evil glee in her voice.

I'd taken her measure and decided the best route was to avoid giving Cecily any ammunition. "Lady Kaldaire needs my help to get her new house ready." Well, that was a lie, but not a big one. "Once it's done, I doubt she'll need my assistance for anything."

"And won't you be a sad little thing then, forced back into selling hats."

Ladies were glad to buy my hats. They were well made, well fitted, and stylish. I'd hardly consider myself forced to sell hats, but her words stung nevertheless. "I am a milliner by trade."

"One without clients if I have anything to do with it. I think it's shameful the way you take advantage of Roberta."

"I don't think anyone can take advantage of Lady Kaldaire. Not you. Not me. Not the police."

I saw the door start to open behind Cecily as she said, "You've taken advantage of her in her poor, widowed state. I find that shameful."

"I find that unlikely." Detective Inspector Russell spoke from behind the "poor, widowed" Lady Kaldaire.

The present Lady Kaldaire spun around. "Roberta. I was just watching out for your best interests."

"I know what you were doing, Cecily. Your husband is looking for you." Lady Kaldaire strode in and sat down. "Sit down, Inspector. Emily."

Once I made sure the door was shut behind Cecily, I said, "I don't know what I can add to what everyone's told you so far."

"You entered the breakfast room after Lady

Kaldaire."

"Yes. The two Ladies Kaldaire were sitting at the table with the remains of their meal in front of them when I walked in."

"No Lord Kaldaire?" the inspector asked.

"No."

"Where was Gregson?" Lady Kaldaire asked.

"Upstairs about to be murdered," I said, and then tried to cover my outspokenness by adding, "Too bad we don't know who he was with." I suspected I'd just made things worse.

"No." She waved a hand at me. "He shouldn't have been upstairs. He should have been seeing to clearing the table. He should have been in there with us. I was so aggravated with Cecily I just realized he was missing."

"Did Gregson open the door to you, Miss Gates?"

"Yes, but then he told me I knew the way to the breakfast room, and I came in here alone while he answered Lord Kaldaire's call from the study."

"His lordship said he had him show out a visitor," the detective said. "How long from the time you entered the house until you saw Gregson fall?"

"Less than ten minutes."

"Can you be more precise?"

Not really. "Five minutes, more or less. After I phoned the police station, Lord Kaldaire came in the front door complaining that Gregson wasn't answering the door. I don't know where he'd been."

"I didn't know he'd left," Lady Kaldaire said, sounding as if she should have been informed of his movements.

Once again, I was glad that I wasn't a member of this family.

"He said he thought he saw a friend of his on the

pavement, so he went out to speak to him. Turned out it wasn't his friend at all," the inspector said, flipping over a page in his notebook. "Miss Gates, did you see anyone upstairs when you went up to the green bedroom?"

"No one on the stairs or in the room until the bobby came up. And there was no sign that anyone had been in the room besides the window broken out and the blood and the glass in the draperies."

"Blood?" Lady Kaldaire asked.

"Yes, and I saw a nasty wound on the side of Gregson's head opposite the side he landed on. I think he was hit first and thrown out the window afterward." I looked at the inspector for confirmation.

"We'll need to wait on the results of the postmortem," he said, his face lacking expression.

I decided I must be right. "We're looking for someone who could lift Gregson and heave him out the window with some force," I told Lady Kaldaire.

"Gregson was hardly a lightweight. It would take both of us and one of the maids to lift him up and toss him through the window," Lady Kaldaire said, "and I wouldn't trust any of the maids to keep their mouths shut about something like that."

"We were both downstairs when it happened," I reminded her while looking at the inspector. I felt guilty and I'd had nothing to do with it.

"This could be a suicide," the inspector said. "He was despondent and took a run at the window. It gave way and the blood was from cuts he received as the glass broke."

"He wasn't despondent. If anything, he seemed pleased with himself when he told me he was staying at Kaldaire House rather than moving with me." Lady Kaldaire sounded disgruntled. Even though she knew he'd be better off staying, she couldn't understand why anyone would not want to work for her, even as she bribed, threatened, and encouraged me to help find her husband's murderer. I felt certain everyone received the same treatment.

"Is this true?" I received Russell's gray-eyed stare.

"I had little to do with Gregson, but I didn't see any change in him." I thought I answered him reasonably.

Russell's expression was grim. "If I find you in the vicinity of one more crime, I'm taking you in."

My heart took a dive into my knees. Finally finding my voice, I asked, "On what charge, Inspector?"

"Consorting with known criminals."

"But Lady Kaldaire has been around both crimes."

"She had a reason to be. You didn't."

"Don't be difficult, Inspector," Lady Kaldaire said. "You need our help."

"And I suspect you need mine." He leaned forward in his chair, his knee nearly hitting mine. "How long until your new house is ready, my lady?"

"Perhaps a week or a little more. Why?"

"There have already been two murders in this household, and by now everyone must know you are looking for the killer. I'd be just as happy if you were elsewhere."

"Unavailable for the murderer to do away with you," I added.

"That goes for you too, Miss Gates."

I glanced back at the inspector. "Why me?"

"You were first to come upon the crime both times. If I were the killer, I'd wonder what else you've discovered. And I wonder why your shop front door has a new windowpane and your shop assistant was attacked."

I found him staring at me and deliberately held his gaze. His eyes darkened. Something—magnetism, fate, call it what you will—caused our bodies to lean toward each other. I finally said, "I don't live here."

"The killer knows where you live. Or did you think that was an unhappy customer who tore apart your shop?"

Fear trickled through my veins as I thought of the mysterious summons the day before. "We can't just stop living."

"I have an idea," Lady Kaldaire said, causing us both to jump. I'd forgotten she was there, since I was busy studying Inspector Russell's mercurial eyes, solid jaw, and tempting lips.

I had no idea what he was looking at. And I really didn't need to be studying anything tempting. Not when a Scotland Yard detective thought a killer was watching me.

"Emily, how would you like to spend a few days in the country? It will give you a chance to try your hand at selling hats to lady motorists while we talk to Lady Taylor."

"I don't have time to spend in the country. I have a business to run. I can't go." Both Lady Kaldaire and the inspector tried to convince me, but my mind was made up. Especially since she'd given me an idea of a new product to sell to lady motorists. Hat veils.

CHAPTER SIXTEEN

I spent the rest of the day, when I wasn't working on current orders, sketching ideas for a new style of veil to protect the hats and faces of female automobile passengers. By that night, I had a workable design.

After dinner and talking over everything that had happened at Kaldaire House with Noah, I went out to the workshop alone to try out my idea with a piece of fine net and different styles of hat frames. I measured how much fabric would be needed to cover the crown and decorations.

Once I cut a piece of net and sewed in a drawstring that would leave enough fabric to cover any crown, I studied the rest of the net. I realized the long tails of net on either side would allow for tying my creation around the neck or under the chin.

I was sewing drawstrings around a half-dozen more veils when I heard a banging on the door to the street. The door was barred, as it was every night. No doubt someone outside could see the lights on in our high windows, but I was not going to answer the door.

The banging stopped. Then I heard the distinctive click of lock picks, a sound I remembered all too well from my games with my grandfather. I sat motionless watching the lock, wishing the burglar would go away. When I heard the snick of the lock releasing, I jumped. Something shoved against the door, but the bar across the doorway held.

Finally, all was silent again. I was about to resume sewing when I realized I hadn't bolted the alley door behind me. I ran over and tried to slide the bar across the door, but it was stiff. We seldom used the bar on this door, coming and going from the shop across the alley. I pulled as hard as I could and after what felt like hours, moved it into place.

The next moment, something slammed into that door. I took a step back, staring at the entry. When that didn't work for the burglar, he tried his lock picks again. The door was unlocked, but he couldn't get in. The bolt stopped him.

Eventually, all was quiet. I sat at the worktable, too shaken to sew. After a short, unproductive time, I gave up. I relocked the street door from inside, slid the bar off the alley door, and walked out carrying the biggest pair of scissors we owned.

No one was there.

After my eyes adjusted to the dark, I locked up the alley door to the workshop, unlocked the shop door, and went in.

I had to cross the storeroom to reach the light switch. Something I did frequently, so I had arranged the space to ensure nothing would be in my way.

I sensed rather than saw something move in the dark. I jumped out of the way and screamed.

Someone shoved me and I lashed out with my scissors. I heard footsteps running down the inside staircase and Noah saying, "Emily? Emily?"

The shadowed figure ran for the door and pulled it open. I ran after him, my scissors again ready. He must have known I was there, because he swung with a solid fist and hit my left shoulder. The pain took my breath away.

I swung around to clutch my shoulder and my scissors connected with something in front of me. The lights came on as Noah raced into the storeroom, Matthew and Annie behind him.

I got a good look at my attacker as he fled out the storeroom door. Big man, maybe thirty, with dark hair. And a long, ugly scar running down his left cheek. He matched the description of the man who'd attacked first Noah and then Jane.

Noah came over and put an arm around me, taking the scissors out of my hand. "Did you cut yourself?"

"No." I looked. There was blood on the tip and a piece of dark wool fabric stuck in the blades. I had wounded him.

Noah put the bar on the back door and we all went upstairs. Annie was first and had disappeared by the time I reached our flat. "Did you hear anyone in the alley?" I asked Noah.

"Yes. I looked out the window but didn't see anyone. What is going on?"

"Someone tried to break into the workshop through both doors."

Matthew couldn't hear our words, but he sensed our shock and he kept a hand on my arm as if afraid I'd disappear.

"What?" Noah dropped onto a kitchen chair. "We've never had any trouble in this neighborhood."

Not until the first note came in through the shop window. Before the butler was murdered. After I saw that rat-faced man with the new Lord Kaldaire. "When I came into the storeroom, someone was waiting for me. I saw him for an instant when you turned on the light. He looked like Jane's description of the man who attacked her."

Noah must have read my thoughts. "Inspector Russell is a sensible man. I think after you report this, you should take up Lady Kaldaire's offer to go with her until all this blows over and the police make an arrest."

"You think so?" I'd be leaving Noah to run the business on his own. A heavy burden.

Noah didn't appear to mind. "Yes. Give the police time to find this killer. I want you safe."

"You, and Jane, need to be very careful while I'm gone. Matthew and Annie, too." I'd feel guilty if anyone was injured after I ran away to the countryside with Lady Kaldaire.

He shook his head. "I'm sure they'll know you've left, whoever they are. And I doubt they'll want to come back after you marked them."

"Did anyone try to break in through the shop?"

"No, but someone did ring our bell after you'd gone across the alley," Noah said. "I sent Annie to find out what they wanted."

Fear flashed through me like lightning. Annie was a timid thing, and we'd not been able to pry anything out of her about her background. If anything happened to her because of this investigation, I'd never forgive myself. "Is she all right?"

"Of course. He wouldn't leave his name and she didn't recognize him, so she told him you were out and slammed the door in his face."

Wherever Annie was before we found her, she'd learned to be cautious. "Where is she?"

We found her shivering, hiding under her bed. I spent the next hour sitting on the floor with her on my lap, assuring her she was safe.

* * *

Two days later, Lady Kaldaire and I alighted from the train in the lovely market town of Rolling Badger to find the Dowager Marchioness of Linchester and a youngish man waiting on the platform for us.

"Marjorie," Lady Kaldaire said, stepping forward and giving her friend an air-kiss, "thank you so much for meeting our train and putting us up."

"It's my pleasure, Roberta. This is my son, Lord George Whitaker. George, will you see to their luggage?"

"Yes, Mama." Lord George gave me a smile and walked off toward the porters.

"George is my younger son. He's frightfully keen on motor carriages. He's one of the organizers for this road rally, so we'll be having lots of company." Marjorie looked fondly in the direction of her son.

He appeared to be confused by the sheer volume of our luggage. His directions to the porters made it difficult for Lady Kaldaire's lady's maid to get any help from the men. Or maybe it was Lady Kaldaire's arrival with myriad trunks that was causing the commotion. I worried again that she hadn't been quite truthful when she said we'd only be here for a couple of days. "Perhaps I could help by pointing out which are ours." I gave the ladies a curtsy and walked over. "My lord, would it be of some help if Lady Kaldaire's maid and I told the porters what is ours?"

"That would be a tremendous help, Miss—?"

"Gates." I pointed out our luggage to the increasingly irritated porters. They seemed both annoyed and amazed by the number of trunks and hatboxes we'd brought.

"You're not Lady Kaldaire's companion, are you? I mean, that would make things difficult."

"No, I'm not Lady Kaldaire's companion. Why do

you ask?"

But George's attention had already drifted to another subject. "Golly, what is all that netting on your hat, Miss Gates?" He sounded like this was a concept that confounded all his brainpower. I hoped his horseless carriage engine had more vigor.

"It's designed to protect me from the dust and insects while riding in a motorcar," I said as I finished claiming our luggage. "Could you direct the porters to the baggage wagon?"

I was glad to discover that wasn't beyond George's abilities. The maid, Mary, was even happier to find the baggage wagon was horse-drawn and she'd be riding back with the driver. She kept looking at Lord George's motoring garb and shuddering. Leaving Mary to sort out the luggage, I went back to the two ladies.

The dowager marchioness was explaining some program to Lady Kaldaire. "They go out at different times and drive the same route. There are stops en route, at various homes and public houses, where they sign in and the time is noted. And everyone should travel no faster than the legal speed limit of twelve miles per hour."

"How is this a challenge?" Lady Kaldaire asked. "Would they want to go faster?"

"Well, my dear, all these young men do. But the problem is the motorcars are always breaking down and getting punctures in their tires. And every day, it's a different route with different stops. Cars breaking down. Drivers getting lost. It's total chaos." Lady Linchester sounded completely exhausted from all the commotion.

"If they all leave at different times, how can they know who won?" Lady Kaldaire persisted.

Marjorie, Lady Linchester, looked uncertain. "It has

to do with how much time it takes to get from one point to the next. They have a marking system to determine the winner each day."

"It sounds wonderfully exciting," I said. I came to sell veils to be used for motoring, so I felt obligated to be enthusiastic. And as long as my uncle Thomas wasn't driving, it would probably be safe.

"Are you keen on motors, Miss Gates?" George asked, coming up next to me.

"I don't know. I've only ridden in omnibuses in London."

"Oh, good. You can ride back to the house in my car. Find out how much fun it is. Mummy?"

"Of course." She turned to Lady Kaldaire. "It's really quite simple, Roberta. You just close your eyes and pray."

Lady Kaldaire glanced from Lady Linchester to her son, clearly unimpressed. "I think I can handle that."

"Oh, good." George signaled the wagon driver to take our cases to the house and then helped us into the car. I was given the front seat next to him.

"Lady Linchester," I said when I was seated, "I have a veil for you. Just like Lady Kaldaire's and mine." I took off my veil to demonstrate. "You set the veil over your hat like this, with the band around the crown. Then you pull the netting over your face and hair."

I showed her and then said, "You take the two ends of the sash around the bottom of the veil, circle your neck, and tie the fabric under your chin in a bow. And there you have it."

Lady Kaldaire had experimented with hers on the train and only needed to lower her veil and find the two ends of the narrow sash and tie them. Lady Linchester needed both of us to help her, but we finally had her secured and ready.

"Roberta, you are so smart not to wear a widow's veil. It wouldn't keep the dust out of your face and those long ends might snag in a tree branch," Lady Linchester said.

"Yes, I am rather pleased with Emily's hats." She gave me a smile.

"Well, you ladies look ready for the rally. Shall we go?" George had been cranking the engine while we'd prepared our hats for the dusty ride and we started off with a jerk.

I gasped. I was used to omnibuses and trains, but I'd never sat so close to the front of the vehicle. The macadamized road was rushing toward us and disappearing under the bonnet, taking my breath with it. A great wind blew in my face. I pressed my back into the seat to put a little more distance between me and the world galloping straight at us.

"Jolly fun, isn't it?" he shouted over the noise of the motor.

I thought the contraption would shake us to pieces when we took off on a rutted dirt road after we'd left the village behind. Fence posts raced past on either side of us. This was faster than the omnibuses could drive along the crowded streets of London.

"I bet you could really speed on paved roads. Do you have any of those outside of towns?" I shouted back. We were sending a dust cloud behind us, but with the veil, I wasn't having any difficulties with dirt or bugs in my eyes or mouth.

A tap on my shoulder made me turn to see Lady Kaldaire shake her head, her eyes shut. Apparently, she'd heard my comment about speed and didn't want me to suggest anything so horrifying.

Lord George, staring straight ahead with a tight grip on the steering wheel and the gear lever, didn't notice. "We've designed the rallies so a part of each day is driven on hard surface. Are you having fun?"

"Yes. Very much so. Thank you." The air rushing past me became exhilarating as I grew used to it. Since we weren't enclosed like we were in a train carriage, the speed made my heart pound. I could see why people called it wicked and dangerous, but it was also adventurous and joyous.

I felt that with the next bump, I might fly out of my seat. My hands gripped the leather cushion on either side of my skirt in hopes I would stay put. I couldn't take my eyes off the road as the engine seemed to gobble up the terrain. As a city girl, I could only guess horseback riding at a gallop must be as exciting.

I glanced back at the two older ladies. They both had their eyes shut and their lips moving. "Are the veils protecting you from dust and insects?" I called back at them.

Lady Kaldaire opened her eyes in a squint. After a moment, she opened them fully. "Yes." We hit a bump and her eyes snapped shut again.

"Are you speeding again, George?" Lady Linchester asked without opening her eyes.

"No, Mama," he said and then gave me a big grin that let me know he was lying. "Let me open it up the whole way so you can see what she can do."

"No," came in two wails from the back seat, but George had already shifted, and the automobile roared down the lane. Birds flew away and large animals began to stampede in the fields, but I found the ride thrilling.

Too bad the noise, the jolts, and the choking exhaust smells were giving me a headache.

The engine made a grinding noise as we slowed and turned onto a long drive heading toward a magnificent house. Georgian, I guessed, with great wings on each side. What caught my attention were the horseless carriages in the forecourt.

"Are you having a lot of the drivers staying here?" I shouted. Even though our speed had slowed, the engine noise prevented normal conversation.

"Oh, my. We're here," Lady Linchester said, opening her eyes. "Yes, we're having a few here. Others are staying with friends in the area or in the village at the pub."

"The Taylors live near here, don't they?" Lady Kaldaire asked after taking a deep breath. She seemed pleased to have arrived.

"Yes. Just over that way about a mile. Taylor is racing his new motor, too," George said as he gestured vaguely in my direction. Then he had to grab one of the controls again as the vehicle started to buck like an angry horse.

Settling down, the contraption delivered us safely to the front steps. Several men in overalls looked up from various automobile bonnets as we drove in but, disinterested, went back to work.

I climbed unaided from the vehicle, but the ladies needed the help of George and the butler. Once inside, Lady Kaldaire and I slipped off our veils, but Lady Linchester was still fighting with hers when a plain young woman with brown hair and lovely brown eyes came into the hall. She joined in the confusion that seemed to wrap itself around the older lady and we soon had her separated from the veil.

"Oh, Deborah, there you are," Lady Linchester said. "The current Marchioness of Linchester, this is Lady

Kaldaire and Miss Gates."

"I wish you wouldn't put current in front of my title. It makes it sound like James has me here on trial," the younger Lady Linchester said to her mother-in-law with a shake of her head.

The dowager barely slowed down. "I invited them since they're having a bit of trouble with people getting murdered at Kaldaire House. The police think they'll be next."

What had Lady Kaldaire written her? My stomach felt like we'd just hit another bump in Lord George's motorcar.

CHAPTER SEVENTEEN

"How do you do? I'm sure you'll be perfectly safe here," Deborah, Lady Linchester, assured us.

We exchanged curtsies.

"Miss Gates has invented this contraption for riding in that horrible horseless machine of George's," the dowager said, holding up the veil. "It almost makes it palatable."

"Oh, what is it?" Deborah, Lady Linchester, studied it for a minute before she took the dowager Lady Linchester's discarded hat and tried putting the two together. I held my hand under the hat and demonstrated with my other hand.

"How clever. I'd like one, too. Where did you find it?"

"I'm a milliner, so I thought I'd expand my business into something new that ladies could use. Although I admit this was the first time I'd used one on a country road, it worked better than I expected."

"May I have one? I can definitely use one, since George is always taking James and me out in his new machine."

"Of course," I said, pulling another one out. "It's my gift to you and your mother-in-law. You're being very kind to let Lady Kaldaire and me stay out here for a few days."

"I'll put the servants on watch for any London

killers." She sounded quite serious.

"Please don't bother. The detective thinks we'll be safe enough away from London. The only problem is being away from my shop for that long."

A surprised look crossed her ordinary features. "You don't find it difficult saying you're in trade?"

"Not at all. I grew up working in our millinery shop with my mother. It's as natural to me as being a debutante is to you."

"Miss Gates, you are a breath of fresh air. Everyone around here is afraid to mention business or money or trade for fear of seeming crass. I can't help but think it's a perfectly normal part of life."

"Deborah, please. None of your free thinking around here," her mother-in-law said.

"Thank you for the covering," Deborah, Lady Linchester, said. In a lower voice, she added, "We'll talk later."

I thought I might like to get to know the current Marchioness of Linchester.

We were shown to our rooms and then Lady Kaldaire said she would lie down before tea. Since I normally did a great deal more in a day than sit on a train, I asked if I could walk around the grounds. The young marchioness said she'd accompany me.

Once we got outside, she gave a deep sigh and said, "My mother-in-law doesn't think there's anything strange about Lady Kaldaire suddenly asking us to put the two of you up for a few days just because an unknown assailant killed her husband, but I do. And since you seem to have the freedom to say things none of the rest of us dare, I thought I'd ask you. It's not too presumptuous of me, is it, Miss Gates?"

"Not at all. I'd wonder too, if I were in your position.

You know the details of Lord Kaldaire's murder?"

"Of course."

"Two days ago, the Kaldaire butler was thrown out an upper-story window to his death."

She gasped.

"The police thought it would be safer if Lady Kaldaire and I left London for a little while."

Her eyes narrowed. "I understand them thinking Lady Kaldaire might be in danger, but why you?"

"Because I was the first to discover both crimes. And because Lady Kaldaire asked me to find out who killed her husband."

"Gracious. Are you some sort of private investigator?"

"No. I am a milliner. Lady Kaldaire, however, sees people as capable of carrying out more than one function." I hoped it wasn't a case of her seeing everyone from the point of view of what they could do for her.

"Did you design her hat? As a new widow, I expected to see her in a veil or a bonnet. Something more traditional."

"Lady Kaldaire doesn't feel she can put on all the trappings of mourning until her husband's killer is found."

We walked in silence for a minute before Lady Linchester said, "Do you know who killed him?"

"I haven't any idea. I feel like Doctor Watson."

"I guess you could use Sherlock Holmes."

"I could. Do you read Conan Doyle's stories?"

"I do. And love them."

I smiled at her. "So do I." We began a discussion of his stories that carried us around the house twice. We found ourselves talking as if we were old friends.

I stopped and looked out at fields green with half-grown plants. "I've never been to a house like yours before. I've never been in the country. Everything is so beautiful. So perfect."

"You wouldn't say that if you spent any amount of time here." She gave me a smile, but there was sadness in her eyes.

"Is my presence here a problem? Is that why Lord George asked if I were Lady Kaldaire's companion?"

"Did he? You see, to George's way of thinking, if you're stuck out here in the countryside, either you're landed gentry, one of us, or you're someone who works for us. The tenant farmers, the vicar, the schoolteacher, the postmistress and her shop, the publican, they're all tenants for one or another of the landed families."

"That's a lot different from city life."

"I love the few chances I get to travel to London with James. To me it's an exciting change." She took a few more steps before she said, "If you don't mind, I'll call you Miss Gates rather than Emily as Lady Kaldaire does. That way I can give you status in everyone's eyes so you can eat meals with us and be treated as a true guest."

I grinned at her. "Thank you for your consideration. There is no place to eat around here if your family decides not to feed me, and it's a long walk back to the train station."

"If you're called Emily, even Miss Emily, you'll be thought of as Lady Kaldaire's companion, and you'd only be marginally tolerated. If it's Miss Emily Gates, called Miss Gates, people will be less likely to question your exact role here."

"As if I'm an old school friend or a distant relation?"

"Exactly. Actually, I think your frankness is

refreshing."

"Thank you." That would make my task easier. As long as she was being helpful, I decided to press my luck. "Do you know Lady Taylor?"

"The new one? The former Mrs. Dennison? Yes. She's absolutely beautiful, but she's not conceited about it." Her eyes widened. "You want to question her about Lord Kaldaire's death? She wouldn't have done it. She's not that kind."

"I don't believe she did. I think she may have some information she doesn't realize is important."

"Why?"

"Because Lord Taylor was one of the last people to see Lord Kaldaire alive."

"Oh, he wouldn't have—"

I put out a hand. "I know, but they were speaking that night about Lady Taylor, and I want to know her husband's mood when he returned home. Or if he mentioned whether anyone else was about."

Lady Linchester shook her head. "That can be tricky, getting a husband to tell you what he considers to be 'men's business.' We're still thought of strictly in terms of our womanly virtues. We're not given credit for our brains, even by men as forward thinking as James and Lord Taylor."

"You don't think she'd know if something had been wrong when he returned?"

"Oh, she'd know, all right," Lady Linchester said, "but whether she could get him to tell her about it or whether anyone else was present is something else again."

A footman came toward us. "My lady, tea is served in the red parlor."

With a nod, Lady Linchester led me inside.

I didn't believe the dowager Lady Linchester when she said this was an unimportant parlor, used for family and friends but not formal occasions. The fabrics on the chair cushions and the draperies were new, bright, and unsullied, and the patterned carpets were thick. I'd seldom seen anything so lovely in the homes of my London customers.

Of course, the air here was much cleaner than London's sooty smog. The sky was blue. I could get used to life in the country, as long as I had money and a title.

We sat down and tea was served. The two older women caught up on news of some of their friends before I could ask, "Do many of the motorcar racers travel with their wives?"

"Some do. We don't have any staying with us. Just men clomping about the house in the evening. And the conversation at dinner is all about ratchets and gears and ratios. But don't worry. They won't disturb your peace, Miss Gates," the dowager Lady Linchester said.

It wasn't my peace that concerned me. My hopes for advertising my motoring veils fell.

"Perhaps we could visit Lady Taylor tomorrow," Lady Kaldaire said. "I want to introduce her to Emily."

Marjorie, Lady Linchester, set down her teacup and smoothed her skirts. "Roberta, what is going on?"

The old woman was sharper than I had thought.

"Lord Taylor was one of the last people to see Horace before his death. My hope is Emily can learn from Lady Taylor what they discussed and if their discussion can shed any light on who so cruelly ended Horace's life." Lady Kaldaire could have given more drama to her statement if she'd pulled out a handkerchief and dabbed at her eyes, but she didn't need to. Her emotions were evident in her voice.

Marjorie, Lady Linchester, raised an eyebrow. "Really, Roberta, that is most extraordinary. Do you really think Lady Taylor can help?"

"Yes, and Emily is just the person to accomplish this."

"Emily? Really?" Three pairs of eyes focused on me.

I swallowed, straightened my shoulders, and said, "That is what Lady Kaldaire expects of me. And this would give me a chance to show off my motoring veils to someone else who might find them of use."

"Then I'll send her a note and suggest we stop by in the morning while the men are all out racing about the countryside. Oh, I feel like I'm playing a role in a gothic novel."

The dowager Lady Linchester spoke with such enthusiasm that her daughter-in-law had to bite back a smile. "There's no need. The Taylors are the noon stop tomorrow on the racing circuit. They're hosting a picnic lunch at their home for all the racers and their guests."

The picnic would make it difficult to talk to Lady Taylor away from a houseful of guests. How would I get to speak to her alone?

The dressing gong sounded, removing any chance I had to ask my question as the ladies rose and headed to their individual rooms and maids to get ready for dinner. I had a new concern.

I was as vain as any other woman. I immediately began worrying whether my gowns would be adequate, and what would I do with my hair?

Just before I needed to go down to dinner in my emerald green gown, the fanciest and practically the only one I owned, there was a knock on my door. Mary, Lady Kaldaire's maid, popped her head in and said, "Her ladyship wanted me to check and see if I could do something with your hair."

That almost sounded like a command to make myself more presentable. I thought my hair always looked nice, but good manners made me say, "That would be nice. Thank you."

Using green ribbon, a brooch, and talent I didn't possess, Mary soon had me looking like I belonged in the upper class. "You're an artist, Mary."

She grinned. "Just let my mistress know you're pleased."

"I will."

I went downstairs to find we were all gathering in the blue room to go into dinner. Deborah, Lady Linchester, came over and said, "We're going in family style, since there are many more men than women tonight. No worrying about precedence, thank goodness."

Since no one was within hearing distance, I dared to say, "I thought all of you knew that system from the cradle."

"I wish. It's when you get into the nuances, such as whose title is older, that it gets to be worrisome. And some of these men are unknown to any of us. George invites just anyone along."

I hoped none of them had followed us from London.

CHAPTER EIGHTEEN

Lord George, Deborah's brother-in-law, came over to me and silently smiled. I had no idea if I was supposed to speak first or if he simply had nothing to say.

"How was your racing this afternoon?"

I'd apparently chosen the right topic, because I didn't have to say another word while we waited to go in to dinner, or for the first two courses. Lord George told me everything there was to know about his vehicle, all the other racers, their families, and the course. Some of the other drivers sitting near us joined in the conversation from time to time, and dinner became a jolly event.

I didn't understand the first word any of them said, but I managed to smile and nod and exclaim at the proper times.

Somewhere in the third course, Lord George said, "Golly. I'm not boring you, am I?"

Oh, dear. I thought I had hidden my complete lack of comprehension or interest. I might as well sound like a simpleton. "Oh, no. I think you're frightfully clever. I'm afraid this is all over my head, but I'm glad you're enjoying it so much. I like to see people enjoy their pursuits."

"Golly." He gazed on me with adoration. "Mummy thinks it's dangerous and James thinks it's a passing lark. You're the first person to see how important it is to me."

"Oh, I'm sure others see how important—"

"I was never very good at school. Father said it was good James came first to get the title. I'd be swindled out of the house and grounds in no time." He looked down and took my hand. Then he glanced up into my eyes and said, "It's nice to meet someone who thinks I'm clever."

"Oh, you must have mechanical talents to keep your motor running through these races. I'm sure you're quite clever." I tried to unobtrusively tug my hand away with no luck.

Mercifully, one of the other motor carriage mad young men said something to him and my hand was forgotten. I slid it away.

At the end of the meal, the ladies left for their coffee elsewhere, and I was spared hearing the end of a long discourse on brakes.

Lord George didn't speak to me after dinner, just smiled in passing. My ears needed a rest. I thought I'd had a lucky escape. But if we could travel so quickly to Rolling Badger, so could the killer in a fast motorcar.

* * *

The next morning, it took Lady Kaldaire, the Marchioness of Linchester, and the dowager's lady's maid to get the dowager marchioness moving at an early hour. To me, it felt like the middle of the day, but I was the only one of us who had to work for a living.

We took the carriage over since Lord George was driving the motorcar in the race. James Whitaker, the Marquess of Linchester, was riding as his partner in case of breakdowns or becoming lost. Apparently, the race required teams of two in the motor carriages.

When we arrived, we found Lady Taylor in the

breakfast room with her female guests. Lady Linchester had been right. Lady Taylor was beautiful. Although she was near forty, her alabaster skin was as smooth as a girl's. Her features were in perfect proportion, her figure slim, her movements graceful, and she had the longest eyelashes I'd ever seen. Nature had been much too kind to her.

The female guests were all married to racing drivers and found it odd Lady Kaldaire and I were there without any connection to any of the automobiles in the race. But all of them had heard about Lord Kaldaire's recent demise. Lady Kaldaire had no problem telling anyone who would listen that her dear friend Marjorie invited her to get her away from the unfeeling new Lord Kaldaire.

Lady Kaldaire could spin stories out of thin air. She introduced me as a friend of the family who had tried to save the late Lord Kaldaire's life and was now under threat by his killer. Scotland Yard had suggested we both leave London for a short time while they searched for the murderer.

That was at least partially true, which seemed to suit Lady Kaldaire's purposes. At least here she had dropped the pretense that I was going to design the interior of her new home.

Except for thanking someone for handing me a cup of tea, I kept my mouth shut.

The ladies chatted for a half hour, talking about people I either didn't know or who were clients. I decided there was nothing I dare add to the conversation.

The guests went upstairs to change for luncheon while Lady Taylor greeted women who were arriving from neighboring country houses for the picnic. A few minutes later, Lady Taylor excused herself to get ready. Lady Kaldaire rose and followed her out of the room.

I waited with the two Ladies Linchester and the women who had just arrived. After a minute or two, a maid came in and asked me to follow her. I excused myself and left the room.

I was led upstairs to Lady Taylor's boudoir, where I found Lady Taylor staring at Lady Kaldaire with a look that mixed fear and fury. Her lady's maid stood off to the side, unsure of what to do.

Lady Kaldaire focused her solemn gaze at Lady Taylor. "The question is how far will your husband go to protect your good name. Would he resort to murder?"

I would have gladly put my hand over Lady Kaldaire's mouth. This wasn't how we should proceed if we wanted to learn the Taylors' secrets.

Amanda, Lady Taylor's jaw dropped. Then she recovered, stepping toward Lady Kaldaire with an angry glare. "He most certainly would not. My reputation has never been in question. Who would he murder?"

"My husband. I know your husband was in my house the night my husband was killed. I know they argued about whether you ended up with the proceeds from the DMLR railway stock." Lady Kaldaire wore the expression of an avenging angel. "Did he kill my husband, Amanda?"

Lady Taylor looked around the room, I suspected for an escape route from a lunatic. I couldn't blame her. Lady Kaldaire certainly sounded mad. "No. Of course not. No one ended up with the proceeds from the stock. There was no money after the bankruptcy."

She looked at me for help, but I wasn't going to save her. Keeping my tone level and quiet, I pointed out, "Other people were in financial straits because of the collapse of the stock. You weren't." And then it hit me. "Unless Commander Dennison sold his stock before the news got out about the bridge and the quicksand. He didn't have any losses, and therefore neither did you."

She sighed and signaled to her maid which dress she wanted. Her maid slipped her into a dazzling white gown of muslin and lace, perfect for a picnic or garden party. While the maid buttoned her dress, Lady Taylor asked, "How did you find out?"

"It was a safe guess. I've had—experience in this area." Actually, I had relatives who made their living by knowing when to get out of bad deals. Since my grandfather couldn't imagine a way for Dennison to have made money, the only answer was he didn't lose any.

"The commander was always hard up. He needed to raise cash, so he sold his stock long before anyone realized the extent of the problems. Then when the project failed..." She lowered gracefully onto a stool.

"Does Lord Taylor know?" Lady Kaldaire asked.

"Yes. That's what he went over that night to tell your husband. They argued, but Edward finally convinced him of the truth. When he left, all was well between them. How much did your husband lose in the railroad stock crash?"

"Not much. He didn't have much to gamble with," Lady Kaldaire said.

"Then why was he hounding me? The commander left me with little. I couldn't have paid anyone back." Lady Amanda looked from one of us to the other.

"My late husband was tenacious like that. He believed everyone should be honest and aboveboard, and no one should swindle their friends." Lady Kaldaire walked over to the dressing table and looked at the jewelry spread out for that day.

Lady Taylor reached out one tapered hand and touched Lady Kaldaire's arm. "But I didn't swindle anyone, and I don't believe the commander did either."

"I'm afraid Horace assumed you had. Once he got an idea into his head, it was hard to get him to change his mind. He had been a great believer in the DMLR railway and refused for the longest time to believe the company had gone bankrupt. When he finally accepted the truth, he decided he had been swindled. It couldn't just be bad luck. Not with Horace." Lady Kaldaire shook her head, but a small smile of remembrance appeared.

"How did Lord Taylor convince Lord Kaldaire that he'd been unlucky?" I had never understood how my swindling relatives routinely convinced their marks of their bad luck.

"The Taylors had lost more money than the Kaldaires, and yet he married me. Edward's belief in my innocence is what convinced Lord Kaldaire. At least that's what Edward told me when he came home."

"How did he seem when he arrived? And what time did he get there?"

Amanda, Lady Taylor stared at me. I'd pushed too hard. "What interest is it of yours?"

I sighed and watched her as I said, "I found Lord Kaldaire injured, and I know what time that was. I feel duty-bound to give Lady Kaldaire the answers she's seeking about her husband's murder. The more facts I can discover, the sooner I'll find out the truth."

I could see in her eyes when she accepted my story. "He seemed fine. Relieved that the two of them were no longer quarreling. And he returned about eleven."

I nodded.

"What time did you find him?"

"A few minutes after eleven."

She looked worried. "There must have been someone there after Edward and before you arrived."

I gave her a smile. "I'm sure of it. I just have to figure out who it was."

"Now, we need a plausible excuse as to why we've holed ourselves up away from the guests for so long," Lady Kaldaire said.

Lady Taylor smiled at me. "I need to buy one of your wonderful motoring veils I've been hearing about."

I took one out of the bag I had with me and showed her how to drape the veil for a hat with either a low or high crown, with either a wide or narrow brim, protecting the hat as well as the wearer. Fortunately, Lady Taylor was a quick study, her maid was a quick worker, and we soon left the boudoir.

We walked downstairs to the morning room where we found both Ladies Linchester with the other ladies. "Wherever did you go?" Marjorie, Lady Linchester asked us.

"She bought one of Miss Gates' motoring veils. It's very clever, and since Lord Taylor has become enamored of these machines, I expect Amanda will be using hers often," Lady Kaldaire said.

"They're frightfully ingenious," the younger Lady Linchester said. "I wore mine for a quick spin yesterday—"

I didn't hear anything else because I looked past her into the entrance area where several rally teams were standing, shed of their goggles and dusters. Two of the men looked very familiar. Too familiar.

What were Uncle Thomas and Cousin Tommy doing there?

And how would I avoid them at the luncheon?

CHAPTER NINETEEN

Before I came up with an excuse to hide in the house, several ladies professed an interest in my motoring veils. I was swept up by women chatting to me about hats while they walked out of doors. By the time we reached the gardens for the picnic luncheon, I had orders for several motoring veils to deliver when we returned to London.

The tables and chairs were set up under tents and trees on the manicured lawn. The food and drink were laid out on long tables under a separate tent with maids and footmen in silent attendance.

Viscount and Lady Taylor had ordered up a feast. Roast beef, chicken, salads of every description, dainty rolls, lemonade, sherry, coffee and tea—the bounty went on and on.

There wasn't a cloud in the sky. It appeared the Taylors had even ordered the weather.

I'd filled my plate and begun to wander in the direction of my uncle when Lord George Whitaker came up to me. "Hello, Miss Gates. Wonderful day, isn't it?"

"Yes, the weather is lovely. How did you do in the rally this morning?"

"Oh, we won't count up points until tonight. But we've done smashing in the first legs. I don't think anyone has beaten our times, and they've been clean."

"Clean?"

"We haven't speeded. If your time is too fast, they know you've been speeding and they deduct points for that." He went on and on.

I wondered how long I needed to keep up this conversation when a familiar male voice said, "Well, my lord, the morning's racing has been fine."

"Indeed it has. Oh, Miss Gates, may I present Mr. Longacre."

"How do you do?" I said, staring into my uncle's eyes. At least I didn't have to worry about anyone knowing these men were my relatives. They were here under a false name, no doubt with some theft in mind.

The only questions were: where, and had they already taken what they came for?

"It's a pleasure to meet you, Miss Gates. I've heard about your wonderful veils for ladies who motor. Where did you get your inspiration? Do you travel by motor carriage often?"

"No. My first journey by horseless carriage was just the other day with Lord George. Are you local to these parts, Mr. Longacre?"

"Oh my, no. I'm from London myself. Motored up here with my son. I enjoy it, but I'm afraid I'm finding that road rallying is a young man's game. I'm staying at the White Horse in Rolling Badger. Lovely town. So quiet. So peaceful. Have you seen it?"

I was glad the cousin was Tommy and not Petey. Tommy had some sense. "I haven't spent any time there, but I plan to. I've heard the church is lovely."

"Yes. Yes, it is."

We had a meeting place if it became necessary. I really hoped it wouldn't, because I did not want to be sucked into my father's family's larcenous schemes.

And I had no way of knowing if Inspector Russell

had sent someone here to spy on me.

* * *

Once we returned to the Linchester estate, I was bored. Since I was accustomed to working all day every day, and half the night when necessary, this enforced idleness was wearing on my nerves. We'd learned what we'd come for from Lady Taylor. I'd received a few orders for my motoring veils, although I'd given away nearly as many as I'd sold.

I could leave a happy woman, but Lady Kaldaire wasn't ready.

"Emily, it would look odd for us to leave after only a day's visit. We need to stay for the rest of the race, to give Marjorie moral support." She was dressing for tea, as were both Ladies Linchester.

Not having the extensive collection of clothing they had, I planned to wear the dress I wore to lunch again to tea. "My business needs practical support. I need to return to town." I smiled at Lady Kaldaire's maid. "You can return to town with Mary."

"And what will you be doing while I'm here?" Lady Kaldaire's gaze was icy.

"Running a millinery shop. That is my occupation."

"I need you to find out what happened to my husband. And that letter. That must be the key to this business." She thrust her arm into a sleeve, nearly hitting Mary.

"Whatever happened must have occurred between the time Lord Taylor left and I arrived. It was only a matter of minutes, but any other clues or witnesses must be in London. You need to go back there as much as I do, no matter what Inspector Russell says about our safety."

The longer I was away from London, the less

threatened I felt by the unknown assailant. In another day or two I would convince myself I'd dreamed any threats I feared.

My expression must have been hard, because Lady Kaldaire waved away Mary's suggestion of a very plain mourning skirt and jacket for tea and said, "Give it one more day. If we haven't learned anything more by tomorrow night, we'll return the following morning."

"Agreed." How much could happen in a day?

We went down to tea, an exceedingly tedious affair with only the four of us present. Lady Deborah, at my insistence, had little Lord William, affectionately called "Billy-billy-boo" by his besotted mother, brought in for us to meet.

His nurse handed him off and Lady Deborah and I fussed over the baby. The older two ladies made pleasant comments from a distance, but Deborah and I got right into it, singing nursery songs and playing with his fingers and toes. He liked my version of a spider, smashing my fingers with his little fist.

After a half hour, the nurse returned and tranquility, and boredom, settled on the parlor once more. We were discussing literature, something I couldn't add much to, when Lord George came into the parlor.

After a brief greeting and even briefer bow, he said, "I have the best news, Mummy. The Prince of Wales is coming for the motor rally tomorrow. It's an unofficial visit, but he'll be at Willows for the lunch break to look over the motor carriages. Wouldn't it be swell if he took up road rallying? I'd love to have a go at racing the Prince of Wales."

"How did the duchess get to be so lucky?" the Dowager Marchioness of Linchester asked the room.

"Jonas Henry wrote to the prince and invited him. Turns out they've known each other since they were youngsters in the Navy," George said.

"Lord Jonas Henry is the duke and duchess's second son," Lady Deborah explained.

"Are we invited, or is this a gentleman-only event?" Lady Kaldaire asked.

"Oh, no. The entire party is invited, from here and Taylor's, at least. I couldn't have the prince eating lunch with us without having my best girl along." Lord George gave his mother a vacant smile.

"I wouldn't think the duchess wants to face thirty ravenous men and the Prince of Wales on her front lawn without female company," Deborah, the Marchioness of Linchester, said. She appeared to be fighting down a smile.

I appreciated my chance to meet Lady Deborah on this trip. I enjoyed her unvarnished honesty and subtle sense of humor. I also thought it providential for the aristocracy that James was born first and had chosen Deborah for his wife.

Her mother-in-law didn't sound thrilled with Lady Linchester's comment when she replied, "Hosting the Prince of Wales is an honor, no matter if it is unofficial."

"Yes, I would say it is," Deborah replied. "It gives a shine of respectability to motor racing. I know James will be delighted. How did you make out today on the road course?"

There was a pause because Lord George had just stuffed two teacakes into his mouth.

Into the silence, Lady Kaldaire said, "I suppose it's white dresses and wide-brimmed straw hats for all. That's all right for you young ladies, but it leaves the matrons looking rather washed out. I'm almost happy I have to wear mourning."

* * *

As it turned out, Lady Deborah was the only one wearing unsmudged white in our carriage the next morning. I wore my dark blue skirt with a white shirt, while Lady Kaldaire was in unrelieved black and Marjorie, Lady Linchester, wore the gloomy colors of a long-established widow.

The laundering necessary to keep a skirt white when all around me was grass, or more often street dust and coal soot, was prohibitive. The style was only for the very vain or very rich, and I was neither. I didn't even have a lady's maid, a deficit ignored by the other two ladies and supplied by Lady Kaldaire, who lent me the use of Mary when necessary on this visit.

Lady Kaldaire had been in a state, truly bad-tempered, until I suggested she wear the newest hat I'd designed for her with a curved-down brim, black roses, netting to symbolize mourning, and a high crown. My own hat, in dark blue to match my skirt, had a wide brim with white ribbons and trimmings. With my auburn hair, and wearing dark blue, I would stand out in a whitewashed crowd.

Marjorie, Lady Linchester, was horrified that I didn't fit in and unsure of what she thought of Lady Kaldaire's hat. Deborah, Lady Linchester, looked pleased and told us how much she liked our outfits.

We were almost there, clopping along the lane at trotting speed, when the driver started to slow the carriage. "Ma'am, one of the machines seems to have broken down ahead."

"Well, see if they need anything," the dowager marchioness said. "Really, all these terrible machines do is break down."

We pulled alongside the motor carriage, which sat between the lane and a high wall, and our driver said, "Do you need any help?"

"No, no. We're fine. Won't take but a few minutes more, will it, Tom?" I heard a familiar voice say. After a pause, the same voice said, "No. We'll be along soon. Thank you for asking."

I peeked out the carriage window. It was indeed my grandfather, disguised by a duster, goggles, and a plain motoring cap, but I saw no sign of Uncle Thomas or Tommy.

Another carriage pulled up on the outside, the two carriage drivers conversed for a moment, and then the other carriage drove on. After a "good day," our driver put his team into motion.

I was facing backward and on the side of the carriage closest to the broken-down motor vehicle. I watched out the window long after we were past, but I didn't see any sign of anyone but Grandpapa. Then, just as we turned into another lane and some trees were about to block our view, I thought I saw a head appear over the top of the wall.

I didn't want to ask what they were up to.

CHAPTER TWENTY

We didn't travel far before we made one more turn, and we were on the drive up to The Willows. The house was a pale mansion of classical grace in the midst of normally placid lawns. Now, it stood as a backdrop to the hubbub of drivers and servants and princely retinue. Motorized carriages were lined up in the forecourt, and tents were set up in a grassy field beyond the gravel.

"Oh, dear. The prince has arrived and we're late," the dowager Lady Linchester said.

"He's not here to see us, Marjorie. I'm afraid we're reminders of his grandmother." Then Lady Kaldaire looked at me and smiled.

Lady Kaldaire would never remind me of Queen Victoria. I'd never met the queen. I'd never even seen her. But I couldn't imagine her sneaking around a palace, sending her servants searching for clues to a murder.

The carriage crawled up to a spot for the ladies to descend, the carriage in front of us just pulling away. As always, I was the last one down.

"Emily, wander around and see if you can hear anything about any of our suspects," Lady Kaldaire murmured as she pulled me aside.

"I'd think murder would be the last thing on their minds. The sun is shining, the next king is here, and they're celebrating a marvelous new invention."

"Well, that's not why we're here."

"We've ruled out Viscount Taylor. There's nothing keeping us here. We need to get back to London and continue our search there," I reminded her as firmly as I could in a whisper. I didn't want to be anywhere in the area when my father's family pulled whatever theft they had in mind.

"You're right, Emily. It's looking more and more like Prince Maximilian, and he's in London. We'll leave in the morning. I'll tell Marjorie I need to organize my move from Kaldaire House. She'll understand. Former householders aren't the most popular of tenants."

"Especially when it's the previous tenant who has the fortune?" I asked, raising my eyebrows.

"Emily, you're being impertinent." Lady Kaldaire tapped me with her parasol, but she was smiling.

We fixed our plates and sat at a distance from the prince, who was surrounded by the duke and duchess, their motoring son Lord Jonas, and some other men whose names and faces meant something to the other ladies there, but nothing to me.

In honor of Prince George, King Edward's heir, we had both hot and cold dishes at this picnic along with champagne, three types of wine, and tea. The servants must have been run off their feet with the well-rehearsed delivery of everything anyone might want.

I stuck with tea and sandwiches, eating them off delicate china, since I never knew when a customer or potential customer might be watching my behavior. I would never occur to them I might be watching theirs.

I was glad we'd catch a train tomorrow morning and be out of here before there was a hue and cry over some crime. How long would it be before they realized there was no one named Longacre here?

And then the criminals rounded the corner and chugged up the drive. With a belch of smoke, they came to a stop in the forecourt, fortunately far enough away not to send smoke toward the picnic. Several of the drivers went over to greet them and commiserate over their bad luck.

I watched them, wondering what they were up to, when I realized there were only two climbing out of the machine and removing their goggles and dusters. My uncle and my cousin. Where was my grandfather?

I was staring at them from my chair when Lady Kaldaire tapped me on the shoulder and said, "This man wants to take you to meet the prince."

I looked at the ladies, trying to wipe the guilty thoughts from my face. "Me? Doesn't he mean you, Lady Kaldaire? Lady Linchester?"

"No. He wants to speak to you, Miss Gates. And take a motoring scarf with you," the marchioness suggested.

My first thought was they'd captured my grandfather doing something illegal. Swallowing, I rose, nodded to the ladies, and followed the man in the morning coat and patent leather shoes as he picked his way across the grass.

I was left to stand waiting near the prince's chair while he talked to some distinguished-looking men, smoked a cigar, and drank brandy. The man who brought me over finally walked up behind the Prince of Wales and spoke into his ear.

"Excellent," the prince said and rose to face me.

I managed the deepest curtsy I had ever attempted and did so without falling on my face.

When I was upright again, the prince said, "I understand you've invented a scarf that is handy for ladies who are riding in a motorcar."

"Yes, Your Highness." I pulled a scarf out of my bag and held it up, demonstrating how it was worn by using my hand. Then I said, "Does the princess motor with you?"

"On occasion."

"Then you might give this to her from me with my compliments, that she might enjoy its use while riding with you. If she has any questions about how to attach it to her hat, she has only to contact me at my London shop." I handed him my business card with the scarf.

"Thank you very much," the prince said, handing my gift and card to the fellow in the morning coat. "How long have you been motoring?"

"Not long, sir. But I could quickly see that women passengers needed protection both for their hats and their faces."

"Indeed. Well, thank you. I'll pass this on to May." The prince nodded to me and turned back to one of the men in his group.

I made another curtsy, not quite so deep this time and walked back to where Lady Kaldaire was sitting with some ladies.

"What did he want?" the dowager Lady Linchester asked.

"One of my scarves."

The younger Lady Linchester nodded. "I think your name has been made in fashion."

"I hope so. It's a good design and well made. I'm proud of my work." My tone must have made clear I was serious.

"Well, it's good fortune for you, Emily, that the prince came today. We're leaving in the morning," Lady Kaldaire said.

"Oh, Roberta, no."

"Marjorie, you of all people should know what work it is to create a new home after I've lived in Kaldaire House all these years."

"Cecily doesn't want to share?" the younger Linchester lady asked.

"Deborah, you know Cecily."

She chuckled. "Yes, I daresay I do."

I definitely liked the young marchioness.

We all rose when the prince made his way to the carriage that would take him back to the railway station. He made a few brief remarks praising the enterprising spirit of the designers and racers of the motor vehicles and thanking his host and hostess. Then he climbed in, followed by the man who had summoned me to the prince's side and another similarly dressed servant. Their driver wasted no time in leaving.

"Wonderful to see the Prince of Wales taking an interest in motorcars," a voice said beside me.

"Yes, it is," I responded as I faced my cousin Tommy. He'd shed his duster and goggles, but still wore his motoring cap.

"Miss Gates, is it? I hear you've come up with a scarf designed to protect ladies' hats when they're riding in a motorcar."

"Yes. You must be one of the racers."

"Thomas Longacre, at your service."

"Good luck, Mr. Longacre. You have a lot of competition in this field."

"No competition at all, miss."

His cheeky grin told me all I needed to know. They'd already done whatever they came here to do. I really didn't want to know what it was.

"Have you been into Rolling Badger?" he asked me.

"No, I'm afraid I've not had the pleasure."

"You should see the church. It's a beautiful medieval building with a marvelous organ. They have evensong every night at five. You should try to attend tonight."

What were they up to?

Cousin Tommy gave me a brief bow, his body posture satirical, and walked off.

"Who was that?" Lady Kaldaire asked as she joined me.

"One of the racers. He was kind enough to tell me when evensong is held in the Rolling Badger church."

"Really, Emily, I didn't know you had a religious interest."

"No. A musical one. I've heard the organ in the church here is magnificent. I want to hear it for myself. I'll ask Lady Linchester for a ride in the carriage to service."

"I should go along to chaperone."

"I don't think it will be necessary. I'm sure none of the drivers will be there." It would be the young man's grandfather who'd attend the service, and I didn't want Lady Kaldaire to meet him. "And the vicar and congregation will be present. I'll be perfectly safe."

Deborah, Lady Linchester, was happy to lend me the use of the carriage and driver for evensong, since it would be our last evening there and my last chance to hear the organ. However, her brother-in-law, Lord George, overheard us.

"I say. Our afternoon program is pretty short. I'd be glad to take you to evensong in the motor. Give you a chance to ride in it again."

"That's terribly nice of you, but won't it interfere with your racing? I'd hate to do anything to hurt your chances for a victory." Going to the church with Lord George Whitaker could be almost as big a disaster as going with Lady Kaldaire.

"Oh, no. Won't hurt a thing. Be ready for church at twenty to five and I'll drive you into Rolling Badger. I like that old pile of stones. It's the vicar's sermons I can't stand."

"George." His mother looked scandalized.

Everyone was staring at me. I couldn't come up with a solitary excuse. "That's very kind of you. If you're certain I'm not interfering with the race—"

"That's settled then. Twenty to five, and wear your scarf." Lord George strolled back to the grounds where drivers were readying their motorcars for the afternoon excursion.

We returned to Linchester House a short time later. At twenty to five, I went into the front hall where the butler told me Lord George was waiting out front. I spotted him sitting in the idling vehicle. When he saw me, he waved and beeped the horn. The most embarrassing sound split the air and birds scattered overhead.

I climbed in unaided and gave Lord Whitaker a smile. "Thank you for taking me," I shouted over the engine noise.

"My pleasure. It's not often I get a chance to take the motor to church. Mummy doesn't approve."

I sat on the front passenger seat, watching trees and fence posts speed past. I gripped the seat as we banged and jolted over ruts in the dirt.

"With Mummy not here, we can go as fast as the old motor will take us."

I tried to give him a smile while gritting my teeth. Lord George only believed in one gear. The fastest one.

I was still trying to catch my breath and calm my shaken nerves when I spotted Grandpapa studying a stained-glass window inside the church. Lord George wanted to sit in the front row, but I shook my head and shifted the veil on my hat. "I won't be able to hear all the tones of the organ if we sit too close to the front. At least halfway back would be better—here, this should be good."

I chose a pew more than halfway from the altar and George obediently sat next to me on the center aisle. Grandpapa walked up shortly after I did and sat at the other end of the pew on a side aisle. He leaned toward me. "Could you help me find the first prayers in the book? My eyesight isn't what it was," he said.

I slid over and opened his prayer book. "There's nothing wrong with your eyesight," I muttered to him.

"Point it out to me. Now, what are you doing here?"

I held the book out to him and pointed. "Selling veils to cover ladies' hats and faces while riding in a horseless carriage, and hiding from Lord Kaldaire's killer."

"What?" came out as a strangled whisper.

"There have been two murders at Kaldaire House, and three attacks on the shop. It seemed to be the time to go into hiding. What are you doing here?"

The organ began the processional. The sound filled the space, bouncing off the stone walls and stained glass.

We stood up, and looking at his prayer book, Grandpapa pointed at a page. "Your uncle Thomas has taken a shine to motorcars. Thinks they'll improve our business. Always forward thinking, your uncle Thomas." The organ music and the choir covered the sound of his words for anyone nearby.

I turned a couple of pages and pointed again. "They're expensive and unreliable. You saw that this afternoon."

"You saw what everyone was supposed to see. There was nothing wrong with the vehicle. And it's borrowed."

That meant stolen.

"When do you go back to London?" he continued.

"Tomorrow morning."

"That's good, pet. Try to stay out of trouble. And away from killers."

I forgot to act as I stared at him. "Grandpapa, why are you here? What was on the other side of that wall where you broke down?"

"The Willows, of course."

CHAPTER TWENTY-ONE

I saw it all in a flash. Uncle Thomas and Tommy went in the back of The Willows while everyone was focused on the front and the arrival of the Prince of Wales. No one wondered what they were doing. They all assumed the Longacre vehicle had broken down while engaging in a motor race.

Meanwhile, The Willows had been robbed.

I couldn't help it. I worried about them. I began my act again with another flip of the pages. "Are you all safe?"

"Nothing to worry about, pet. Everything is fine."

I wasn't sure if I believed him or not. "When do you go back to town?"

"The last day of races is tomorrow. The day after, there'll be no trace of the Longacres."

"Be careful you don't leave anything behind. Country people aren't fools, you know."

"Neither are we, pet."

The prayers began then and I moved back to stand next to Lord George as we both recited the responses. I thought the cool, towering stones might collapse with both Grandpapa and me in church, but the church, or God, was tougher than I thought.

Vespers was a short service, but when I looked over at the end, Grandpapa had disappeared.

"Who was he?" Lord George asked.

"Some man who's blind as a bat. Poor old thing."

"You're a kind woman, Miss Gates."

We walked out to the motorcar parked on the verge of the road. It was a fine evening, and people were walking by or riding past on horseback, carriage, or automobile. Two young men, probably one of the teams in the race, stopped next to Lord George's motor. After brief introductions, one of them said, "We thought you'd be home with all the excitement."

"What excitement?" Lord George said as I thought, *Oh, no.*

"The duke's steward has been phoning around to find out if anyone else's house has been burgled. It seems The Willows was robbed this afternoon. Some of the duchess's jewelry has been taken along with that of one of her guests. Miss Vanlanden."

Lord George couldn't get his jaws and his voice to work in harmony for a moment. "Wow—oh, my—but what—isn't she—?"

"Yes. That American heiress. First the prince. Now the burglary. This is the most exciting race ever." The driver of the other car sounded thrilled with these events.

I was horrified. How close were they to catching my father's relatives?

We spent the entire ride back to the Linchester estate with George shouting about gypsies and Scotland Yard and how the robbers could be in Wales by now. I clung to the doorframe and the seat and shouted one-word replies as necessary.

I was in time to discover from the butler that the ladies were talking in the music room rather than dressing for dinner. I walked in as I unpinned my hat, but my hands stilled when I saw Inspector Russell standing in the center of the room facing Lady Kaldaire.

Blast. He'd caught my father's relatives. The room grew cold and dark and blurry as I realized my business would be ruined and my dreams of sending Matthew to school were over.

"It's absurd," Lady Kaldaire said, turning to face me. "He says Newton pushed Gregson out the window."

For a moment, I was so relieved I couldn't form coherent speech. Too much time spent with Lord George, I decided. I took a breath to slow my hammering heart and said, "Are you certain, Inspector? What reason could he possibly have?"

"Gregson had caught Newton stealing the house silver. Gregson turned him in so he was fired and thrown out without references. The current Lord Kaldaire has confirmed this."

"When did this happen?" Lady Kaldaire demanded in a tone worthy of our king.

"The morning of Gregson's death."

"Nonsense, Inspector. I was there. Nobody informed me."

"They didn't want to bother your ladyship."

"That would be a first." Lady Kaldaire looked down her nose at the inspector. "Lord Kaldaire only fired Newton to make me move out of Kaldaire House faster. I'd already hired Newton to be my butler. He didn't need references, nor did he need his position in Kaldaire House. This is all nonsense."

"Would your ladyship hire a thief?"

"Of course not."

"The stolen items were found among Newton's possessions. So apparently, he would have lost his new job, too." Russell gave the ladies a small bow. "Just wanted to keep you informed, your ladyship."

"You don't think he killed Lord Kaldaire, do you?" I asked as he passed me.

"No. We're still working on that."

I looked him over carefully. His collar and cuffs were pristine. His suit had been pressed, his bowler hat brushed, his shoes shined. His style was middle-class, but he was clean and neat. He knew how to appear presentable. In that instant, I knew he'd studied these people as closely as I had.

But that didn't answer my question. "Why did you come down here? You could have told Lady Kaldaire about the arrest of a servant when we returned to town."

He stopped then and lowered his voice. "I came to Rolling Badger on another matter. But I also have to ask myself, where is your family, Miss Gates?" With that, the inspector strode out of the room. I turned to find all eyes following him. His physique did have that effect on women.

On the other hand, it was his parting words that made my heart pound.

"I must get back to London in the morning. Something must be done," Lady Kaldaire said.

"What time is the first train?" I asked. I couldn't wait to get out of Rolling Badger, now that I knew my father's relatives had struck and Inspector Russell was here.

I'd successfully advertised my hat shop and added a new product to help pay for Matthew's schooling. Now I needed to put as much distance as possible between my family, Inspector Russell, and me.

* * *

Lady Kaldaire and I waved as the motors left for their last day of racing before we took the Linchester carriage and baggage wagon into Rolling Badger to the train station. Unimpeded by Lord George, Mary took care of having our baggage loaded while Lady Kaldaire and I said our good-byes and thank-yous to the Linchester ladies.

We were in front of the station when Inspector Russell walked by. "Lady Kaldaire, ladies," he said, doffing his bowler. "Heading back to London?"

"Since you've arrested the wrong man for Gregson's death, yes, it is necessary for me to return to London at once." Lady Kaldaire gave him the aristocratic stare.

Marjorie, Lady Linchester, moved next to her and gave him the exact same look.

You couldn't deny the solidarity among the aristocracy.

Apparently, Inspector Russell recognized it, too. "Don't let me delay your ladyship."

"Aren't you traveling back to London?" I asked.

He stared into my eyes. I couldn't miss his suspicious look. "No, I'm still hunting the criminals who burgled The Willows yesterday. And I'm working on another matter."

"Another burglary, Inspector?" I hoped so. That would keep his attention off my relatives. I doubted they'd been here before.

"Yes. Nothing like the incident at The Willows, though. This was a local, a servant, who stole money from his master." He was eyeing me suspiciously. Or maybe I was just imagining it.

"That could have been what happened at The Willows. One of the servants saw the chance and grabbed some jewels while everyone's attention was elsewhere." I forced my voice to sound indifferent as if I was spouting off ideas.

"I'd hoped to escape the criminal elements by

spending time in the country," the dowager said, "and then they plundered a well-ordered house like The Willows."

"It's these new motorcars. Criminals can go anywhere," the inspector told her, not taking his eyes off me.

"That must make your job more difficult," Deborah, Lady Linchester, said.

"Not if I know who to keep an eye on."

He suspected my relatives because I was here. *Blast*.

I stared back at him. "Lady Kaldaire and I came out to Rolling Badger because you suggested we'd be safer here than in London. Instead of worrying about her husband's killer, we should have been worried about burglars."

"You weren't robbed, were you?"

"No. The only people I know who had anything stolen were at The Willows," Lady Kaldaire said.

"It was as if they were the targets of a band of thieves," the dowager marchioness said. "Of course, it is the grandest house for miles around. I suppose it's a miracle it hasn't happened before."

"With this road rally going on, no one would notice an extra motor. I don't suppose you ladies noticed anyone suspicious."

We all shook our heads. I kept my expression innocent.

They announced our train was coming into the station and the inspector walked off. Lady Kaldaire and I, after hugs and curtsies with the Linchester ladies, hurried through the station and out onto the platform. I was relieved. The inspector might suspect my relatives, but he hadn't yet realized they were in the rally.

* * *

I won myself a two-day reprieve from chasing after Lord Kaldaire's murderer while I saw to my business and filled more orders for motoring veils than I had expected. Apparently, word had traveled about the wonder I'd designed.

I set aside all of the proceeds from the veils to send Matthew to the School for the Deaf.

The trip had been a success in that regard. I only wished we'd found out more about Lord Kaldaire's death so I could go back, unimpeded, to my business.

On the morning of the third day, I received a summons from Lady Kaldaire to call on her after church. I waited until after Sunday dinner was finished before I went over to Kaldaire House. Rawlings, the former second footman, answered the door.

"Is Roberta, Lady Kaldaire, at home?"

"The lady is a new widow and not receiving visitors."

His stuffy tone told me Gregson and Newton's misfortunes had been good for someone before I asked, "Are you the new butler, Rawlings?"

"I am."

"Congratulations. Lady Kaldaire sent me a note requesting my presence after church. Would you please have someone tell her ladyship I'm here?"

He glanced quickly over his shoulder, took a deep breath, and said, "Wait here."

He disappeared inside. Fortunately, it was a pleasant day and I didn't mind the wait. A minute or two later, he reopened the door, a maid at his side. "Lucy will take you to her."

I stepped inside and took a few steps following Lucy, no doubt toward the back of the house, when Lord Kaldaire appeared. "What are you doing here?" he boomed as he swelled his chest.

I used my unimpressed tone. "Lady Kaldaire asked me to come."

The aristocratic sneer didn't leave his voice as he said, "Can't you get her out of here? We simply don't have room for her and her household. The servants are confused as to whose orders to follow. It's a disaster."

"I'm sure she'll be moving soon."

"Are you? Well, I'm not. Tell her to get packing." He turned and stormed off.

I looked at Lucy and raised my eyebrows. She grinned and led me to the morning room. As she opened the door, I heard, "Who—oh, Emily. Thank goodness. I was afraid it was Laurence or Cecily again. They simply must invade this room every half hour."

"He did just order me to tell you to get packing."

"He's odious." Lady Kaldaire glanced over and focused on the maid. "I'm sorry, Lucy. You shouldn't have had to hear that."

The maid stood by the door. "I imagine he's still angry about the man who came here earlier."

I saw the possibility immediately. The late Lord Kaldaire was struck down by a caller at an odd time. Now, the new Lord Kaldaire was visited by a caller on a Sunday morning. "Lucy. Wait. What man?"

"Come in and shut the door, girl," Lady Kaldaire said.

She shut the door but shook her head. "I don't know who he was, but Lord Kaldaire was very angry with him. Something about a note and not doing any more business with him. The other man was angry, too, but he kept his voice down."

"Thank you, Lucy. Oh, Emily, I need to get out of this asylum."

Lucy slipped back out as I said, "How are the decorators doing?"

"Just a few more days. Which means I need to know if I should hire a footman or not. Go see Inspector Russell and find out what is happening to Newton," she said, making a shooing gesture with her fingers.

"He stole from you. Well, the house." I still had trouble separating Lady Kaldaire from Kaldaire House.

She gave me a level stare. "No, he didn't. Gregson was the butler and the house silver was his responsibility and kept under his guard. He'd have caught Newton in a moment. Whatever Newton is, he isn't stupid. Well, not that kind of stupid."

"Do you plan to rehire him?"

She placed one hand on her chest and sighed. "If I must. I hope Newton saw something that night. Something that meant Gregson needed to get him out of the house. No one but Gregson could have planted that evidence on him."

"Unless Gregson knew who hid the silver in Newton's room and tried to blackmail him or her."

"Not her. Can you imagine trying to pick Gregson up and throw him out the window?"

I shuddered at the image. The man had weighed a great deal more than I did. "No."

"I want you to visit the prison and talk to Newton. Find out what he and Gregson knew."

"Russell's not going to let me in there." He didn't trust me. My last name was Gates.

"Of course he will, Emily. He's a man. A man who is falling for your charms. I saw the way he looked at you at the train station. He didn't run into us by accident."

If Lady Kaldaire thought an attraction was what was between us, I'd let her think it. Better that than discovering he thought I was involved in robbing a duchess.

"Now, I want you to go see Russell and convince him Newton has information both of you can use to find my husband's murderer."

CHAPTER TWENTY-TWO

"I'm not trying to break Newton out of prison. I only want to talk to him." I stood in Inspector Russell's office the next morning, my police escort hovering in the doorway, and stared up into the inspector's gray eyes. Eyes that didn't look welcoming.

Russell leaned over his desk toward me. His dark gray three-piece suit was clean and pressed. His maroon tie was knotted properly. Time in Rolling Badger had done wonders for his dress. He could have passed for a bank manager or a solicitor. "There is nothing to be gained by your speaking to him. No."

"On the contrary. I believe he has vital evidence in the death of Lord Kaldaire. That is why someone framed him for this theft and had him fired." I kept staring into his eyes, hoping to see them soften.

"Bl—" he began, biting off the curse and stalking away from me.

"Inspector, I need to speak to Newton," I patiently explained. Again. Matthew wasn't this stubborn, and he was still half in his childhood.

"No, you don't. This discussion is concluded. Good day." He walked over and threw himself into his desk chair. It screeched in response but didn't fail.

"Then I shall have to find another way to discover what he knows." I kept my tone sweet as I twirled around to march out of the office, making my skirt swing. My gray gown might have been somber if not for the wide lavender waistband that was copied in my high collar and cuffs. My hat was a demure wide-brimmed lavender with gray feathers. Inspector Russell wouldn't realize the care I'd chosen in my dress, but I hoped he felt the effects.

"He doesn't know anything," Russell snapped out behind my back.

I turned back and stomped to his desk, no longer interested in the effect I had on him. "That's where you're making your mistake. You believe what titled people tell you rather than what servants say."

"Why would Lord Kaldaire lie to me?"

"He wants to get even with the elder Lady Kaldaire for some past slight. Lord Kaldaire might be passing lies on to you he'd been told by Gregson. His lordship hoped this would move Lady Kaldaire out of his house faster. He had a hand in this, whatever this is." I ticked suggestions off on my fingers. "Do you want me to continue?"

"No." He groaned softly. After he was silent for a minute, he said, "I suppose I need to go with you to the prison."

I gave him a bright smile. "You may learn something useful, too."

He grumbled, but he rose from his desk and picked up his bowler hat. As we walked down the corridors of Scotland Yard, uniformed constables and suitcoat-wearing staff turned and looked. I knew we made a handsome couple and enjoyed the attention. Russell hurried me along as he stared straight ahead. Soon, we were in a hansom cab on our way to see Newton.

"Have you ever ridden in a motorcar, Inspector?" I asked as we clopped and plodded our way across

London.

"Yes, once. We soon broke down and spent a fun afternoon in a downpour trying to repair the engine."

"You have terrible luck, don't you, Inspector?"

He gave me a rueful smile. "Have you? Ridden in a motorcar?"

"Yes. But only on sunny days and we never broke down. We sped along as if on a galloping horse. It was great fun." The smile on my face as I thought about those trips must have said it all.

"I congratulate you on your good fortune." Despite his serious nature, he finally grinned at me. "Was this in Rolling Badger?"

"Yes. The son of our hostess had an automobile and he enjoyed giving us rides."

"Ah. Lord George Whitaker. Your suitor."

Looking at his gloomy expression, I burst into laughter. "Lord George? Oh, dear me, no."

"How do you like being back in London with regular people?" He studied me across the narrow confines of the cab.

"It's nice to be home, but people are the same all over. Some are good, some are bad, and some never show us who they really are."

"And who are you, Miss Gates?" His voice gentled to a breath of air.

I turned away, not wanting my face to give away my fears for my grandfather, and found Brixton Prison loomed over the barren landscape ahead of us. I gave a silent sigh of relief.

Among its inmates, Brixton Prison housed those unfortunates still awaiting trial. The fences, tall and unyielding, were ominous; the buildings of sooty gray brick were cold and impenetrable. I followed Russell closely as we went through gates and walked down halls, our footsteps echoing around us.

Despite the warmth outside, we were shown into a cold, dank room. I sat on the chair on my side of the heavy table. Russell leaned against the wall behind me. A minute later, Newton was led in and his handcuffs removed.

He sat down across the table from me and said, "Aren't you that hatmaker her ladyship holds such store by?"

"Yes. That's why I'm here. Neither of us believes you killed Mr. Gregson."

"Ask him. He's sure of it," Newton sneered, looking past me at Russell.

I had to deal with men who overlooked me on a daily basis at the millinery shop. Suppliers, creditors, husbands of customers. I wasn't about to allow an imprisoned footman to do the same. "You're here to talk to me. Not him. So, tell me what happened, starting with the night Lord Kaldaire was murdered."

Newton dragged his gaze back to me. "Why? Won't make no difference."

"It can't hurt. And right now, you need all the friends you can get."

"Those aristocrats aren't our friends, no matter what her ladyship has convinced you of."

"Maybe not, but she can be helpful when she chooses. And she thinks you have something to tell her about the night her husband was killed."

"I didn't do it. I wasn't even in the house."

"Just tell me what happened."

"You heard me tell her ladyship."

"I heard you tell her half-truths. I'm not your employer. You don't need to make it sound like you followed the rules."

He sat back and scratched his jaw. "I'm not really sure when I got back. I ran into a friend at the pub and we were talking and drinking–"

"Drinking what?" Russell asked.

"Ale. Gin. And a lot of it. I'm not really certain when I got back, but I do know Gregson was waiting by the door for me to come in."

"Did you exchange words?"

"He said I was late and started to give me a lecture. Then he said, never mind, you're in no fit state. Go to bed. At least I can lock up now."

"Did you say anything?"

"Good night, maybe. Nothing else. Wouldn't have been smart. Gregson was that angry."

"Did you see anyone else?"

"Rawlings, the second footman, laughed when I stumbled on a step. I just wandered off to my bed and left them to stay up if they wanted. And I didn't wake up until the police came through and found me in my bed."

"So did you really see what you said you saw outside on your way home?" I watched him closely.

"I think so. I remember seeing a chap in a top hat as I was trying to sneak around to the servants' entrance without being seen."

"Are you sure it was that night? Are you sure he was by Kaldaire House?" Russell asked in a scoffing tone.

Newton sat up straighter and glared at the inspector. "Yes. I mighta had more than my share, but that man was there hanging around the house that night. Don't know who he was or where he'd come from, but he was there."

"Was it Prince Maximilian?" I asked.

"Who?" Newton asked.

"Never mind." It would be wonderful to have someone tell us when Prince Maximilian left Kaldaire House, but Newton wasn't that person. "And you heard nothing until the police woke you up after Lord Kaldaire was attacked?"

"Dead to the world."

"Now, tell us about this theft you were accused of."

"I didn't do it." He slammed his fist against the table.

"I've not heard anything about this. What are you accused of stealing?" I said without inflection.

The lie seemed to work, because he settled down enough to say, "A silver pitcher and some candlesticks."

"Were they found in your things?"

"Yes. Gregson grabbed me when I walked into the servants' hall. He took me to Lord Kaldaire and then we went to the room I shared with Rawlings. There was a sack in the back under my bed. I'd never seen it before. I swear I hadn't." He banged both hands against the table, but weakly this time.

"Did Gregson say how he knew it was there?"

"He didn't say a thing. He just ordered me to follow him. I did as I was told. And once his lordship got involved, there was nothing I could do or say."

"Were you asked to explain?"

"Yes. I told them I couldn't. I didn't know how those things got there. Lord Kaldaire kept asking me questions, one right after the other. It was worse than being questioned by your lot," he added, looking past me to where I knew Russell stood.

"When were you told you were fired?"

"Right then. Lord Kaldaire told me to pack up my things and get out."

"When was this?" I could hear Russell shift his position behind me.

"Shortly before Gregson took a header out the window." Newton gave me a sly grin.

"What time that morning were you fired?" I planned to keep pressing until I heard some actual times.

"It was eight-thirty or pretty close to it when Gregson told me to follow him. It only took a few minutes to get his lordship and then go up to my room. I almost thought Lord Kaldaire was waiting for us. A few minutes to fire me, a few minutes to pack with Mr. Gregson standing over me, and I was out the door as the clock struck nine."

Times, at least, could be checked with Lord Kaldaire. "How did you learn about Gregson's fall so quickly?"

"The bobbies that picked me up in the Rat and Cat told me about it. But I wasn't in the house when he fell and I got witnesses."

"So you don't claim he jumped," Russell said in a very quiet voice.

"No. Not him. He was always too full of himself." Newton scowled at the table. I could hear the cogwheels in his brain moving.

"I can see on your face you've thought of something. A reason why someone murdered him. What is it?" I demanded.

"I don't know who, but I know why. Gregson was always after getting a percentage for himself."

"You mean money?" I asked.

"He means blackmail," Russell said, walking toward the table. "He'd done this before?"

"Yeah. He was getting a bit extra from old Lord Kaldaire for some secret or other. Something about a woman. It was probably innocent enough, but Gregson could always make things look bad. He had a couple of the maids doing favors for him, doing his laundry for free, running errands he should have run for the household, because of broken china or being out late."

"And yourself?" Russell pressed, now leaning palms flat on the table staring down at Newton.

"He tried a time or two. I told him I'd take my chances with Lady Kaldaire."

"You seem to think Lady Kaldaire has a good opinion of you." Russell didn't move a muscle or raise his voice. Somehow, it made him more ominous.

"She must. She's here," he said, pointing at me.

"What she wants to know is who killed Lord Kaldaire. She thinks Gregson's death is a clue," I told him.

"Nah. Somebody got tired of paying him off."

"Or Gregson knew who killed Lord Kaldaire and was blackmailing the murderer." I glanced up at Russell. "Now we just have to figure out what Gregson knew."

"Good luck with that," Newton said. "Gregson would never let go of a piece of information that he thought would be of use to him someday."

I held Newton's gaze. "But if he were going to tell someone, or even hint about knowing something, who would he tell?" Oh, please. Let there be someone who knows what Gregson knew.

Because Gregson knew who killed Lord Kaldaire. I was certain that was why he had to die.

CHAPTER TWENTY-THREE

Newton looked at me across the scarred wooden prison table and said, "Not anyone in the house. Gregson didn't think any of us were too bright."

I agreed with his assessment. "Outside of the house?"

"The landlord at the Broken Bugle. I've seen the two of them talk, heads close together, many a time as if they were plotting something."

It turned out Newton had nothing else of use to tell us. He just kept whining about his own troubles. Once we left that cold, grimy pile of bricks and climbed into a hansom cab, I asked Russell, "Are you going to have a talk with the landlord of that pub?"

"It's worth a try."

"May I sit in?"

He turned to give me a sharp look. "Why would I let you do that?"

"Because I got more out of Newton than you did."

"Beginner's luck."

I gave him a grin. "Probably. I would like to hear what the publican has to say."

"That would be breaking even more rules than I broke by letting you speak to Newton."

The inspector broke rules? Interesting. "How did you get me in there?"

"I said you were his sister," he mumbled, his face

reddening.

"Thank you." My smile widened. It was good to know even Russell could ignore regulations when it was necessary. "How would you like to come for dinner and tell me what the landlord says?"

"Dinner with the Gateses. No, thank you."

"Only two Gateses. Matthew and me. And Matthew is deaf, so he can't repeat what you tell me. Cousin Noah isn't a Gates and falls asleep right after dinner. And Annie, last name unknown, is only a child."

"Why are you so determined to follow this investigation?" His tone was quiet. Serious.

I held his gaze, the two of us unblinking as we rattled along in the cab. "Because Lady Kaldaire wants to know who killed her husband and won't leave me alone until the truth is discovered. I want my life back."

"Tell her to leave finding her husband's killer to the police. That's our job."

"She doesn't trust you. Oh, not you personally," I amended when I saw his expression change. "She believes the police are too trusting of the upper classes. Lord Kaldaire says Gregson told him Newton stole, and you believe Newton stole. You can't question Gregson, and you didn't ask anyone else. If Newton was a thief, Lady Kaldaire would know about it."

"And you don't trust the upper classes." He watched me closely.

"No. They don't feel they have to be on their best behavior around me. I'm a tradesman. It's acceptable to cheat and lie to me. And I'm not the police, so they can be indiscreet around me without repercussions."

He leaned back and folded his arms. "What exactly did you learn in Rolling Badger? Who did you talk to while you were in the countryside with Lady Kaldaire?"

I gave him the bare bones of what I had learned, leaving out anything to do with my relatives. Inspector Russell didn't say a word until I finished.

"You've been busy."

I nodded.

"And you're certain Viscount Taylor is in the clear, and Prince Maximilian is involved?"

"Yes, but I think there might be a third party."

"Why?"

"I think Newton returned later than we've been told. Gregson said now that Newton was back he could lock up and go to bed. A good butler, and Gregson was good, wouldn't have followed his boss's directions to go to bed until he was certain the upstairs was locked up properly, including the study. Therefore, the man in the top hat left the house later than the time Gregson gave us for the prince's departure."

Russell nodded, his expression somber. "I'll let you know what the landlord says."

"Do you think the landlord will tell you as much as he'd tell me?"

"You're a female, Miss Gates."

"Your powers of deduction never fail to amaze me, Inspector." My tone was dry.

He shook his head. "The landlord won't say anything of a risqué nature in front of a woman. Especially with a constable listening. He'll be free to at least allude to certain subjects without your presence."

"Someday, Inspector, women will shock you." Something told me that day was a long time off, and I suspected Russell was one man who was unlikely to be shocked. "Hopefully, the landlord won't fail you."

After a lengthy silence, Russell said, "What time's dinner?"

* * *

Inspector Russell was punctual. He'd also shaved, changed his collar and cuffs, and brought a bouquet of flowers. Noah's eyebrows rose before he shook his head and went to wash up for dinner. Matthew laughed. Although it sounded like a donkey braying, the inspector showed no surprise and even made an attempt to converse by using hand gestures. Annie occasionally peeked up at him from the doorway.

I put the flowers in a vase and placed it on the sideboard. Then I brought in the dinner prepared by our neighbor, Mrs. McCauley, and we sat down together, with Noah showing up at the last minute.

The inspector kept the conversation to general subjects while we ate, I guessed to avoid having to discuss police matters in front of Noah. Noah watched him carefully and didn't say much.

After dinner, Russell offered to help me with washing dishes. Annie smiled and flew from the table. When Matthew understood, he folded his hands in prayer and bowed to Russell for sparing him that chore. Then he slapped the inspector on the back and hurried away wearing a big grin.

We carried the dishes into the kitchen, followed by Noah. "Why are you involving her in your work?" my cousin asked, taking an aggressive stance and looking up the few inches he lacked against Russell.

"I'm not. She's involving herself. I thought if I told her what she wanted to know from my interview, she wouldn't go out looking for trouble."

"I'm glad you both have such faith in me," I said, scrubbing a cup with more vigor than necessary.

"You and Lady Kaldaire are running a race to see who's going to be first to get Emily hurt," Noah said, ignoring me.

"Nobody wants to see Miss Gates hurt." The inspector was still sounding placating.

"Then act like it. Get out of her life."

"No." I spun around from the sink to face them both. "I'll decide who I help and who I don't. Neither of you found Lord Kaldaire lying there with his head all bashed in and bloody. I did, and it's not something I'll quickly forget."

I took a step toward them, waving the cup. "I want Inspector Russell to find the person responsible. I want to help Lady Kaldaire discover who killed her husband. So don't try to stop me from seeing Mr. Russell, Noah. And don't try to hold information back from me, Inspector."

Both men stared at me in amazement. It felt good.

"Inspector, take that towel and dry this cup. Noah, you'd better get out of here before I put you to work."

He stalked out of the kitchen.

As I washed, the inspector dried and stacked the dishes on the table. "The landlord of the Broken Bugle is a man called Jack McDowell. He admitted he and Gregson were good friends, but he claimed he didn't know any secrets of Gregson's."

"Did you believe him?"

"No. And I told him he wouldn't want the Bugle closed down for being a bawdy house. He blustered a bit, but he finally saw reason and told me what Gregson said to him."

I stopped washing. "Well?"

"A week or so ago, they were complaining to each other about how people don't do their work carefully or properly. A serving maid had just dropped a pint of ale and made a mess. Then Gregson said, 'Sometimes, though, someone failing to do their job properly can be a windfall for someone else.' McDowell asked what he meant. Gregson said a doorman at a club had mixed up two notes and passed them to the wrong members. One contained a very incriminating message."

"What did it say?"

"He swears Gregson never told him."

"What club? Who received the note and who did it belong to?"

"All McDowell said was Gregson told him Lord Kaldaire put it in his safe until he could decide what to do about it. Then a third party learned about the mix-up and had a different way to put the note to use."

"Gregson? But if he killed Kaldaire for the note, who killed him?" That made no sense to me.

Russell set a dried plate on the table and faced me with his arms folded. "No. From what McDowell understood, apparently this unnamed third party saw the usefulness of the note and stole it to put it to use. I believe Gregson then saw his opening to blackmail this third party."

"That sounds like a dangerous thing to do." Particularly since it led to his death.

"Gregson had nerve, I'll give him that. But I feel confident his murderer was the person who removed the misdirected note from the safe and then objected to being blackmailed."

"Someone who can enter and leave Kaldaire House without drawing attention to himself." I leaned on the sink.

"Someone who knows how to enter through the breakfast room doors?" He looked at me, his eyebrows raised.

I scrunched up my face. "Not me. I couldn't lift

Gregson and I've never been any good at breaking into safes."

"Never been any good at breaking into safes? What kind of a childhood did you have, raised among the Gates family?"

I stared into the inspector's face and saw a look of amazement start to spread. There was no point in lying to him. "Grandpapa used to entertain us by teaching us—things. It was a game. Nothing else."

With a start, I remembered the dishes in the sink and discovered water spreading onto my apron.

"Until you used your knowledge to break into Kaldaire House." He took a step toward me and lifted my chin with one hand. "Miss Emily, that was a dangerous thing to do. And it's led to your taking ever-bigger risks for Lady Kaldaire."

"And for you," I added.

"All I've asked you to do is keep an eye on your family for me. I wouldn't have asked if I thought you could be in danger from them. You are your grandfather's only granddaughter. They won't hurt you." He smiled at me, his gray eyes twinkling.

I stared into those mesmerizing eyes and, suddenly, I saw his plan. "Inspector, have you asked me to keep an eye on them so they would keep an eye on me?"

The smile never left his face. "Your wash water's getting cold."

I rinsed the soapy plate. "Inspector, do you have a Christian name?"

He took the plate from my hand and began to rub it with the towel. "James."

"Why, Detective Inspector James Russell, did you tell me what the publican told you?"

"To keep you from going there on your own. It's a

rough place. Cousin Noah would not approve."

"You would not approve."

"No."

I studied him for a moment. "So what's the next step?"

"Dogged police work. We'll get this crime solved eventually. My bosses demand it. Lord Kaldaire was a peer, murdered in a household full of people. The household was just as full, and it was daytime, when Gregson was thrown from the window. Those are the cases that are easiest to solve. Or so you'd think." He finally set down the plate to take a platter from me.

"You realize the killer must be able to enter and leave Kaldaire House without being noticed. But who could be a killer and fit that requirement?"

"Whoever it is, we'll find them." His expression was grim.

"You don't want me to continue to investigate this with Lady Kaldaire?"

"Convince her to let us do our job. We'll get there."

"She won't listen. And that means I have to help her." I found I was facing him again, standing very close, staring into his expressive eyes.

"Don't put yourself in danger, Miss Gates. If you even imagine there might be some risk involved, call me. Or call your grandfather. I don't want to see you hurt."

"Why? Because you might still want to arrest me for the hatpin murder by the Underground station?" I smiled at him.

"I will if it will save your life." He looked serious.

"Tell me about the victim of that murder."

He moved ever closer, as if he wanted to grab me. "You're not going to—"

"No." I continued to smile. "I just want to talk about something we won't argue over."

He appeared to consider this for a moment. "This is all in strictest confidence."

"Of course, Inspector."

He nodded. "The victim was stabbed between ten-thirty and ten-forty p.m. His name was Jeremiah Pruitt. Son of a wealthy and respected family, but he was from all reports a bit of a wastrel. There were a few scandals in his past. Cheating at cards. Getting a housemaid in trouble. Everything hushed up by his family."

"Sounds like a fool. Or a rogue."

"Lately, however, he'd apparently turned over a new leaf. He was seeing Miss Annabelle Wyatt, the daughter of Isaiah, Lord Wyatt of the Admiralty. His friends thought an engagement would be announced soon. His family was pushing it, but that might have been in an effort to settle him down."

"How sad, to be killed when he was beginning to improve his life."

"If he was."

I heard the skepticism in his tone. "There was some question of this?" Jeremiah Pruitt sounded like an interesting case. And someone my grandfather would know about.

"Yes. Recent gambling debts. A flirtation with another young lady of society. Some less-than-reputable friends."

"Why are you telling me about this?"

"You asked me to." He must have seen my skeptical expression, because he sighed and continued. "It helps me clarify my cases in my own mind by talking about them aloud. You have a sharp mind and can keep your own counsel. I can't think of anyone I'd rather talk to about these crimes than you."

He gave me such a heartwarming smile that I couldn't help but return it. "I'm honored that you value my acquaintance so highly."

We were standing very close to each other, smiling into each other's eyes, when Matthew dashed into the kitchen.

Matthew stopped, looked at us in surprise, gave a braying laugh, and hurried away again, but the spell was broken.

CHAPTER TWENTY-FOUR

By lunchtime the next day, I had done final fittings on two hats and presented bills to some of my stubbornest customers before calling at Kaldaire House. Rawlings led me to the morning room, where Lady Kaldaire was overseeing the packing of the knickknacks that had covered the shelves.

"Wait, Rawlings," I said before he shut the door between us. "Lady Kaldaire has a question for you."

"Yes, please wait, Rawlings. Mary, Lucy, you've worked past your lunchtime. Get your lunch now and come back to finish this afterward."

The lady's maid and housemaid stopped their packing, bobbed curtsies, and slipped past Rawlings and out the door.

"Go ahead, Emily," Lady Kaldaire said and pinned Rawlings with a look.

Rawlings shut the door and came further into the room, looking from one of us to the other as if ready to bolt at any moment.

"There's no reason to look so worried, Rawlings. You're not in any trouble. It's only that you can straighten out a point for her ladyship," I said in a soothing voice.

He nodded, his eyes darting from one of us to the other.

"Her ladyship just wants you to tell her the truth

about what time Newton returned to the house the night Lord Kaldaire died."

"I did."

"We know you were trying to protect a friend. That's commendable, Rawlings, but her ladyship wants the truth. We know Newton returned later than you told us. When did he return?"

"The clock in the hall had already chimed the hour a few minutes before. Mr. Gregson came back downstairs after that and said, 'Has Newton returned yet?' I said no and Mr. Gregson was most cross."

"Why?" Lady Kaldaire said.

"Apparently, Lord Kaldaire had finally gone upstairs. Mr. Gregson had to wait on him for a few minutes before he could lock the front door and only then could he come back down."

"That's perfectly normal. Why was he cross?" Lady Kaldaire repeated.

"Because he still had to leave the servants' entrance unlocked until Newton returned. He was threatening to lock him out when Newton finally returned. He stumbled in then and Mr. Gregson snapped at him as he locked the door. I'd finished cleaning the silver and asked if I was excused. Mr. Gregson told us both to go to bed."

I was confused by his explanation. "When the clock struck eleven, where was Mr. Gregson?"

"He was upstairs."

"How long was he gone?"

"Five minutes. Maybe a little more."

"And how long was he back before Newton came in?"

"No more than a minute. Another minute and Newton would have been locked out."

"Thank you, Rawlings."

Looking relieved, the young man bolted from the room, remembering to shut the door silently behind him. Lady Kaldaire gave me a level look and said, "What made you question him about that?"

"When I spoke to Newton at the jail, he said he tripped over a step and Rawlings laughed at him. Rawlings was there, sober, and in possession of the information we need."

"And did it do us any good?"

I nodded to a chair and she gestured for me to sit. Once I did, I said, "Did this sound completely normal to you? The amount of time Gregson was gone to lock the front door? Five minutes? Possibly a minute or two more?"

"It does seem excessive."

"Newton still swears he saw the man in the top hat in front of this house, but he doesn't know if he had been inside or not. Gregson was inside the house on the ground floor at the same time, judging by when Newton came in. Gregson knew if this person had been inside, and probably who it was. He could have spent the extra time watching to identify this person."

"Prince Maximilian," Lady Kaldaire said with conviction.

"Maybe. Or maybe a third person. Remember, Gregson saw the prince out."

"Perhaps he was lying about the time when he said he saw the prince leave."

"Or perhaps he was telling the truth."

"But who gains from my husband's death?"

I took her question literally. "His brother, his brother's wife, Prince Maximilian if it gained him the contents of the safe, an unknown person retrieving an unknown item from the safe—"

"Thank you. I get the point," Lady Kaldaire said drily. "I wonder if the unknown person is the same man who's been visiting the new Lord Kaldaire. Not the sort of man I'd think Laurence would have any time for. Rather flashy. Oily. Large. Very middle-class and not very tidy about it. Rather rat-faced. Not a gentleman, if you understand my meaning."

I made hats for the aristocracy, as well as those with "new money," and those with just the pretense of new money as they crawled into the middle and the upper-middle class. The hats that the ladies of these three groups wanted, and how much they were willing to pay, and how they acted in my shop, were miles apart. "I understand. And you have no idea who he is?"

"None. Laurence has made a point not to introduce us. He's not the type of man I'd expect Laurence to welcome into this house, but they spend time together in the study. I wonder what he wants."

* * *

Two days later, I received a message from Lady Kaldaire to meet her at her new townhouse. I didn't have time. From the moment I walked into the shop, I was rushed off my feet.

Customers came in who needed hats for mourning, for garden parties, for afternoon calls, for walking, for cycling, veils for motoring, and for every other aspect of their lives. I drew, redid trimmings on hats in stock, ran orders over to the factory, and waited on customers. Jane hurried too, but we couldn't quite keep up.

I knew I'd hear from Lady Kaldaire demanding my presence. She'd have to wait until I closed the shop for the day if business kept up like this. She wouldn't like it, but then, she had no idea what it was like to run a business.

Of course, she hadn't told me what was so important. I knew she'd let me know what she wanted sooner or later.

Sometime after Jane and I caught separate hurried lunches, a mother and daughter entered, their footman waiting by the carriage. The girl was a blonde but seemed sickly pale rather than fashionably delicate. She stood just inside the door while the mother walked forward. Free of customers for the moment, I hurried over to greet them.

"We're looking for something subdued. A friend of my daughter recently died and she wants to wear mourning for her friend for a few weeks."

"What style are you looking for, Mrs.—?"

"*Lady* Wyatt. This is my daughter, Miss Annabelle Wyatt."

Where had I heard that name recently? The girl and I exchanged curtsies. "I'm sorry for the loss of your friend. What styles do you usually fancy?" I asked. "I should be able to do something similar but in a suitable color."

"She likes styles appropriate for a young girl," her mother said. "And no veils. The friend was not a relative, so any veiling would be unsuitable."

The daughter looked furious, or perhaps mutinous.

"The hat you're wearing. Would you like something like this?"

"T-this hat was h-his favorite," she said and burst into tears.

I led her to a bench and sat down next to her, putting my arm around her shoulders while she fished out a handkerchief.

Her mother huffed out "Annabelle" as the bell over

the door rang. In walked Roberta, Lady Kaldaire, modeling the latest in mourning fashion, one of my wide-brimmed hats in black with the veil over her face.

Annabelle forgot her tears as she stared for a moment. "I love that hat."

"Without the veil," her mother snapped.

The daughter opened her mouth, clearly ready to blast her mother.

"Lady Kaldaire, do you know Lady Wyatt?" I said into what was becoming an awkward moment with a family row ready to break out in my shop. I stood and moved between the combatants to introduce the two ladies.

Lady Kaldaire gracefully lifted her veil over the crown of her hat to make it part of the cascade down her back and set about finding acquaintances in common with Lady Wyatt. This group included Prince Maximilian, and harmony reigned in my shop again as Annabelle kept her mouth mulishly shut.

"Miss Annabelle lost a friend and will be wearing mourning for a few weeks," I said, taking the girl's hat and mentally running through my inventory for similar styles.

Lady Kaldaire nodded at my words and sat down next to the girl. "I'm mourning a husband of many years, but I think it must be harder to lose someone in the prime of life. All that promise ahead of them. I'm very sorry. You'll always remember them, but also remember they wouldn't want to see you sorrowing."

The girl, possibly because of the new audience, said, "He was my dearest friend. We hoped to be married."

The mother cleared her throat. Obviously not a marriage she hoped for.

"You won't believe this today, but twenty years

from now, you'll think back on him and smile." Lady Kaldaire used a soothing tone I'd never heard from her before.

"I don't think I'll ever smile again." The girl sighed.

"That's because you've not been eating properly."

"However did you—?" She gave Lady Kaldaire a sharp look before she sniffed. "I've lost my appetite."

"Nevertheless, you must eat. Otherwise, your complexion will become dry and sallow. The other young ladies will laugh at you behind your back. No, you must resume eating and keep your head held high. Otherwise, when you're ready to reenter society, you will lack for invitations."

That must have been her mother's refrain, because the girl's mouth thinned stubbornly. "I'll never want to reenter society."

"And do what? Sit around the house while all your friends are out having a good time dancing and going to concerts and parties? You want to cut yourself off from pleasure?"

"But it was so horrible. He was murdered." Annabelle could certainly wail dramatically.

Lady Kaldaire gave a small shrug. "So was my husband. Am I cutting myself off from society and starving myself? No. I'm trying to find the villain who killed him so I may see him hang. Even an old lady like myself can savor such satisfactory results."

The girl looked surprised at first, but then you could see the beginning of a plan on her face. "I understand."

"You'll do nothing of the sort," her mother insisted.

Lady Kaldaire and Miss Annabelle both looked at me.

I shook my head, holding my palms out. "I have my hands full taking care of my shop."

"Leave it to me," Lady Kaldaire told the girl. "In the meantime, call on me after you've stopped looking so sickly and have begun to go out in society again."

Lady Wyatt looked at Lady Kaldaire as if not certain whether to thank her or murder her.

Miss Annabelle took one of Lady Kaldaire's cards and gave her one of her own.

The older woman said, "Call on me any day after luncheon. We'll see what can be done. What was your friend's name?"

"Jeremiah Pruitt."

My jaw dropped as Inspector Russell's words came back to me. Pruitt's family had wanted to marry him off. Now I learned the other side of the story. Her family was not happy with the situation. And Pruitt had been murdered down the street from and about the same time that someone had bashed Lord Kaldaire over the head.

We were entering the land of too many coincidences, and I wanted to run. If there was any connection between the two deaths, this was too dangerous for a mere milliner to investigate.

"I believe Miss Gates knows something about the case already," Lady Kaldaire said, watching me.

I wished my expression hadn't given me away. "I've heard about it from the inspector. I know they're working very hard to find his killer."

"Then why haven't they found him yet?" Miss Annabelle sounded petulant. If she acted like this all the time, I pitied her mother. Or blamed her.

"Catching a murderer and building a case that will stand up in court takes time," I told her.

Lady Kaldaire patted her hand and said, "Pick out a hat, something Mr. Pruitt would have approved of, and wear it with a smile on your face. And when you're more yourself, come visit me."

Thus began the longest hour of my life as Miss Annabelle and Lady Wyatt fought over every design in my shop. Jane took over the other customers who came in during that time, at one point glancing over and giving me a sympathetic smile.

As we started on the second hour, I began by getting them to agree to a shape, wide-brimmed with a low crown. Then I asked Miss Annabelle what she wanted to decorate the hat with. That argument between mother and daughter only lasted fifteen minutes, as they shared the Victorian mindset of "more is better." Then we came to the color.

"Black," Annabelle insisted.

"A pastel shade," Lady Wyatt countered.

"What do you think of blue? Blue roses signify mystery, and as you are embarking on a mystery, Miss Annabelle, this might be appropriate. A pale shade for the hat with darker flowers, feathers, netting, and so on." I thought it was a brilliant solution.

Lady Kaldaire, who'd waited patiently for the pair to finish while giving her opinions on everything going on in my shop and thereby unnerving Jane, immediately voiced her agreement and assured them both that they would love the result.

I doubted that very much, but as long as they paid me for my creation, I'd be happy.

With grumbling agreement from both mother and daughter, I whipped out my order pad and started writing.

Once they finally left, their deposit in my cash box, I gave a loud sigh and asked Lady Kaldaire why she'd come.

"Today is moving day. Kaldaire House has been my home since I was a new bride of eighteen. When I tried to thank the servants for their service, Laurence told me I was interrupting their duties and to leave. He ordered everyone back to work."

Lord Kaldaire's behavior sounded repugnant. Unfeeling. And selfish.

My dismay must have shown on my face, for she smiled and signaled me to join her in one of the mirrored booths for ladies to try on hats. Each booth was designed to minimize the ability of other customers to overhear a conversation.

Sitting in the chair in front of the mirror, she said, "Cook turned in her notice on the spot. Told him he could fix his own luncheon and left to pack. When he told her he wouldn't give her a reference, I said I would. Someone, I'm not certain who, gave an abruptly silenced cheer."

"And so you came here to help me out?" Amazingly, she had saved the day. In one case.

"Not at all. You can handle this on your own. I wanted to get out of the way of the movers and let Lyle and Mary organize the household."

"Who's Lyle?"

"Wallace Lyle. My new footman. Or butler. We'll have to see how everything works out with Newton."

"Newton sounded very convincing when he said he didn't kill Gregson," I told her. "It seems Gregson was a blackmailer. Newton did tell us the name of someone who might know what secrets Gregson was holding over someone's head when he died so gruesomely."

"Gregson was a blackmailer? In that case, I can understand why he would want to stay at Kaldaire House. There wouldn't be enough secrets in a widow's house to keep a blackmailer in pin money." She tsked. "So, have you talked to this person?"

I gave her a suitably tailored version of what Detective Inspector James Russell had told me.

She listened carefully, and when I finished, said, "So the police think someone who can enter and leave Kaldaire House without arousing suspicion called on my husband late on the evening he died. I would have said there were very few who could do this until you broke into the breakfast room."

"There are a great many people who can break into a house. The problem comes when you need a certain person who not only can enter Kaldaire House without attracting attention but also would know to search the safe for this mystery note. This person has to be familiar enough with your house to know where the safe is and how to get into it." I stopped, hoping she understood what I meant.

"If someone knew Horace had this note, I suppose it would be easy to get in and force him to hand it over. But then why kill him?"

CHAPTER TWENTY-FIVE

That night after work, I received an urgent request to come to Lady Kaldaire's new home. I ate a hurried dinner and had Matthew and Annie wash the dishes while I rode a wheezing, smoking omnibus to find out what Lady Kaldaire meant by writing she knew *who must have killed my Horace.*

A gray-haired man I'd not seen at Kaldaire House answered the door in an old-fashioned frock coat. "Lady Kaldaire, please?"

"Are you Miss Gates?"

"Yes."

"She's expecting you, miss." He held the door wide for me and I walked in.

"Are you Mr. Lyle?" I handed him my cloak.

"Yes, miss."

Before I could say any more, "Emily. I'm in the music room," floated down the staircase from the first floor.

I nodded to Lyle and walked up the staircase, noting the crates in the front hall. When I reached the next floor, I found Lady Kaldaire in the back room of the pair. She was filling shelves with books and sheets of music. Other than the shelves and two armless chairs, the room was empty. I couldn't imagine how she'd fill so large a space.

She stopped what she was doing and spun around

to face me. "I've been thinking about what you said earlier. Who could enter and leave Kaldaire House without attracting attention. The answer is...someone who's already been admitted."

"Then you think the murderer is...?" I had no idea.

"Prince Maximilian, of course. He'd been admitted, so no one would be surprised to see him there. He wanted the letter in the safe. He would have no qualms about bullying Horace into opening the safe for him. And he might have taken anything else inside to throw suspicion away from him."

"So you want to...?" This was the part I didn't want to hear. I suspected whatever her plan was, it involved me doing something illegal and risky.

"I want you to break into the prince's house when no one is home and search the hidden compartments in the cabinet."

"Do you have any idea how hard it is to know when everyone is gone from a house? And how seldom people in Prince Maximilian's position send all their servants away at once?" It was time to stop this nonsense. I'd helped her, but I wasn't about to do anything so dangerous. And I was convinced the prince was dangerous.

"I'll take care of that."

"How? Do you think he'll tell you—?"

"Yes, I do. Don't worry. I'll make sure his house is empty, and then you can get in, retrieve the letter, and get out again without anyone being the wiser."

"That won't help you learn if he killed your husband. And if he were going to use that silly letter, he'd have done it by now. There's no reason to do this."

She was deaf to my logic. "It's either this, Emily, or I will go to that nice Inspector Russell and tell him I'll testify against you for breaking and entering. That I have no idea why you were in my house that night and Horace never played games like that." She gave a sniff as her nose and chin rose and turned away from me.

My stomach felt like I had eaten iron weights. I saw no way to avoid prison and the loss of my business. I'd found myself warming to James Russell. Finding out everything I'd told him when I'd first met him was a lie would destroy his trust in me forever. I would be embarrassed. Ruined.

Worse, while Noah would take care of Matthew, there was no way he could afford to send him to the School for the Deaf in Doncaster by himself.

"No. Please. Think of Matthew." I was begging and I didn't care.

"You must think of Matthew. I need to think of Horace and the mess he's left behind. His killer must be unmasked and this letter destroyed. A letter that must be hidden in one of the compartments in the prince's cabinet. I'm certain of it."

"Which letter? The Queen Victoria or the one that went astray from his club? Your husband supposedly had both in his safe."

"If that friend of Gregson's is to be believed, I suspect the killer has both notes. If you find both in the prince's desk, then we can be sure he killed my husband." Lady Kaldaire gave me a sorrowful look as she reached out and clasped my hands. "I must find Horace's killer. I feel him calling to me to unmask his murderer. Please, Emily, help me. I know we're getting close to the answer."

There was no doubt she planned to use me to hunt down her husband's killer. If I resisted, I felt confident she would destroy me, and she had the power to do so.

She was, after all, an aristocrat.

I needed some insurance.

* * *

I traveled across town and arrived on my grandfather's steps well after dark. He answered the door while adjusting his braces. As soon as he saw me in the dim light from the hallway, he said, "Pet. Come in. Is something wrong?"

"I need your help."

"Come in. We're all in the parlor."

I followed him down the hall and into the largest room in the old building. My grandmother sat by the fire knitting something in very dark wool and barely glanced up when I entered. My uncle Thomas sat on the sofa, one of my cousins on either side. Petey sat on the floor at my grandmother's feet, which told me someone had tried to correct him since he was half hidden by her skirts. My uncle Victor was rocking slowly in a rocker. A couple of cousins stopped their card game and stared at me.

The house smelled of coal fires and expensive cigars and the pie Grandmother had baked for after dinner. The room was crowded and cozy and I felt safe there among these crooks. They were my family.

"What is she doing here?" Petey asked.

"I need your help."

"That's a laugh," my grandmother said.

"Now, Aggie," my grandfather said. "Let's hear her out."

"I'm being forced to break into a house to look for two letters in a cabinet that is a sort of giant puzzle box." I could tell by the silence and the lack of movement that I had caught their attention.

"One of the letters purports to prove Queen Victoria

was illegitimate. We don't know the contents of the other letter, only that it fell into the hands of a murdered man by accident. Both letters are thought to have been in a safe in the murdered man's study that was found open and empty when his body was discovered."

"I think you better tell us all, pet, and then tell us what you want," my grandfather said.

"I'll make a pot of tea," my grandmother said, setting aside her knitting.

Two cups of strong tea with plenty of sugar and a half hour later, I'd told them all that had happened. Well, I downplayed Inspector Russell's role, of which only Grandpapa seemed aware.

"Now, pet, what do you want us to do?"

"I want your help making certain no one is in the house and warning me if anyone returns."

"You don't trust Lady Kaldaire to know whether all the servants are out of the house or not?" Uncle Victor asked.

"No. She doesn't know what she's doing. She thinks you ask a lot of questions and people tell you the truth."

"Oh. An amateur." He nodded.

"So, first you don't want anything to do with us. Now, all of a sudden, you need us and our talents, so you come and expect us to drop everything and help you," Petey said.

I suspected his pique was because he'd hidden his share of the loot from three jobs in my hat factory and the police had come and taken it all away. I decided to let someone else point that out. "I need your help. Either you'll help me or you won't. That's your choice."

"I'd like to see the cabinet," Uncle Victor said. Puzzle boxes had always been his specialty. That and safe cracking.

"That would mean coming inside with me."

"Not a good idea," Uncle Thomas said. "This isn't our caper. We won't get anything out of it. We'll keep you safe Emily, you're family, but we won't get involved in your break-in."

"I appreciate it. I'll let you know when it'll happen. All I can say is it'll be soon and in the evening. Lady Kaldaire would never dream of a break-in during the day."

This brought a round of laughter from the professionals.

"Hey, I'm here," a man's voice called from the hallway. "I hope you saved me some pie."

I knew that voice. I sprang to my feet and headed toward the door.

I met my father at the doorway, my grandfather right behind me.

"Emily? What are you doing here?" my father asked in a tone of disbelief. He didn't sound happy to see me.

Well, I wasn't happy to see him either. "I'll talk to you later, Grandpapa," I said as I squeezed past and dashed out into the night.

* * *

Sunday morning, Lady Kaldaire sent her manservant, Lyle, with a message.

Prince Maximilian has given all his servants the evening off. He is dining out and then going to a musicale. There won't be a better chance than tonight to find those notes.
Roberta, Lady Kaldaire

I contacted my grandfather. We agreed on eight in

the evening as it would still be light out and everyone in Mayfair society would be sitting down to dinner.

At the appointed time, I spotted one of my cousins in the communal gardens. He gave me the "house is empty" signal and I walked up to the servants' entrance.

I used the lock picks the way Grandpapa had taught me, feeling for the click of metal releasing metal. Fortunately, I didn't need any light. I'd been taught that using a lantern called attention that I didn't need and could be a giveaway that something wasn't right.

I entered the back door after only a few moments. The house was silent as only an empty building could be. I was home free.

I hoped. Any mistake could land me in jail. Ruin my reputation. Destroy my millinery. Eliminate all my hopes for my brother.

Light came in the curtainless kitchen window, allowing me to find the stairs without tripping over furniture. Upstairs, I opened the parlor draperies and let the light filter in so I could find my way around. Opening the curtains also told whichever family member was watching the front of the house that I was inside at work.

I didn't need light to find the secret drawers in the cabinet that held the scandalous letter. They could only be opened by sense of touch.

I started at the top left-hand corner and worked my way to the right and then down. The wood was cool and smooth under my fingers, the gaps between the drawers tiny. After what I guessed was fifteen minutes, I'd found two compartments in addition to the one I'd found the first time I saw the cabinet. All were empty.

The prince said there were four hidden places. The letter had to be in the last one.

I worked on in desperation. A servant might return at any time and I didn't want to be caught. Prince Maximilian was the type to call the police on housebreakers and I didn't need to join my family as another convicted felon.

And I didn't want to add to their troubles.

The last opening sprang open and with a surge of triumph, I reached inside.

Nothing.

A light came on, making me suck in my breath as I jumped. A man's voice said, "Well done, Miss Gates. I think that's a record. That last one is terribly difficult to discover."

I collapsed against the cabinet for a moment before I looked over to find the prince standing perhaps six feet away, holding a pistol aimed at my chest. My heart galloped out the door while my feet remained rooted to the carpet. "Your Highness. I couldn't resist trying to find the other openings."

"You could have asked."

"Where's the challenge in that?" I tried to sound sassy. I'm afraid I sounded pitiful.

"Does Lady Kaldaire know of your talents?"

"Of course. She encourages me." I forced a smile to remain on my face, but the pistol frightened me. I didn't think he'd use it, but I wasn't sure. I wished I'd thought to work out an "I'm in danger" signal to my family. A mistake I wouldn't make again. If there was an *again*.

"I would have thought you were smarter than to get involved in national affairs."

"What?" It sounded like he knew everything.

"I'm disappointed in you." His eyes were cold. Demonic. But then, in nearly half an hour, he'd never moved a foot or breathed deeply. If he had, I would have known I wasn't alone. He was inhuman.

"I opened all four of the secret compartments in your cabinet. I succeeded at my challenge. I'm proud of myself." Despite my trembling, I gave him a cheeky grin.

"Pride goeth before a fall, Miss Gates." He gestured me away from the cabinet with the barrel of the pistol. He probably didn't want to chance hitting it with a bullet and damaging the finish.

I moved into the center of the room. "You knew I'd come here tonight and try to open those secret compartments."

"I know what Lady Kaldaire wants. And so I sent my servants off for the evening, told Lady Kaldaire that ridiculous story about plans for this evening, and settled in to wait for you. Too bad she had to go out, but that will save her having to see your body when I shoot an intruder."

"Isn't that a little drastic? No harm was done. And I've satisfied my curiosity, so you know I won't be back." I hoped I could talk my way out of this.

His rock cliff of a face didn't look like that would be possible. He reached into the inside pocket of his jacket and pulled out a piece of paper. "Is that what you were looking for?"

"Looking for?" I squeaked.

"Don't become a parrot, Miss Gates. It's not flattering."

I marshaled my shaking nerves and asked, "What do you have there?"

"I said I know what Lady Kaldaire wants. A letter written by Victoria's mother to a friend. Unfortunately for Lord Kaldaire, it was written in German. The translator he hired has long been a supporter of my family. He told me about the contents. And where it was kept."

"Why would anyone want the letter? Nobody will believe it, and it doesn't make any difference. Not a century later." It didn't make any sense to me.

"The letter has political uses, whether or not it's believed. Some of us have plans that you don't need to know." With those words, the prince sounded like the great-grandson of a king.

"So you stole the letter and killed Lord Kaldaire." I felt my eyes widen. *Blast.* I refused to give him the satisfaction of seeing me faint, scream, or beg. I hoped he couldn't see me quake.

If he killed Lord Kaldaire, I didn't like my chances to leave here alive.

CHAPTER TWENTY-SIX

"I stole the letter, yes, but Lord Kaldaire was already dead when I entered the room. Or so I thought. Before I could make sure, I heard someone coming and I stepped back into a dark corner near the door. Imagine my surprise to see you enter. You look quite daring in trousers." Prince Maximilian's smile was more of a leer. "At that time, I didn't know you wanted the letter."

"I didn't. I was after the painting of the *Lady in Blue*."

"An art thief." He was still leering.

"No. Yes. It's a long story."

"We have time."

I certainly hoped so. "Lord Kaldaire owed me for several hats Lady Kaldaire had purchased. He wouldn't pay me. I knew how much he liked the painting of his great-grandmother, so I was going to take it and hold it for ransom until he paid Lady Kaldaire's bills."

"I watched you. You never glanced toward the painting that hid the safe. But then you found Lord Kaldaire and aroused the household. Why?"

"He groaned. He was still alive."

"You're a good person. I would hate to have to shoot a good person." He spoke as if he meant it, but the pistol was still aimed at me. "After the servant answered your ring, you looked away and I slipped out of the room. With the letter. I was gone before the police arrived."

"How did you open the safe?"

"It was already open."

"The safe was already open and Lord Kaldaire was already struck down when you entered the study." I gave a loud sigh. "This makes no sense. There was very little time for anyone to commit a crime. Did you see anyone outside the house walking away? Any sign of anyone moving around the house?"

"The painting had been pulled away from the wall, showing the inside of the safe. The only thing in it was this letter." He waved the yellowing paper in his hand.

"There were no other papers?" What about the note Lord Kaldaire supposedly received by accident?

"None. All I had time to do was take the letter and swing the painting back over the safe before I had to hide," he told me. "And I saw no one either inside or outside the house before you entered."

I think better when I pace. I hadn't realized I'd started this habit until the prince cleared his throat and I found myself ten feet from where I'd stood before and the pistol still aimed at me. I swallowed and told him, "The safe was open and a valuable letter was left inside. Whoever the murderer was, he must have come for something else that was in the safe."

"And Lady Kaldaire has no idea what." He sounded certain of this. He must have asked her. I was surprised the lady could lie so convincingly. Unless he asked her before I told her what Gregson's publican friend told Inspector Russell, in which case she had been telling the truth.

I resumed pacing, certain at this point Prince Maximilian wouldn't shoot me. But he was certainly enjoying tormenting me.

"When we find out what else was in the safe, we'll

know who killed him. Lord Kaldaire never mentioned anything to you, did he?" I asked the prince.

"No. The translator came to his study and saw where he put the letter after they finished with it. He said he didn't see inside the safe."

"Do you trust this translator?"

"Yes."

Curiosity made me ask, "How would you have opened the safe if it hadn't already been unlocked?"

He smiled. "You are not the only one with the skill to enter locked buildings and to hide and wait to get what you want."

"Why would a prince need to learn such things?" His upbringing was definitely different than Lady Kaldaire's.

"I grew up in a time and place where such skills were necessary to survive political intrigue. However, I wouldn't have needed to use my skills if I could persuade Lord Kaldaire to open the safe for me."

"Could you do that?"

"There are many ways to convince a man to do what you want." He was still smiling in a way that made me nervous.

"My grandfather would like you," I told him. "Neither of us struck down Lord Kaldaire—"

"Are you sure?"

"Yes."

He shook his head. "You are more trusting than I."

"Perhaps, but I think if you have the skill to escape that room without me or anyone else seeing you, you wouldn't have bludgeoned Lord Kaldaire. You wouldn't have needed to." Then I remembered Gregson's words. "You were shown out of the house by the butler. How did you enter the second time?"

"What makes you think I left the first time?"

I stopped pacing. Had Gregson lied about shutting the front door after the prince? "If you didn't leave and come back, you saw who killed Lord Kaldaire. I can't believe you witnessed a murder and haven't said anything to the police."

Again the smile of a wolf. "You credit me with more scruples than I possess."

"You disappoint me, Your Highness. I would have thought with your talents, you'd have left and come back later surreptitiously."

"In this case, you are wrong." He watched me in silence for a moment. "When I was ready to leave, I heard someone in another room on the ground floor. I thought at first it was the butler, but then I heard him come up from the basement. I admit to a certain curiosity, especially since Lord Kaldaire wouldn't give me the letter I wanted. I thought perhaps there was another bidder."

"You were going to pay him for the note?"

"If necessary. I grabbed the front-door handle, snapped a good night at the butler so he'd keep his distance, and shut the door. The butler hadn't closed up the house for the night yet, so I knew the door wouldn't lock. I just waited outside for the butler to leave the front hall."

"So you came back inside after only a minute?"

"Perhaps, certainly no longer than that. I slipped into the dining room and listened for my chance. Other than voices in the study, no one seemed to be on the ground floor."

"Could you hear what they said?"

"No. The sound was muffled by the closed doors."

"Then what happened?" It was as though he was telling me a story.

"After a few minutes, the clock struck the hour. I heard footsteps in the front hall go out the front door and the door shut. Then someone else walked along the front hall and turned off the light in the hall. This second person sounded as though he moved away to another part of the house. A minute later, another set of footsteps went past the dining room door. Then I heard the front door open and close once more."

"So two people went out the front door in the matter of a minute or two?" I was trying to picture all this activity.

"Yes. After the door closed a second time, I heard someone else walking down the front hallway. A third person. Instead of going out the door, the footsteps stopped. After another minute, that person walked away and went down an echoing, uncarpeted staircase rather than out the front door."

"No one spoke as they walked down the front hall?"

"Not a word from any of them. I had the impression they were trying to be quiet. Once the house was silent, I left my hiding place and went into the study where one light was still on. I saw the safe open and when I went over to examine the contents, I found Lord Kaldaire on the rug. I retrieved my letter and then I heard someone at the door. You."

I was confused by his description of footsteps going every which way. I thought that was his intention, but there must have been at least three people besides the late Lord Kaldaire and the prince walking around the ground floor at the critical time.

"So you hid until the house was in turmoil." I took a deep breath and said with as much authority as I could muster, "Now, will you please put away that absurd pistol?"

"I haven't decided yet."

"Decided what?"

"Whether to kill you, turn you in to the police, or let you go."

"Letting me go would be the honorable thing to do."

The smirk on his face told me I was going to have to try harder. "No. The honorable thing would be to turn you over to the constables."

"Then you can't be certain I won't claim you kidnapped me or some other fanciful tale."

He snorted at my lie. "You won't be able to prove anything."

"The police already know that I'm here. And I've had people watching the house. If I don't come out..."

My words wiped the smile off his face. The expression that appeared in its place sent winter winds dancing across my flesh. "Why would the police know you are here?"

"They've been following me for days." I couldn't hide my smile. This was the first time I was glad they were watching me.

"They suspect you in Lord Kaldaire's death."

I shook my head, pacing his polished wooden floors. "They expect me to lead them to his killer."

"Won't they be disappointed when they find your body instead?" The menace in his tone left me frozen in place.

And then I grew annoyed with him toying with me like a cat with a mouse. "What could that possibly gain you?"

"I won't have to worry about what you will reveal."

"But you know you don't have to worry. I already said I don't think you killed Lord Kaldaire. And I don't believe you can topple the monarchy with that ridiculous letter."

His cold smile didn't reach his eyes. "Perhaps."

Did he mean he didn't have to worry, or he couldn't remove King Edward VII from the throne? I watched him, wondering what he'd decide. And again wondering if I would manage to get out of there alive if I walked away.

His expression was grave. "Go back to Lady Kaldaire and tell her I will not give her the letter."

I stood there, amazement making me slow.

"Go. *Now.*"

Freed, I rushed out of the front of his house, down the pavement, and up to Lady Kaldaire's door, all the time hoping my family and the police saw my exit. My frantic hammering brought her footman, Lyle, to open the door. "Oh, it's you, Miss Emily. Her ladyship isn't home yet."

"May I come in and leave her a note?"

"Of course." As I stepped into the light of the hall, Lyle said, "Are you all right? You look as if you've seen a ghost."

I'd almost been turned into one, but I didn't need to explain that to the servant. "There should be paper and ink in the morning room." I headed in that direction.

I hadn't finished composing my note when I heard the bell and then the voices of Lady Kaldaire and Lyle. I walked into the hall, holding the half-finished note in my hand.

"Emily," her ladyship said as she took off her wrap. "Did you have a successful evening?"

"We need to talk."

"Lyle, I'd like tea for two in the morning room. And perhaps some of Cook's biscuits." Lady Kaldaire walked toward me, pulling a long hatpin out of her favorite mourning hat.

Remembering my recent experience facing Prince Maximilian's pistol and the murder of Mr. Pruitt, I jumped back at the sight of Lady Kaldaire's hatpin.

"Really. Emily. If I were going to use a hatpin on you, I'd have done it long before now. Besides, you're too valuable."

"No, I'm not. I opened all the hidden drawers, but the letter you want was in Prince Maximilian's pocket. He was waiting for me. With a pistol."

"Really." She turned around, marched past Lyle as he quickly opened the front door again, and continued down the steps.

I raced after her and caught up to her on the pavement. "You don't want to challenge the prince about this. He's not the killer."

"I'm not going to challenge him, Emily." She continued her stately march to his front door where she ran the bell.

Maximilian opened the door. "As you know, my servants are all out this evening, so you will have to do with my humble welcome."

"I'm not here for your welcome, Prince. I want to see the letter that my husband put in the safe."

Lady Kaldaire and Prince Maximilian stared at each other for a long time. Neither blinked.

A skill I'd like to learn.

"I have no intention of bargaining with you, dear lady."

"Every man has his price."

"Not this time." Maximilian sounded certain. Of course, he had the letter.

"Stealing a letter from a dying man. That was not kind." Queen Alexandra couldn't have delivered those words with more regal disdain.

"My apologies, dear lady."

"Tell her about the other two people who entered Kaldaire House that night," I said.

She must have picked up on my eagerness, because she said, "Two other people? Who were they?"

"I don't know."

Her voice turned icy. "Prince, if you would, please tell us about your visit with my husband on the night he died."

"Not tonight, and not on the doorstep."

"Of course. Forgive me. Perhaps you will come for tea tomorrow and we can discuss this. I have some other questions I'd like to put to you."

"I am at your service," the prince said.

We exchanged bows and curtsies before Lady Kaldaire turned and marched down his steps and up her own. I was impressed that she could walk that distance with that much vigor without knocking her unpinned hat loose.

Obviously, she had a very good milliner.

As I left for home, I gave the area a discreet glance, but I didn't spot any of my relatives or a constable. They must have thought the danger was over.

I hoped they stuck around long enough to listen to the information Prince Maximilian shared.

CHAPTER TWENTY-SEVEN

I had nearly reached the omnibus route when a pleasant male voice behind me said, "The prince apparently told you everything he knew. We should have you teach us interrogation techniques."

I jumped when he first spoke, but as I turned and looked at Inspector Russell, my heartbeat sped rather than slowed. "What are you doing here?"

"Seeing you get home safely."

"That's kind of you, but I'll be fine."

He smiled and took my arm. "I don't want to risk such a valuable property."

Now he'd made me angry. "Do you mean like a carriage horse? Or perhaps my workshop?"

"Don't be daft. Gregson was killed for what he knew. Now you've demonstrated to all and sundry on the street tonight that you're learning his secrets."

I thought of our talk on the doorstep where anyone could have overheard us and shivered, despite the warmth of the evening.

We took an omnibus, this one motorized, toward my home. After we sat, I asked, "Are you a Londoner by birth?"

"No. Outside Cambridge. My father was a country vicar."

"A vicar?" My surprise leaped out of my voice.

"Is it that hard to believe? Have I become so heavy-handed that I must be a Londoner?"

"It's hard to picture a detective inspector being the son of a vicar." I thought all offspring of vicars were pale, soft creatures. Inspector Russell was sharp, hard, and bright. There was more to him than I expected and I found him fascinating.

"Why? Because my upbringing gave me an education and a polish that most members of the constabulary don't possess?"

"Is that why you're a detective inspector?"

He grinned. "In part."

"In part? What other attributes do you have?"

His grin widened. "Perhaps you'll find out."

Neither of us spoke during the rest of the journey, but we sat squeezed together on the seat. It wasn't until we'd alighted and nearly reached my door that I said, "Lady Kaldaire has invited Prince Maximilian over for tea tomorrow. Do you want me to tell you anything I learn?"

"Yes. Don't worry. I'll appear sometime after tea."

As I opened my door, he doffed his bowler and walked off into the night.

* * *

I arrived at Lady Kaldaire's new house after a full day of work to find the prince sitting in her unfinished parlor with her, both of them drinking tea.

After she called for another cup for me, she said, "Now that Emily is here, tell us about your visit to Kaldaire House the night of Horace's death."

"My first visit concerned a difference of opinion on the House of Saxe-Coburg-Gotha expressed in your husband's letter to a scholarly journal. Actually, that reason was a ruse. I was familiarizing myself with the study for a later visit."

"To what purpose?" Lady Kaldaire asked.

A sardonic smile hovered on his lips. "To steal the letter you sent Miss Gates to steal back from me yesterday."

"And since you're not such a fool as my husband, you took precautions to safeguard it."

He gave her one assured nod.

"How did you reenter the house?"

"The front door was unlocked. I simply waited a minute and let myself back inside."

"At least you didn't use the breakfast room doors. That seems to be the popular route." She glared at me.

"Before you ask, I did not see your husband's killer," the prince said. "When I returned to the study, he'd already been struck down and the safe opened. I took the letter and made certain the room was empty except for the two of us. I then had to hide in the shadows when Miss Gates arrived."

"Didn't his killer pass you on the front steps?"

"No. While two different sets of footsteps left, I was hiding in your dining room." He gave her a hint of a bow. "I beg your pardon for using the room for such an inappropriate purpose."

"My," Lady Kaldaire replied in a sarcastic tone, "the house was simply swarming with visitors that night."

This conversation was bizarre. The evening before, the prince had pointed a gun at my chest and threatened to use it. Now he was apologizing for hiding inside the Kaldaire House dining room uninvited. I was grateful that the prince was clearing my name with Lady Kaldaire, but I wished our earlier conversation had been less frightening.

I might as well get as much information as I could to bring to Inspector Russell's attention.

"Prince Maximilian told me he heard a third set of footsteps follow whoever left by the front door. This third set of footsteps went to the front of the house but didn't go outside. Gregson, perhaps?" I said.

"That would explain how he could have blackmailed the killer. And in turn been murdered." Lady Kaldaire looked from one of us to the other. "As we had already guessed, someone entered the house between the prince's official visit and Emily's unofficial arrival. Someone who was seen by Gregson."

"But who was it?" I knew Lady Kaldaire wouldn't release me from my job as her investigator until we discovered the killer's identity. "You heard two visitors come out of Lord Kaldaire's study? Two visitors who arrived together but left separately?"

"They left separately. I don't know if they arrived together or not. I never saw either of them." The prince gave me a small shrug.

"You didn't look out a window? The dining room overlooks the street." I was amazed the prince didn't display more curiosity. I'd have had my nose pressed to the windowpane.

"It wasn't until I saw Lord Kaldaire that I realized I should have made an effort to learn their identities." He sounded annoyed with himself.

"So it's possible they came in the unlocked front door and hid while you were in the study the first time on your official visit. Then they went into the study unannounced during the short time you were outside." I was trying to account for all the activity before I arrived at Kaldaire House.

"People seemed to have slipped by Gregson on a regular basis." Roberta, Lady Kaldaire sounded irritated. "Doesn't anyone ring the bell anymore?"

Then she said, "Leaving that matter aside, I believe you're acquainted with Lord Wyatt."

"Yes. I know the family quite well," he said.

Oh, wonderful. Now her ladyship was going to start trying to solve Jeremiah Pruitt's murder, no doubt using me as her sleuth. I was tempted to get up and leave.

She ignored my dismay and raised an eyebrow at the prince. "I think the family was not happy with Miss Annabelle's choice of male companions."

He laughed. I was surprised at the spontaneous, amused sound that rumbled from deep inside him, and it stopped any thought of my leaving. "That is putting it mildly. I thought Isaiah, Lord Wyatt, would murder young Mr. Pruitt. Not that any father would blame him. He was a nasty piece of work."

"Did they ever come to blows?" I asked.

"Nearly, once or twice. Mr. Pruitt had quite a reputation for gambling. He owed money all over town, and his family was on the point of cutting him off from further funds. Rumor said one of the stipulations for more funds was that he marry respectably."

He stretched his long legs and made himself more comfortable. "There was another young lady he also paid court to, but her family wisely turned him away. Probably something to do with a child born to one of the former Pruitt servants. The maid caused a scene at the worst possible moment, forcing the family to buy her off. It was all hushed up, of course."

"Not a young man of good reputation," Lady Kaldaire said.

"Even worse after he and another young man showed up at a ball, having imbibed too much beforehand, and embarrassed themselves, their parents, and several young ladies." The prince's tone made clear his low opinion of the murdered man.

"And yet Lady Wyatt considered allowing her daughter wear mourning for the idiot." It seemed odd to me.

"Miss Annabelle is an only daughter. Lady Wyatt always gives in to her in the end." His tone said he didn't think much of the two women, either.

"Dear me. No wonder the girl is the way she is." Lady Kaldaire picked up the teapot. "Would anyone like some more?"

I quickly held my cup out. "How serious was Miss Annabelle about Mr. Pruitt?"

"Far too serious. The family feared she planned to elope with the fellow. I heard Lord Wyatt threaten his life at our club."

"What was Mr. Pruitt's reaction?"

"He wasn't there. You don't think the Imperial would allow someone like Pruitt in? He'd be blackballed in an instant."

"So who was Lord Wyatt talking to when he threatened Mr. Pruitt's life?" I knew I shouldn't have asked as soon as I saw Lady Kaldaire's eyes light up. She wanted to get me involved in solving Pruitt's murder, and now I found myself helping her toward her goal.

Curiosity was the bane of my life. I'd never get home tonight if I kept helping Lady Kaldaire with her ever-expanding investigation.

"He was talking to a group of members who were all agreeing the young man should be horsewhipped. With them was a man with a dangerous reputation who comes to the club sometimes as a guest of the new Lord Kaldaire."

"Laurence brings men of low repute to the Imperial? I can imagine what Horace would have said about that." Lady Kaldaire nearly overfilled my cup as her gaze flew to the prince.

I carefully lifted my cup to my lips and sipped off the excess before setting it down and asking, "Does this shady man have a name?"

"Of course he does," the prince said with a hint of a smile.

I stared at him, eyebrows raised.

"Denby. Jonathan Denby. He's a gambler who's rumored to have ties to nefarious characters. Criminals. And for this or for some other reason, he frightens a few members of the club. I suspect he's a blackmailer, although I have no proof. No one has actually said so."

I couldn't resist saying, "Really. Members of the Imperial Club leaving themselves open to blackmail like ordinary mortals."

"Emily." Lady Kaldaire looked askance at me.

I thought it worth asking her, "Have you ever met Jonathan Denby through the new Lord Kaldaire?"

"I believe Laurence called a man Denby when he greeted him in the front hall of Kaldaire House. We haven't been introduced. I must say I didn't care for him."

"Did anyone mention a reason for him to be there?" There might have been a perfectly harmless reason for this man to be there. At least, I hoped there was.

"No, but then, Laurence has never shown any interest in explaining himself about anything."

I turned to the prince. "Is it possible Jonathan Denby was the person Your Highness heard that night? The late Lord Kaldaire was apparently short of cash. Could they have argued and Mr. Denby attacked him?" It made as much sense as any other theory we'd concocted.

"What would they have argued about?" Lady

Kaldaire asked. Now that she knew Prince Maximilian hadn't killed her husband, she was trying to find another villain.

"Perhaps someone at the Imperial Club knows." I looked at the prince, hoping he would volunteer.

"No, Miss Gates. I've assured you of my innocence in Lord Kaldaire's death, and I have the letter I wanted. I'm finished with this business, but I wish you ladies luck in finding the killer." He rose, bowed to us, and walked out of the room.

We heard Lyle say good-bye to the prince as he shut the door behind him.

"Emily, how will we find out more about Mr. Denby and his connections to Laurence and to Lord Wyatt?"

From the expression on Lady Kaldaire's face, I knew she was giving me another assignment. One I couldn't turn down if I wanted my newly won truce with Inspector Russell to last and Matthew to finally go to school.

I left there as quickly as I could and went to my grandparents' house. My grandmother blocked the door as she greeted me with, "What are you doing here?"

"I want to talk to Grandpapa."

"Stop using him for your silly errands for that lady. He's too good a person for you to use when you need him and then toss him away like rubbish when this family embarrasses you and your respectability."

"I'd never treat Grandpapa that way. He's not like some people around here who make it clear they don't want me around. Me or Matthew. You've never invited us for dinner once since Mama died. Our cousins are over here all the time." I couldn't keep the hurt out of my voice.

"They know they don't need an invitation like some

grand lords and ladies." Her arms were crossed over her narrow bosom as she glared at me.

"But we do, Gran. We know you don't want us around. We remind you too much of Mama. And you called Matthew stupid." Tears formed in my eyes. I was tired from a full day of work and hurt and angry from years of deflecting my grandmother's fury.

"He is stupid."

Every muscle in my body tensed and I saw red. She defended stupid Petey. Why not loyal, trustworthy Matthew?

CHAPTER TWENTY-EIGHT

"He's not stupid. He's as clever as the rest of your grandsons. Smarter than dumb old Petey. But he's deaf." I didn't care that I was shouting at my grandmother. I was about to turn and run when Grandpapa came to the door.

"Go make tea, Aggie," he said in a soft voice. "Come in, pet. How did you do last night?"

I sniffed and swiped at my eyes with my gloved fingers. "I learned some things, but now I'm left with a bigger puzzle."

"Come in to the dining room and tell me about it."

We sat across a corner of the big wooden table from each other. "First of all, thank you and Cousin Will and whoever else watched out for me last night. I was very glad someone was looking out for me when he aimed a pistol at me."

Grandpapa put his head in his hands. He sighed deeply before he shook his head and looked at me sadly. "I wish you'd left as soon as he did that. Or never gone in there at all."

"I wasn't worried. He didn't act like he'd use it. He didn't seem very angry about me being there. He had what Lady Kaldaire sent me to retrieve in his pocket, but I did open all four secret compartments in the desk."

"Well done, pet."

Grandmother came in, set the tea on the table, and

walked out without speaking to either of us.

"Oh, dear. I'm afraid I've made your grandmother angry."

"It's my fault." I hated upsetting Grandpapa's peace.

"No, it's mine. I could have set things right years ago, but your father asked me to keep his secret. I have, but now I think it's time to finish with secrets within the family."

"If it's my father's secret, then I don't want to hear it." I was ready to bolt, and I hadn't yet told him why I was here.

"You won't hear it today. Now, what is this new puzzle?" he asked as he gestured for me to pour the tea.

"I need to learn what you know about Jonathan Denby and Jeremiah Pruitt. I know they both have bad reputations, but little else."

"Denby? No, pet, you'll have nothing more to do with this business." He spoke so firmly I was shocked.

"Why?"

"Officially, Denby runs an illegal gambling den. That's not bad, but it's rumored he's a blackmailer and an assassin who's killed a half-dozen men with a sharp, thin blade. He's said to kill men for hire."

"For hire?" I couldn't imagine hiring someone to murder someone for you. That was more repugnant than strangling someone with your bare hands. I could see wrinkles standing out around Grandpapa's frown and a slight tremor in his hand as he set down his teacup.

"Gentlemen have been rumored to pay him to kill rivals for a woman's hand or competing heirs for an inheritance."

"I can't picture Lady Kaldaire or the new Lord Kaldaire hiring someone to kill Lord Kaldaire."

"You didn't tell me he was stabbed."

"He wasn't. He was bashed over the head."

"Denby stabs his victims. Always. At least that's what's said."

I remembered what Inspector Russell had told me. "Has he ever stabbed anyone with a hatpin?"

"If anyone knows how to efficiently kill someone with a hatpin, it would be Denby. Why, pet?"

"Jeremiah Pruitt was killed with a hatpin. Or something similar. And Denby was seen listening to a young lady's father at the Imperial Club, where Denby is most definitely not a member. Lord Wyatt, the girl's father, was heard to say he wanted Pruitt dead."

"That's circumstantial. We've dodged many a jail sentence because of evidence being that weak."

"If this were more solid, it might be enough to stop Lady Kaldaire from investigating further. She's taken an interest because the young lady, Wyatt's daughter, asked her to. I can't picture her telling a young girl her father might have had her lover murdered."

"Do you want me to sit in the Imperial for an afternoon and see if I can learn anything?"

"Would you mind?"

"Not at all. It's a pleasant place to spend an afternoon, and it's always good for a hint or two that might bring us business."

I could picture what kind of business that would be, and let his words slide past. I told him everything I'd already heard about Pruitt. "But I know nothing about Denby. If anyone gossips about him, I'd like to hear what they say."

"So you'd only be interested in recent gossip about Pruitt, both his death and Lord Kaldaire's." He smiled.

"I suspect that is all you're interested in, too. New

gossip." The kind that meant business opportunities for the Gates gang.

"I think it's time for Mr. Pettigreen to make another appearance at the Imperial. I'm not busy tomorrow afternoon."

"As long as that's all you do," my grandmother said as she walked into the room.

"There's nothing dangerous about an old man going into a club. Particularly one who's a bit absent-minded and hard of hearing." He reached over and patted her hand. "It's one of my favorite disguises."

"And what will you be doing while he's endangering himself?" Grandmother glowered at me.

"Trying to find a way to get Lady Kaldaire off my back and keep my customers happy." Two nearly impossible jobs.

"Then you won't have time to cook dinner. You and Matthew come to dinner tomorrow night, and afterward your grandfather can tell you if he heard anything useful."

I looked at her in shock for a moment, my mouth hanging open. As her words sank in, a smile spread across my face. "Thank you. Matthew and I would love to."

* * *

The sun shone, business was brisk, and I didn't hear from Lady Kaldaire all day. Pleased with life, I was tidying up at closing time when the bell over the door rang and a shadow fell on my shoulder.

I spun around. "Inspector."

"Are we alone?"

When I looked into his intelligent, stormy gray eyes, I'd have been alone with him if the shop were full of people. Fortunately, Jane had just left. I put up the closed sign and said, "We are now."

"Why did your grandfather go into the Imperial Club this afternoon?"

"I asked him to."

"Why?" He took a step closer, standing improperly near.

My breathing was growing shallow. I felt trapped, but I wasn't fearful. The feeling was exhilarating. "I've heard that Lord Wyatt, whose daughter was very close to Jeremiah Pruitt, said he wanted Pruitt dead. He was in the Imperial at the time speaking to Jonathan Denby."

"Denby? He's a…" Those eyes narrowed as they focused on me. "Do you realize how dangerous this is for your grandfather, asking questions about a man like Denby?"

I was trying hard not to think about that possibility. "Denby has also been a guest at Kaldaire House since the new lord took over. Lady Kaldaire has no idea why."

"Nothing honest, I'm sure." He looked at me for a moment. "Will you tell me everything your grandfather tells you about his trip to the Imperial? No holding any details back?"

Since I knew Grandpapa wouldn't tell me what he'd learned of use in the family business, I said, "Of course. I want you to find this murderer, and not only because then I won't be a suspect in Lord Kaldaire's death."

He nodded and took my hand. His skin was warm and rough and his touch was gentle. "Even knowing I'll arrest anyone in your family I catch breaking the law, will you allow me to call on you after this business is over?"

"Yes. Will you want to call on me knowing I'll do what I can to help my family escape?" Then I had to smile. "Well, possibly not Petey. I'm still angry that he involved me by hiding his stolen goods in my factory. The idiot."

"Even if they break the law?"

"They're my family. Until my mother died, I saw them quite often. I'm very fond of some of them." I saw his expression change. "Oh, dear. I've disappointed you."

And that hurt. I wanted to be as law-abiding and reputable as James Russell. I needed to be, but I was tied by childhood memories and blood to a family who made their living illegally.

"Yes, but I'd expect no less. God help me, but I still want to call on you."

"And knowing your stand on the Gates family, I'll still welcome your visits."

We stood very close, smiling at each other. Then he stepped back and executed a bow worthy of a courtier. I felt a whisper- soft pressure as he kissed the back of my hand.

When he straightened, releasing my hand, I gasped in delight. "I'm having dinner with the family tonight, so I'll see you tomorrow?"

"Count on it." He smiled before he strode out the door, setting his bowler hat on his head with a pat as he left.

I dropped into one of the backless seats available for our customers and pressed the back of my hand to my lips. Oh, my. James Russell was not your usual policeman.

* * *

When we walked into my grandparents' house, I saw the dining room table and knew we were in for an ordeal. It had been extended to seat all of our aunts, uncles, and cousins. That meant my father would be there. Matthew stared at the table with wide eyes as he tugged backward on my arm. His signal that he was ready to leave.

I put my arm around him, gave him a hug, and smiled as I looked into his face. His expression said he wasn't buying it.

Grandpapa came over with a pad of paper and a pencil. On the first sheet, he'd written, "Welcome Matthew. I'm your Grandpa."

Matthew took the pad and pencil and wrote, "I remember you."

"Good boy," Grandpapa said and ruffled Matthew's hair.

Everyone stood around awkwardly until Grandmother said, "Sit down. The food's getting cold."

Matthew and I were seated next to each other in the middle of a long side of the table. Grandpapa blessed the food and then platters and serving bowls came around at a rapid rate. When we finally were able to taste our dinner, Matthew tried a couple of bites and then looked at me with an expression of pure joy.

I wrote, "Grandma cooked this."

He wrote, "Where?"

I pointed her out at the end of the table. He rose, dashed over, and gave her a big hug and a kiss.

She looked at him, startled.

He pointed to the food on her plate and nodded as he smiled.

"You like my cooking?" She pointed to go along with her words.

He nodded again and kept smiling.

"Well, Matthew, I'm very pleased. Very pleased, indeed. You have your sister bring you over more often." Then she looked at me as if I'd deliberately kept him away from his loving grandma.

I guessed she'd rather forget the terrible things she'd said when Mama died and we learned Matthew was deaf. I couldn't forget them, but for Matthew's sake, I could act as if they no longer mattered.

"As often as we're welcome," I said.

"You're always welcome, pet," Grandpapa said.

After we finished eating, Grandmother and my aunts went into the kitchen to see to the washing up. I didn't know if Grandmother had a scullery maid yet as well as a chambermaid, but I was sure she didn't have a cook. The food was too good.

"Boys, take Matthew into the parlor and teach him some card games. And no gambling! He's your cousin." Grandpapa turned to me and said, "We'll go into the office and talk."

"I didn't know you had an office."

"There's a lot of things you don't know, pet."

I followed him to the strangest office I'd ever seen. Ledgers everywhere. I counted four safes of different sizes in the crowded space. A number of exquisite paintings propped up against bookcases or hung from the walls. A board with several locks attached. Several old, brightly colored rugs in the center of the floor. Local maps scattered everywhere. There was barely room for the huge, battered desk and two chairs.

We sat down and I said, "Did you learn anything at the Imperial today?"

"Oh, yes. If you're old, people expect you to be potty and deaf. I'd ask a question, making it sound like I'd misunderstood what someone else said, and then let them talk. Some of them are as potty as I pretended to be, and they said the most extraordinary things."

"How did you get inside?"

"Enter a members-only club? The secret, pet, is to

look and act like you belong. There are only two clubs that have less than one thousand members, and I stay away from them. What doorman, or member, is going to recognize every member by sight when there are fifteen hundred or two thousand of them and some live in the country and don't visit often?"

"Still, what if they question you? Or ask you to sign in?"

"An old man with shaky limbs and poor eyesight is not going to have clear handwriting. I write down, say, 'Herman Pettigreen,' but it could as easily say 'a dozen radishes.' I've learned a cheery 'Good day' to the doorman or perhaps greeting a well-known, elderly member of the club as if we'd known each other for ages establishes my bona fides."

"What if the well-known man asks your name or says he doesn't know you?"

"I tell him, 'Herman Pettigreen. Don't tell me you've forgotten me, old boy, after all these years?' I only do this with the elderly, because they are more likely to believe they're slipping and have truly forgotten me."

"What if Herman Pettigreen is spotted at more than one club?"

"One old man looks like every other old man. And I use a different name at every club I frequent."

"How many—?"

"Only the ones that produce usable information for our line of work. And I make sure never to run up a bar tab. Perhaps a cup of tea, but nothing more."

I leaned back in my chair, amazed at what I'd heard. I'd never guessed it was so easy to get into places that claimed to be exclusive. "What did you discover about Denby and Pruitt?"

"Shortly before Lord Kaldaire was murdered, there

was an almighty commotion about a lost note. Apparently, a note was meant for Lord Wyatt, but the man behind the desk mixed up two notes and gave Lord Wyatt's message to Lord Kaldaire." Grandpapa's expression was grim. "The note was from Jonathan Denby."

CHAPTER TWENTY-NINE

"So Denby left a note at the Imperial Club for Lord Wyatt, but Lord Kaldaire received it by mistake. If they were planning something illegal or morally questionable, Lord Kaldaire now knew about it. He would expect Lord Wyatt, if not Denby, to do the right thing." I looked at Grandpapa and slowly shook my head. This had the makings of a disaster.

"If the right thing was not what they wanted to do, I can picture either of them wanting to clobber Kaldaire for interfering. At the very least, they'd attempt to get the note back before he could take it to the authorities," my grandfather said.

"Which they must have, since the safe was open when Prince Maximilian arrived, and the letter he wanted was still inside. Someone opened that safe for another reason."

"Do any of them have that skill?"

I looked at Grandpapa, hoping he had the answer. "I don't know."

"Both the previous and the current Lord Kaldaire would know the combination." He raised his eyebrows as he stared at me.

"But the new Lord Kaldaire wasn't in town."

"But..." He glanced up and then clambered to his feet as the door creaked open. "Oh, good. Harry, Sarah. I think it's time, Harry, that you and your daughter have an honest talk." His tone said he expected us to comply.

I rose. "I don't think there's anything to say."

"Emmy, love, you need to hear me out." There was a begging tone in my father's voice. Not what I expected to hear.

"No." I tried to push my way out of the room, but my grandfather stopped me. I was surprised at how strong he was.

My father moved to stand directly in front of me. With a hand under my chin to make certain I had to look him in the face, he said, "I couldn't come when your mother was dying. And afterward, you wanted nothing to do with me."

I stopped struggling against my grandfather's grip and said, "Why couldn't you come?"

"I was in hiding. I'd done a job with some acquaintances outside the family. They killed a guard, but not before someone saw us. The coppers were searching for me for murder. Noah found me, tore into me good for hiding instead of being at Elise's bedside where I belonged. He was right. I begged him never to tell you what I'd done. Who wants his daughter to know he worked outside the family with blokes who would kill a man? Who wants his daughter to know he was too afraid of the noose to come out of hiding to comfort his dying wife?"

I struck out, fury in my eyes and in my fists. "Instead, you let me believe all these years that you were a heartless, evil, selfish, rotten—"

My grandfather gripped my shoulders. "He was none of these things. Stupid, perhaps, but not evil."

"And so I lost both my parents." My grief overwhelmed me and I began to sob. Tears rushed down my cheeks.

It was some moments before I realized I was in my father's embrace. He was murmuring how very sorry he was and how much he missed Matthew and me.

"Why aren't you still in hiding? Murder charges don't go away," I asked, swiping at my wet cheeks.

"The coppers caught the men with the gun during another robbery and hanged them. Satisfied, they closed the case." He studied my face. "Now may not be the best time, but I want you to meet Sarah. She's wanted to meet you for ages."

I pulled back, looking into my father's face. The clincher was when Grandmother came in carrying a little boy. He had the face of the woman who stepped next to my father. "You got married and had a child and didn't tell me?"

"It's been six years. You didn't want anything to do with me."

"So now it's my fault?" My voice was close to a scream. And to think I'd almost forgiven him for keeping one secret when he'd sprung two others on me.

"No one thinks it's your fault, pet," my grandfather said.

"You could have written me a letter if you didn't want to see me in person," I told him.

"You would have screamed the house down. Just like your mother," my grandmother said.

"Aggie," Grandpapa said in a warning tone.

"How would I know that you'd read it?" my father said.

"You could have tried. You could have tried telling me the truth for a change." I took two steps away from him and turned toward his wife. "Sarah, is it? How do you put up with his arrogance? With his concealing the truth?"

"He hasn't kept any secrets from me since I hit him with a frying pan. At the time it contained his breakfast." And then she smiled at me.

I smiled back reluctantly. I might not be resigned to my father remarrying, but I thought I'd like Sarah. She was a few years older than me, with brown hair and eyes. There was nothing flashy about her or her dress. "Grandmother, do you have a pan I could borrow?"

"If it'll stop this nonsense, gladly."

My father's eyes widened. I hoped some of that was from fear and not for show.

Sarah took my hand. "Will you introduce me to Matthew, Emily? I want him to meet Sam, and I don't know how to talk to him."

"Written notes will probably work best in this case. We can use gestures for simple things, but this isn't simple."

She nodded. "No, it is not."

I grinned at her. "Come on. And let me take this fellow." I held out my arms and my grandmother reluctantly let go as Sam leaned toward me.

We went out into the parlor where Matthew and some of his cousins were engrossed in a card game. I was glad to see there weren't any coins in evidence. His cousins would have fleeced him.

Matthew took one look at my tear-stained face and set his cards facedown on the table. I set Sam on Matthew's lap and wrote on his paper, "This is your brother Sam."

His face lit up. He grabbed the pencil and wrote, "I have a brother!" while Sam tried to grab the pencil away with his chubby hand.

I took the pencil and wrote, "This is Sam's mother. Father's new wife." I gestured to her.

Matthew, always a better person than I am, took the pencil and scratched out the word "new." Then he grinned at Sarah.

She took the pencil and wrote her name. Then she held out her hand.

Matthew shook it and smiled at her before turning his attention back to his little brother, who was now trying to climb onto his head.

I glanced back to see my father watching us, his eyes moist. "Why did you wait so long?" I asked in a quiet voice, my own eyes wet with unshed tears.

"I don't know. Cowardice?"

* * *

The next morning, Inspector Russell and his unfathomable smile showed up as soon as I opened the shop. I asked Jane to watch for any customers. She raised her eyebrows and smirked behind his back as I led the inspector to the back room.

I glowered at her.

As soon as we settled in the workshop, I told Russell about the misdirected note. He found the information fascinating. I also told him what Prince Maximilian had said about hearing multiple sets of footsteps on the ground floor of Kaldaire House without mentioning the prince's name.

"And you swear the person who was hiding in the dining room listening to people going to and from the front door wasn't a member of your family?"

"Yes. Why must you assume a person in a place he doesn't belong must be related to me?"

"Because they so often are."

I glared at him. "This person is a member of the highest levels of the aristocracy and the reason he was there involved a matter only peers would be interested in." I refused to consider the legitimacy of a dead queen reason to murder anyone. We were no longer in medieval times.

If Prince Maximilian wanted the letter for leverage over someone in the royal family, then that was a motive well understood by my family. However, I believed the prince when he said he didn't murder the nonroyal Lord Kaldaire. "We both know some concerns of the aristocracy are unimportant, and certainly not worth killing for," I told the detective.

Russell leaned on the doorframe, watching me where I stood in the middle of the small space. "All right. I'll believe you when you say the person hiding in the dining room had nothing to do with the murder. I'd also believe Denby was Lord Kaldaire's killer if he'd been stabbed. He wasn't."

I began to pace. "Lord Wyatt wouldn't have needed to steal the note back. He could say that while it was addressed to him, he'd never seen it, and he would have put a stop to whatever it said if he'd known." I felt certain Lord Wyatt was not the killer.

"But having read the note, Lord Kaldaire would have contacted Lord Wyatt, not Denby, and demanded he end whatever was threatened. Wyatt might not have wanted to do that." I stopped and studied Inspector Russell, confused by the various possibilities running through my mind. "Would he have told Denby and then Denby broke into Kaldaire House?"

"Again, if Denby were going to kill Kaldaire, he'd have used a knife. I'll make some inquiries and find out where they both were that night. In fact, I should soon learn where several people were that evening." He smiled as if he couldn't wait for his investigation to bear fruit. "Including the new Lord and Lady Kaldaire and the murdered lord's Lady Kaldaire and all of their servants. They had as much to gain as anyone by the late lord's murder."

I studied him, surprised at the route his thoughts were traveling. "You think it's possible any of them killed Lord Kaldaire?"

"Yes."

"Not his wife. I'm sure of that."

"She was in the house. And she didn't like him," the inspector said.

"She didn't mind him, and she's trying to find his killer."

He raised his eyebrows. "Not the first time someone's used that ruse."

I shook my head and paced. "No, Lady Kaldaire didn't love her husband, but she was used to him. He gave her status she wouldn't have on her own. There was nothing in their lives that would make her angry enough to kill."

"She's still one of many whose alibis must be verified."

I walked close to him and said, "Then we both have a lot to do and need to start our days." I passed by and walked back into the shop as if I had no interest in him at all to hide my real feelings.

He followed me out, tipped his hat, and left without a glance back. I watched the empty doorway for a moment before I shrugged off my disappointment. Walking off first only worked when the other party felt bereft. Russell made clear he didn't feel saddened by my dismissal.

He was the most maddening man I'd ever met.

Lady Kaldaire arrived in the early afternoon and waited through two other customers. They were treated to her praise of my hats as she critiqued their choices and made comments about the angle I set their headgear on.

In one case, I found she was right. The hat did look better tilted to the other side.

Once the two women left looking both flattered and confused, she said, "I want another hat in black in my usual style. It seems to be worn more often than anything else in my wardrobe. Now, what progress have you made?"

I told her about the message that was misdirected to her husband along with Denby's deadly reputation. Then I added, "Everyone who knows him fails to believe he'd kill your husband by bashing him over the head. Denby is believed to always stab his victims."

"Do you think my husband was killed because of this note from Mr. Denby to Lord Wyatt?"

"Well, he wasn't killed for the Queen Victoria letter or because of his threats against Lady Taylor. How many more secrets could he have had?"

Lady Kaldaire tapped her parasol on the floor. "And what was he doing with the money I gave him to pay the bills?"

"The inspector said he's going to find out where Lord Wyatt and Mr. Denby were on the night your husband was murdered. We're going to have to wait on him now," I said. I wouldn't tell her she and her relatives were currently subject to police inquiries.

I was tired of following clues and suspects. I needed to spend more time chasing after the money to send Matthew to school.

She rose. "Marjorie, Lady Linchester, is arriving today for a visit to town and to see her son George. He drove up in that motor carriage of his. It must have been a dreadful trip. Thank goodness Marjorie is coming by train."

I smiled. I liked riding in an automobile, but not for the distance Lord George would be driving.

"I believe it's time for me to mend some fences with Cecily," Lady Kaldaire continued. "I think Marjorie and I will call on her this afternoon. Maybe she knows more about what my husband was up to than I do." She smiled at me. "It can't hurt. And I would like to see the house again. I can't believe I miss that tomb."

Apparently, she did more than see the house, because as I was closing for the night, I received a note.

Dear Emily,
I want you to bring the very stylish red
and white hat with a wide brim and high crown
to Kaldaire House tonight. It was the second
one you showed the ladies this afternoon. It
looked perfect for a garden party. It's for
Cecily, but send me the bill. You have her
measurements from the blue hat with the birds'
wings from last summer. Marjorie and I will
arrive there for dinner at eight. You should
arrive at nine. Then I want you to go into the
study and open the window for later ingress.
Roberta, Lady Kaldaire

Obviously, we were going to search the study again. I hoped we'd have better luck than we did the night the new Lord Kaldaire came home early from the opera. This time, I was going to add some luck of my own.

CHAPTER THIRTY

I responded to Lady Kaldaire's note, told Noah that he, Matthew, and Annie would be on their own for the evening, and went to see my grandfather.

Grandpapa was in the stables when I arrived. "What's up, pet?" he asked as soon as he saw my face.

"I need to have one of my cousins climb in a study window in Mayfair after I open it. He may have an opportunity to remove a small item in the course of the evening, but that's not guaranteed."

He scowled, apparently concerned. "Come inside and tell me what's going on."

I told him what I knew and what I suspected. If I was going to search the study that night, I wanted professional help, including getting in and out of the window. "But not Petey," I added. "I need someone quick-witted."

"Do you think there'll be danger?"

"If Lord Kaldaire's murderer is in the house, then yes." I didn't want to think about that. I only wanted to get in, find the evidence Lady Kaldaire believed was there, and get out in one piece. Apparently, she'd found a way to get everyone out of the house, or at least away from the study.

Grandpapa assured me I'd have assistance, and I headed to the shop to pick up the red and white hat. When I arrived, I found Lady Kaldaire's young footman, a boy of about sixteen, waiting with another note.

She agreed calling in help was a good idea but said we wouldn't need it. She felt sure she knew where the note from Mr. Denby was and we'd only need a few minutes in the study to locate it. I sent a return note saying I'd be there at nine with the new hat. I didn't mention the reinforcements.

I chose my dress with care. I didn't want to ruin a good gown. I wanted freedom of motion in case I had to escape out of a window, but I needed to blend in at an aristocratic dinner party without actually looking like I thought I deserved a place at the table.

I finally decided on a mauve and light blue dress with simple lines that I wore with a small, flexible corset, and which had a skirt with a practical hem that missed the floor by three inches. A velvet toque in a shimmering shade of blue that wouldn't take up much space if I had to climb through a window completed the outfit. I had a bad feeling about our coming adventure. I hoped my costume would let me fade into the background.

With the gift hat in a hatbox, I called a hansom cab and rode to Kaldaire House. When I arrived, I was surprised to see a motor carriage in front of the house. Lord George Whitaker must be at the dinner party. I went up the steps, where Rawlings opened the door to my ring.

"Miss Gates. I'm here for Lady Kaldaire."

"That won't be convenient, Miss Gates."

He must have thought his position gave him more power than he possessed, because I sailed into the front hall before he had a chance to finish speaking and shut the door in my face. He swung around to face me. "Really, Miss Gates, you must leave."

"Your former mistress asked me to bring the current Lady Kaldaire a present. I believe they are both here."

He looked around for help, but we were the only two in the oil painting lined foyer. "Um. Let me... I don't know... You'll have to wait here."

"Fine. Just let them know I'm here." I gave him a contented smile.

He went into the dining room, and I moved closer to the study door, where I waited, hatbox in hand. Almost immediately, Lord George came out. "Golly, Miss Gates. What a pleasant surprise."

"It's good to see you, my lord. Tell me, is Roberta, Lady Kaldaire, here?"

"Oh, my, yes. Mama is with her and they've called for a doctor." He half-whispered his words.

A terrible force squeezed my heart as I realized Lord Kaldaire's and Gregson's murderer might have struck again. "What—what happened?"

"She collapsed during the second course. The footmen carried her out. Mama went with her while Lady Kaldaire was left to carry on with her dinner party. There's royalty here tonight. Well, not our royalty." I realized his quiet voice and glance around the hall was due to guilt. No doubt no one had given him permission to leave the table.

"Prince Maximilian?"

"How did you guess?" He sounded truly surprised that I knew.

Everybody involved in this case seemed to be here. "Mr. Denby, too?"

"That's amazing. You must have seen the guest list."

I had a bigger worry than the guest list. "Is Lady Kaldaire still alive?"

"Yes. I think so. Mama would say something if she dies before the doctor arrives." He spoke solemnly.

Rawlings was not in sight. Time for me to find the evidence before anyone else was hurt. "My lord, go back and enjoy your dinner. I'll wait until things quiet down to speak to Lady Kaldaire. Give my best to your mama."

He kissed my hand in the continental manner and went back to the dining room. I waited a minute to make certain none of the maids or footmen arrived to watch me before I slipped into the study, turning on the one shaded light that had been on the first time I'd entered.

Setting down the hatbox, I went straight to the large window and pulled on the sash. It slid wide open with little effort. The breezeless summer night didn't ruffle the draperies.

Sticking my head out, I saw there was only a small bush outside to trip up a hasty exit and only a five- or six-foot drop to the ground. My cousins thought nothing of climbing that distance to enter a house. Inside, it was only a two-foot drop to the floor.

I was surprised none of my cousins popped in to join me in the curtained recess immediately, but I was sure they were following Grandpapa's orders. After assuring myself the draperies would hide whoever climbed into the room, I walked toward the desk. I was nearly there when I looked at the wall in the recess beyond the desk and saw the *Lady in Blue.*

I stood gazing at it, amazed that my plans to steal it had led to troubles I couldn't have imagined.

As the odor of pipe tobacco reached my nose, I nearly sneezed. A very distinct pipe tobacco that I'd only smelled once before. In this room. The night Lord Kaldaire was attacked.

"You should have waited in the hall, Miss Gates."

I spun around, unable to hide the guilty look on my face. "My lord."

Laurence, the new Lord Kaldaire, worked on keeping his pipe lit as he remained between me and the door. He made a sizable barrier to any escape as he eyed me coldly. When he had the pipe smoldering to his satisfaction, he said, "You take liberties in my house that you shouldn't."

I saw the draperies by the window move slightly in a way no breeze would have caused. My housebreaking cousins were stealthy when necessary. I hadn't heard whichever one it was come in.

And then I risked everything. "The night of the murder was the first time I smelled your pipe tobacco."

Lord Kaldaire laughed, a nasty, depraved sound. "I thought you and Roberta were too close. Just like Gregson."

I tried to look innocent. "Too close to what?"

"Oh, please, Miss Gates. You and my meddling sister-in-law have gone too far. Don't expect her to rescue you. The drops in her sherry have rendered her unable to help anyone, including herself."

My eyes widened as I smothered a gasp. I held on to my fury, ready to spring vengeance on him as soon as I could to save Lady Kaldaire. She might be dictatorial and self-absorbed, but she had a kindness about her that the new Lord Kaldaire would never understand. "What have you done to her?"

"Nothing yet. Just as I've done nothing to you. Yet. But you have a reputation as a housebreaker. With the police. With Prince Maximilian, who's being entertained by my wife while I'm out of the dining room to check on my frail, demented sister-in-law. When another of my guests finds a burglar with my safe open and my wife's jewelry in her hands, he will stop her from escaping."

I stepped back as he came farther into the room, followed by the large, rat-faced man who favored diamonds in his cufflinks. He was the man I'd met entering this house one day who'd looked at me as if I were naked.

The knife in his hand didn't need diamonds to shine. The blade was long and slender, not much wider than a hatpin, with a very sharp point.

"I'm ready," the man with the blade said, leering at me.

I gulped. I wasn't.

"Not yet, Denby. It won't do for me to be here when this happens. Let me get the safe open and the jewelry out first." Kaldaire ignored me as he walked over to the safe, moved the painting away from it, and opened the heavy steel door.

Events became clear. Clear enough that I knew I had to watch both men and not show fear, though they should have been able to hear my heart pound. My palms were soaked. My legs trembled.

"You were the one who opened the safe the night the late Lord Kaldaire died. You were already in town. That's why you ordered your luggage to be brought over from Claridge's and said your wife would come the next day. You came in here that night after Prince Maximilian left and before I arrived. You smoked your pipe and opened the safe. Was it to retrieve Mr. Denby's note to Lord Wyatt?"

"Can I kill her now?" Denby took a step or two toward me, his knife held about waist-high.

"Not yet. How did you learn about that note?" Kaldaire reached in and pulled out a handful of jewelry boxes.

"The same way several others have learned about it. You've done a terrible job of keeping any of this quiet. It won't take long for the police to come knocking on your door. If I were you, I'd cut and run."

"The police can't prove anything." There was a sneer in his aristocratic tones.

"They already know you were in town on the night your brother died. The only question is which one of you killed Lord Kaldaire."

"Can I silence her now?"

"Just a minute, Denby," Kaldaire snapped. For the first time, he seemed nervous. "I won't be accused of murdering my brother. Who have you shared your speculations with?"

"Lots of people," I said, smiling despite my shaking legs, "none of whom shall be named. Since you want to do me harm, I'm not going to make it easy for you."

"Oh, for..." Denby muttered the rest of his words as he stalked toward me.

I backed up in the direction of the window.

Kaldaire took a step or two toward the door, keeping an anxious eye on Denby, when a shadowy figure popped up by the safe, grabbed a handful of jewelry cases, and said, "Got 'em."

"Why, you!" Kaldaire said, spinning around and reaching for the thief.

"Catch!" Jewelry cases shot into Denby's face, toward the painting of the *Lady in Blue*, out the window. Any direction but where Kaldaire could catch them. Two more dark-clad figures leaped into action, snatching jewelry boxes and tossing them around.

"Stop them!" Kaldaire shouted.

Denby swung around, his knife extended, aiming at a dark-clad figure who snatched a jewel case out of midair. Another figure threw a case and hit Denby on the side of the head, ruining his efforts to skewer anything but shadows.

They made a ballet of sudden moves, leaping and ducking, throwing and catching. I knew, at the end, a few valuable pieces would disappear, their "fee" for services rendered.

My cousins would go out the way they entered. I wanted to stay in the house and check on Lady Kaldaire. I shifted around the edge of the room toward the door, staying out of the confusion. I was nearly there when I bumped against a marble bust. I grabbed it before it could fall and shatter.

The thief by the safe opened jewel cases and tossed rings and brooches across the room. He threw a heavy bracelet directly into Kaldaire's face.

"Why, you—" Kaldaire took a step back, raising his arm to fend off the attack just as Denby lunged at a dark shape. The black-dressed thief jumped back and Denby stuck his blade into Kaldaire's arm.

His lordship's scream could have wakened the dead.

CHAPTER THIRTY-ONE

Denby, gripping his bloody knife, rushed toward the door. He sliced the air as he passed me, narrowly missing me. I grabbed the bust by the base and swung it, clipping the side of his head. He sank to the floor, the bust thudding into the thick carpet and his knife falling harmlessly.

Cecily, Lady Kaldaire, arrived a moment later, followed by Prince Maximilian and Lord George Whitaker. She saw the blood soaking her husband's sleeve and fainted. George tried to catch her but missed as she gracefully sank to the carpet next to the rat-faced Jonathan Denby.

When I looked around, the dark-clad thieves were gone. At first glance, it seemed as if all the jewelry and jewelry boxes were scattered across the wooden floor or on the carpet.

"I've been stabbed," Lord Kaldaire groaned.

A moment later, a bobby's whistle could be heard, followed by a pounding on the front door. Rawlings must have opened it immediately, because a moment later, he led two bobbies into the room.

Prince Maximilian was obviously used to taking command. He quickly ascertained that no one had gone for a doctor for Roberta, Lady Kaldaire, and ordered Rawlings to carry out the errand personally. He had a bobby fetch the police surgeon for Lord Kaldaire and reinforcements for locking up Denby.

"And lock up the thieves," Lord Kaldaire commanded.

"What thieves?" the bobby left in the room asked.

"The ones that threw jewelry all over the room."

"You'd better get a doctor quickly. He's hallucinating. It must be the loss of blood," I said.

"What happened, my lady?" the bobby asked.

To my amazement, no one corrected his use of "my lady." "Lord Kaldaire opened the safe to show me a piece of Lady Kaldaire's jewelry. He wasn't certain which Lady Kaldaire it belonged to and he wanted my opinion. Then Mr. Denby burst in waving a knife and demanding the jewelry."

Lord Kaldaire remained slumped in a chair, with a man I suspected was his valet dealing with his wound. His lordship watched me through narrowed eyes in his pudgy face, waiting to see how my story would end.

"The two men struggled and a moment later, jewelry and jewelry cases flew all over the room. Mr. Denby struck Lord Kaldaire with his knife and started to run away with some of the jewelry, so I hit him in the head with the bust."

"Is that true, my lord?" the bobby asked Prince Maximilian.

"I wasn't in here. Lord George and I came in with Lady Kaldaire when we heard a scream."

"Lord Kaldaire?" the bobby said.

He gave me a dark look before he nodded.

"If I may, I'd like to see how Roberta, Lady Kaldaire, is doing and whether the doctor has arrived yet. Prince Maximilian, could you have someone fetch Lady Kaldaire's lady's maid and her smelling salts?"

He bowed to me, a smirk playing on his lips. He

obviously didn't believe a word of my story.

Considering the circumstances, I thought I'd stayed fairly close to the truth. Not wanting to waste any more time, I stepped around Lady Kaldaire and asked, "Where is the other Lady Kaldaire?"

"She's in the morning room with Mama," Lord George said.

"Thank you, my lord."

Lady Kaldaire was laid out on an ugly brown sofa that appeared to be molting. Lady Linchester sat next to her in a side chair, rubbing her wrists and murmuring to her. I hurried to the women, patted Lady Linchester on the shoulder and then felt Lady Kaldaire's forehead and neck. She was still breathing and she had a pulse, but both were very slow and faint.

The doctor came in and asked Lady Linchester a couple of questions about dinner. He gave Lady Kaldaire a cursory examination and sniffed the wine glass, presumably the victim's, that had been brought in by a footman. Then he said, "Do either of you have a strong stomach?"

The elderly Lady Linchester shook her head and nearly ran from the room.

Lady Kaldaire had rescued me from going to jail the night her husband was murdered. Tonight I needed to repay the favor. I straightened my shoulders. "If it means saving her life, then yes, I can stomach anything."

What followed seemed like the longest hours of my life, although it was less than one. Covered with a tablecloth, I held Lady Kaldaire in position while the doctor put a tube down her throat to pour soapy water into her stomach. That came back up along with wine, soup, and presumably the poison.

When it was done, maids carried away the basins

and cloths while murmuring the house was like a hospital with all the sick and injured. Lady Kaldaire was limp as a ribbon but awake and relatively alert.

"Thank you," she said in a hoarse voice as she clutched my hand.

"We'll talk tomorrow," I told her.

"I'm glad to have a tomorrow," came out in a whisper.

"I'm glad you do, too."

She gripped my hand tighter for a moment. "Denby? And Kaldaire? They were here tonight. And the prince."

"Denby has been arrested for stabbing Lord Kaldaire in the arm."

Her drooping eyes sprang open. "Will he live?"

"I think so."

"Pity." Her eyes closed again.

There was a knock on the door and a maid came in and spoke to the doctor. After a minute's consultation, he came to the patient's side and said, "Prince Maximilian has offered to take you home in his carriage. I think you can make the trip without further injury and will feel better once you are in your own home with your own servants."

"You've been talking to Cecily," Lady Kaldaire said to the doctor, struggling to sit up with my help.

"She fainted and landed like a rock on the carpet at the sight of Lord Kaldaire's blood," I told her with a smile.

"Miss Gates was most ingenious," Prince Maximilian said as he walked in with Rawlings and a footman. "After Lord Kaldaire was stabbed, she hit his attacker over the head with a bust of Sophocles."

"Appropriate," Lady Kaldaire murmured. It was slow going, and she needed a great deal of support, but finally she and Prince Maximilian were in his carriage.

"Roberta," Cecily, Lady Kaldaire, said, hurrying outside with the hatbox. "You forgot your newest—"

"It's yours, Cecily. You were complaining you didn't have a hat to match your latest gown for garden parties, so I had Miss Gates bring something stylish as a present."

"Oh, I couldn't accept it. Not after all that's happened tonight." Cecily was still looking pale.

"I suppose a peace offering is in order. Although, next time," Roberta, Lady Kaldaire, added with steel in her tone, "it should come from whoever poisoned me."

"Poisoned you? Don't be—"

"Oh, yes," I said, warming to the notion of scaring the new Lady Kaldaire while I pretended to be amazed. "The doctor was quite clear about that as I helped him save Lady Kaldaire's life. Someone in your household is a poisoner. Can you imagine the gossip about this?"

Cecily paled to the point of looking like a ghost, her eyes glancing around at the bystanders who still lingered. "Something in the food must have gone off. I'll speak to Cook immediately. She could have killed us all."

She turned to run inside when she remembered the hatbox in her hand. "Thank you so much for this, dear sister. I'll call tomorrow and see how you are feeling. Please don't mention this to any of your customers, Miss Gates."

I looked into the carriage at Lady Kaldaire. She nodded. "Nothing will be said if she's content," I told Cecily.

I noticed she slumped as Prince Maximilian said, "Good night," and tapped on the roof of his carriage. His horses immediately began their sprightly pace.

"Good-bye, Miss Gates," Cecily snapped and turned

away to reenter her house, only to find the dowager Lady Linchester and Lord George in the doorway.

Before Cecily could say anything, Lord George passed her and joined me. "Miss Gates, wait. I'd love to give you another ride in my motor. You did so enjoy it before."

I gave him a smile. "I did, indeed." We walked over to his vehicle while he told me all he'd done to improve the automobile and how it rode on the paved streets of London. I didn't understand a word.

"You missed the police taking Mr. Denby away in handcuffs. The detective inspector was very stern with him and with Lord Kaldaire," Lord Whitaker told me.

Detective inspector. Oh, dear. "It wasn't Detective Inspector Russell, was it?"

"Yes, I think that was his name."

"He's the same man who's investigating Lord Kaldaire's murder."

"Golly. Do you think Mr. Denby was responsible for both?"

I was about to say no when I remembered Jeremiah Pruitt was killed a half hour before Lord Kaldaire and very close by. "I don't know. Did you know Jeremiah Pruitt?"

"I'd met him. Why do you ask?"

Then I realized Lord George meant both Lords Kaldaire when he said "both," meaning attacks, not two murders on the same evening. It didn't matter. He had my thinking running through two different possibilities now. Mr. Denby had killed both men, or Mr. Denby knew who killed Lord Kaldaire because he was present or because someone told him.

I'd already judged Denby guilty of murdering Pruitt based on his frighteningly thin, lethal-looking knife.

I dragged my mind back to my conversation with Lord George. "I've heard all sorts of stories about him. He wasn't really a wastrel, was he?"

He nodded, his bland face grave. "I'm afraid he was. My brother warned me not to get involved with him, but it was all right in the end. Jeremiah didn't buy a motor carriage after all."

"Oh, he was a motoring enthusiast."

"No, I'm afraid his heart just wasn't in it." I thought I heard him sigh. "All right, Mummy. In you go. We'll give Miss Gates a lift home on our way to Lady Kaldaire's."

"Oh, good. Someone to ride in front with you, George." Lady Linchester was all smiles as she was handed up into the back seat and put on the motoring scarf I'd given her. She showed such flair with it I guessed she'd been forced to use it frequently.

I dug my own motoring scarf out of my bag and put it on for the first time since I'd returned to London.

"She was poisoned, wasn't she?" Lady Linchester asked just before George started the engine.

"How did you know?" I shouted over the noise of the engine.

"What?"

"How did you—never mind." I kept silent as we drove along, an evening breeze created by our speed. The roar coming out of the bonnet prevented any conversation. I noticed pedestrians didn't stop and gape at the automobile as they would have just a few years before. We even passed a few other vehicles, with Lord George sounding his horn and waving wildly each time. One driver returned his greeting. The others just stared straight ahead as they sped on.

When we pulled up in front of the shop, I turned to Lady Linchester. "How did you know she was poisoned?"

"Because Roberta was right as rain when we arrived. I'm staying with her, you see. After a single glass of sherry, she was slurring her words and then just fell over onto the table and then the floor. That's not normal."

That qualified as quite abnormal. "Who poured her sherry?"

"Lord Kaldaire."

"Not a servant?"

"No."

Why had he done such a thing? "Did he know I was coming to the house?"

"Roberta told Cecily as soon as she arrived. Told her you were bringing a surprise for her. I guess he heard her."

I was glad I'd talked to Grandpapa before going to Kaldaire House. Otherwise, Lady Kaldaire and I would both be dead.

The only question was how were we going to prove Lord Kaldaire, a peer of the realm, had a murderous streak? Or had a murderous friend in Mr. Denby?

* * *

I was up half the night trying to think of a way to prove Lord Kaldaire's guilt or innocence in the death of his brother, the late Lord Kaldaire. Then I rose early to visit Grandpapa. And to thank him.

"Oh, good, pet," he said when I arrived. "Set another place at the table, Aggie. You'll have some breakfast with us?"

"I'd love to. Thank you, Gran."

"I'm 'Gran' now that I'm feeding you, am I?" she said, but I saw her smile before she disappeared into the kitchen.

"So who were the hooded acrobats last night?" I asked.

"Your cousins Garrett, Vince, and Tommy."

"They did splendidly."

"And got away before the police arrived." He spread jam on his toast while he added, "A good thing, since the investigating officer was Detective Inspector Russell."

Gran set a teacup, plate, and utensils at the spot where I sat by Grandpapa. I smiled my thanks. "How do you know who they sent?"

"I waited in the crowd. I had to make sure you were safe."

"Lord Kaldaire fussed about the 'thieves' as he called them, but since he'd been stabbed, I said he was hallucinating. Did they get away with any of the jewelry?" I guessed the answer was yes.

Grandpapa raised his eyebrows and took a bite of his toast.

"I think it was Lord Kaldaire who poisoned Roberta, Lady Kaldaire. When she fell ill, he didn't send for a doctor."

"Pet, I want you to stay away from them. All of them."

"I can't. We're so close to finding out who really is guilty. After the stabbing, Prince Maximilian took over and set things to rights. It's a good thing he did, because none of the Kaldaires were in a position to do anything. And then I helped the doctor clean out Lady Kaldaire's stomach. It was awful." I blinked away the memory. "How could he do that to her? She's his family."

"You like Lady Kaldaire." He didn't say it as a question.

"She reminds me of Gran. Underneath that gruff exterior is a good woman. A kind woman."

"I've always thought of your grandmother as an aristocrat." Grandpapa put on a smug expression as he looked at her.

"Then what am I doing with the likes of you?" she asked him as she set down the eggs and sausage and sat across the table from me.

I began eating my breakfast, staying well out of that discussion.

CHAPTER THIRTY-TWO

When I returned to the shop, I found Jane waiting on a customer and Inspector Russell waiting for me.

One look at his face and I knew we needed to carry on this conversation away from my shop. I led him out to the alley. It was shaded by buildings, cool this early in the morning, and private enough for an argument.

"What did you think you were doing?" he demanded as soon as we were outside.

"Last night? All I did was deliver a hat as requested. The stabbing and poisoning had nothing to do with me."

"Are you certain? Lord Kaldaire says otherwise."

"Really. What does he say? And what does Mr. Denby say?"

"Lord Kaldaire said you let thieves into his study. Thieves who broke into his safe and pulled all the jewelry out. Thieves who ran when he and Mr. Denby entered the room. In trying to apprehend them, Mr. Denby accidentally stabbed Lord Kaldaire."

I shook my head as I paced the alley.

"Don't you have anything to say, Miss Gates?"

I stopped pacing and stared into welcoming eyes. "I wish I could trust you."

"Tell me the truth. I'm not an ogre."

"You want to lock up my father's entire family. That makes you a villain."

"How did you and Matthew enjoy your dinner at

your grandparents' house?" He sounded disappointed.

I sighed, more in aggravation than in sorrow. "We enjoyed it very much. I made peace with my father and met his new wife and their little boy. My little brother. Yes, they live on the wrong side of the law and I disapprove, but they are my family. And Matthew's family, and they were very nice to him. As nice as you were." I smiled at the memory.

He crossed his arms. "Did members of your family open the safe?"

"No. Lord Kaldaire did, saying he would leave the room before Mr. Denby stabbed me. They would say he caught me stealing the jewels and I'd be killed trying to escape."

The inspector looked worried, staring at the cracked bricks beneath his feet. Finally, he looked up with a smile. "Did you or any other Gates touch the lock on the safe?"

I ran the events through my mind. "No one but Lord Kaldaire touched the outside of the safe door. Afterward, it stood wide open. Why?"

"There's a way we might be able to prove it."

I stopped him before he hurried down the alley by stepping into his path. "How?"

He grabbed my shoulders to keep from bowling me over and gave me a devilish smile. "We cleared everyone out of the study and sealed it off. We shut the window and locked it, and told the staff they were not to enter the room on pain of imprisonment. We can go in this morning and take fingerprints. It's not been in use long, but the technique should work since we have specific prints to compare with the ones on the safe."

I found I was all too aware of his touch on my shoulders. So much so, it took me a moment to find my voice. "Will Lord Kaldaire let you take impressions of his fingerprints?"

"We'll tell him they are to eliminate him, since it's his study and his fingerprints should be there. What we won't say is we're interested in learning if his are the only prints on the safe." With a grin, he hurried away.

I spent the morning in the shop trying to work, but all the time, I kept thinking about Inspector Russell and his examination of the safe. Finally, I closed up the shop, sent Jane off to her luncheon, and headed to Lady Kaldaire's new home.

Lady Kaldaire sat bundled in a lap rug, a cup of tea at hand, entertaining the dowager Lady Linchester and the current Lady Kaldaire in her morning room. Lyle knocked, opened the door for me, and then vanished.

"What are you doing here?" Cecily asked the moment I entered the room.

"The same as you, I would imagine." Foolish woman. I gave her a raised brow before I faced the lady of the house. "How are you feeling, Lady Kaldaire?"

"Fine and enjoying all the pampering, thanks to you, Emily."

"No, don't thank me. Thank Prince Maximilian. He took charge and called the doctor. I'm just glad you're all right."

"And I suppose I can thank you for having policemen marching around my house in their heavy boots this morning," Lady Cecily snapped.

"No, I think that was Mr. Denby's doing. He was the one who stabbed your husband. The police take a dim view of maiming people." Inspiration struck and I added, "They must be preparing their case against him."

"Laurence says he won't testify against him. It was only an accident."

"An odd accident, but then, everything about your dinner party last night was odd," the elder Lady Kaldaire said, pulling her lap rug more tightly around her.

"How long has your husband known Mr. Denby?" I asked.

"I don't know. He's one of Laurence's London friends. I rarely came to London before Horace's death."

This was where I had to choose my words carefully. "How soon after you and your husband came to London as the new Lord and Lady Kaldaire did Mr. Denby call at Kaldaire House?"

"Laurence was in London when he became Lord Kaldaire. He told me he and Mr. Denby were to see Horace the evening poor Horace was killed."

I was amazed at how much Cecily admitted.

My gaze flew to Roberta, Lady Kaldaire. Her face was flushed an unhealthy color and her jaw appeared rigid with anger. "Did Laurence see Horace that night?" she asked, her voice cold.

"Well, he must have, mustn't he, since Horace turned Laurence down. Wait, what..." Cecily looked from one of us to the other, a puzzled expression on her face. We all stared at her.

"Turned him down?" the widowed Lady Kaldaire repeated. I was impressed with her control. She kept her voice even and very quiet.

Lady Cecily looked away before facing her sister-in-law with a blush. "For a loan."

They were there to ask Lord Kaldaire for money, but he didn't have any. And Lady Kaldaire couldn't figure out where his funds were going. Could he have been giving the bulk of his money to his brother? Why would he? "When did your husband tell you about Lord

Kaldaire's death?"

"He sent a telegram the next morning, early, telling me to come to London straight away. I was the new Lady Kaldaire." She puffed up when she spoke those words.

"Then when did he say the former Lord Kaldaire turned him down?" I asked.

"That can't possibly be important." She swiveled her body away from me in her chair.

"It is." The ice in the recent widow's tone could have frozen the Thames.

"When I arrived. He said Horace's death had saved his life." Cecily glanced at each of us in turn. "I think Mr. Denby was draining Laurence of cash."

"It sounds very much like Laurence needs to have a long talk with that nice policeman if he wants to avoid hanging for another's crime," Lady Linchester said in a mild voice.

"What are you talking about?" Cecily looked panicked.

"The police will find out about this, and then they're going to think Laurence killed Horace for money and the title to get Mr. Denby off his back." Lady Kaldaire looked up as Lyle knocked and entered the room. "Yes?"

"A message has come from Kaldaire House for her ladyship."

Good luck figuring out who he meant. I was the only commoner in the room.

Roberta, Lady Kaldaire, held out her hand.

"It's for the present Lady Kaldaire. Sent from her husband," Lyle told her.

Cecily took the note, read it, and paled.

"What's wrong?" Lady Linchester asked.

"Inspector Russell is interrogating Laurence about

Horace's murder. He thinks Laurence killed him." She turned to me. "This is all your fault."

"No, but even Lady Linchester warned you of this very thing. If you'd like, I could go with you and see if I can help." I'd take any excuse to see James Russell, despite my family's larcenous ways.

"That's a good idea, Emily. We'll all go. We'll save the inspector a trip to speak to us." The recent widow tossed aside her lap rug, showing she was fully dressed.

After much fussing with putting on hats and gloves, we paraded out to the waiting Kaldaire coach and rode to the house. When we entered, we found a bobby stationed on the front door with the footman.

"Where's Inspector Russell?" I asked.

"Inside with his lordship. Hey, you can't go in there," the bobby said as we marched past him. I couldn't tell if it was his assignment to stay at the front door or his fear of four determined-looking women that held him in place.

I noticed another bobby standing guard on the study door before I followed Rawlings and the other three women in the other direction. The men were in the large formal parlor. Lord Kaldaire sat in a wing chair, his bandaged arm in a sling. Inspector Russell stood in the center of the room, his sergeant in the corner taking notes.

Cecily slid over a side chair to sit next to her husband. Roberta, Lady Kaldaire, sat in a chair on the opposite side but close to Lord Kaldaire. Why was Lady Kaldaire showing support for her brother-in-law when he might have killed her husband?

I hoped this wasn't an example of the aristocracy sticking together or family loyalty. Lady Kaldaire struck me as more intelligent than that. Perhaps she was making certain she was in position to throttle him if she was given an excuse.

Both the inspector and Lord Kaldaire glared when they saw me enter the room, but neither told me to leave. I joined Lady Linchester, where I stood near her chair and kept my distance from the others.

"We know you were the one who opened your safe last night. Yours are the only fingerprints on the lock. We know Jonathan Denby is a blackmailer and a murderer. With your help we can put him away," the inspector said.

"I have nothing to say." Lord Kaldaire didn't look well, but whether it was because of his injury or his fear, I couldn't guess.

"You'd rather hang from the gallows than bring trouble to Denby. You really are afraid of him, aren't you?" I said.

"Miss Gates," the inspector began.

I put up one hand to silence him. "The police must know by now you were in London and visited Lord Kaldaire on the night of his death. Was Mr. Denby with you? Did he see you murder your brother? Is that what he's holding over you?"

Lord Kaldaire turned to the inspector. "I won't put up with this."

"What did you and the former Lord Kaldaire talk about the night he died?" the inspector asked.

"It was a private matter."

"Oh, tell him, Laurence. I refuse to be known as the wife of a criminal just as we finally reach the title."

I felt my eyes widen at Cecily's outburst. Both Roberta, Lady Kaldaire, and the inspector hid their surprise before the inspector made use of her words. "Private enough to die for?"

"All right," Kaldaire said in a gruff voice. "Denby found out I made money on the DMLR railway collapse and was blackmailing me. I could no longer afford his demands and borrowed money from my brother to pay him. He'd already lent me money for the children's schooling. When he learned why Denby was blackmailing me, he turned down my latest request. I came to town to make my plea in person."

"How in the world did you make money on the DMLR railway when everyone else lost?" I might not understand, but I knew my grandfather would want to hear his answer.

"I bought in early. Then when more people wanted to invest, I sold my shares." He reddened and mumbled, "Three times."

"Which no one realized since it went bankrupt." Grandfather would think it was brilliant. The inspector shot me a look that said I'd better warn my relatives not to try this.

"What happened when you came here to make your request?" the inspector asked.

"I found the door unlocked, so we just walked in. Horace was furious that we'd called so late in the evening without an appointment. I begged him, we quarreled, and then I stormed out."

"Who opened the safe?" I asked.

Lord Kaldaire glowered at me. "The safe was locked when I left."

"No. Your brother wouldn't have opened the safe for Mr. Denby. He might for you. Or you could have opened it yourself."

Lord Kaldaire turned his head away, but the inspector stepped into his line of sight. I decided I'd overstepped my place and kept silent, no matter how much I wanted to keep questioning Lord Kaldaire.

After a minute, the wounded man banged his uninjured arm on the wing of the chair. "Denby had just learned Horace received a note meant for Lord Wyatt. Denby was most insistent on getting it back. I told him I'd open the safe if he quit blackmailing me. He agreed. I opened the safe, found the note, and gave it to him."

Lord Kaldaire continued to face the inspector rather than any of the women in the room. "Denby insisted on coming into the study with me. Horace was furious. He tried to stop me from opening the safe. I told him if he wouldn't lend me the money to get Denby off my back, I'd get rid of the man and his blackmailing this way."

Shaking his head, Lord Kaldaire continued. "We argued. The old fool wanted to show the note to Lord Wyatt and demand he control his daughter in a less lethal manner. Denby told him it was too late for Pruitt as he took the note from me. Horace told us both to leave and never return. I left."

"And Denby?" the inspector asked.

"I thought he followed me, but he didn't. I paced up and down the pavement waiting for him out front. He came out a minute later."

"Didn't you wonder why Mr. Denby took so long?" Lady Kaldaire asked.

Kaldaire gave a dry chuckle. "Denby handles people by saying a few words to them in private. Who knows what secrets of Horace's he might have possessed?"

"Horace didn't have secrets," Lady Kaldaire said.

"Don't bet on that," his brother replied.

Cecily reached over and took Kaldaire's uninjured hand. He clasped her hand and gave her a smile. I realized then that they loved each other. To my way of thinking, they deserved each other.

"What time were you at Kaldaire House?" the inspector asked.

Kaldaire seemed to have told us the difficult part of his story. Now he appeared more relaxed, crossing his legs and swinging his free foot. "We arrived a little before eleven and left a few minutes after."

"What time did you meet Mr. Denby?" I asked.

"Perhaps ten minutes before we arrived at the house. We met in front of the church down the street."

Inspector Russell looked at me. "It matches the timeline we've already heard from the servants."

I nodded. "Giving Mr. Denby time to murder Mr. Pruitt a few blocks away before meeting with the soon-to-be Lord Kaldaire. Denby killed Mr. Pruitt with his sharp blade, a blade like the one used by the Central Line killer."

CHAPTER THIRTY-THREE

The inspector gave me a startled look. "You believe Denby killed Jeremiah Pruitt? Why?"

I tried to look innocent. "You need to ask Roberta, Lady Kaldaire, about the note."

"Really, Inspector, it's very simple." Lady Kaldaire commanded his gaze. "I had a long talk with Miss Annabelle Wyatt, a young friend of Mr. Pruitt. Her father feared Mr. Pruitt would lead his only daughter to ruin. He stated in the Imperial Club that he wanted Mr. Pruitt dead. Sometimes, parents say extraordinary things when they are frustrated by their children."

Russell watched her uncertainly. "You believe the note your husband received in error was an offer by Mr. Denby to kill Mr. Pruitt for Lord Wyatt for a sum of money. Where's the proof? And where is the note?"

"Denby took it from me when I opened the safe. I never saw the contents," Lord Kaldaire said.

"And neither has anyone else. Your guess is useless. A dead end." Russell studied the carpet. His voice faded, as if his mind was elsewhere trying to untangle this case.

"Meanwhile, Newton languishes in jail for something he didn't do." That seemed unfair. I walked over to stand between the two men. "It was you, Lord Kaldaire, whom Newton saw out front that night while you waited for Mr. Denby. Meanwhile, Denby was inside killing your brother. No wonder you had to frame Newton for theft and have him thrown in prison. You were afraid he'd identify you to the police." I was finding Lord Kaldaire more annoying by the moment.

"I didn't know Denby was going to kill Horace. And after he saw me outside, I was afraid Newton would blackmail me, too," Lord Kaldaire grumbled, "for something that had nothing to do with me."

"'Too'?" Russell asked.

Kaldaire glowered at the inspector.

"All we need now is to find out who threw Gregson out the window." I smiled at Inspector Russell when he glanced at me and then turned to Lord Kaldaire. "And it sounds like you just gave us the reason."

He ignored me, leaned back in his chair, and closed his eyes.

"My lord, I think you saw Mr. Denby throw your butler out the upstairs window. Then you hustled him out of the house, and when you returned, I caught you sneaking back in as I telephoned the police."

Kaldaire opened his eyes and glared at me. "Why would Denby do that?"

"Because Mr. Gregson saw everything that happened the night Lord Kaldaire was killed. Or at least enough to know you and Mr. Denby were in the house and involved in his death. He decided to blackmail both of you. That was the sort of thing he did. But one of you killed him rather than pay." I'd paced around the room while I spoke and found myself next to the inspector.

"Nonsense."

"That's the real reason he decided to stay as butler at Kaldaire House. He knew you'd never fire him, my lord. In fact, his wages and working conditions would improve."

"He would have been better off taking my offer of employment after all. I was even willing to raise his wages." Lady Kaldaire stared at her brother-in-law. I couldn't tell if I saw anger or hurt feelings in her expression.

When Lord Kaldaire glanced around and saw we were all staring at him, he snapped, "Oh, all right. All Gregson demanded of me was continued employment and an increase in his wages. Denby was his main target. I never expected Denby to strike him and throw him out the window."

Swiveling around to glance at us all, he said, "Denby surprised me. It happened so fast I couldn't stop him. You have to believe me!"

"So you witnessed Mr. Denby kill your butler and you didn't report it," the inspector said.

"I'm frightened of the man. He's a blackmailer and a killer." Kaldaire shrank into his chair.

"Will you testify against him in open court?"

His lordship's eyelids drooped to slits. "Do I have a choice?"

"Not really. We'll take your statement as evidence and then leave you to recover from your wound. And the truth about that wound needs to be mentioned in your statement."

Lord Kaldaire wearily nodded.

I was ready to cheer. Then I realized the truth about his wound would include the "burglars" tossing things about in his study and suddenly, the truth didn't look so appealing. They were family and they'd saved my life. Somehow, I'd have to negate some of that truth.

"Excuse me, Inspector, but who repeatedly broke into my shop and attacked first Noah, and then Jane, and finally me? I'll be happy to swear out a complaint against whichever one of them targeted my home." I stared hard at Lord Kaldaire.

"I don't hang around shops waiting to attack young women," Lord Kaldaire sneered.

"Then you'll be happy to testify that Mr. Denby was the one who attacked us?" I said.

"Don't be ridiculous. He must have had one of his henchmen attack you, trying to scare you off. Denby doesn't bother with trifling matters himself."

"And you knew about it." I swung around and faced Russell. "Inspector, I want him charged with being a party to the attacks on me and my family."

"We'll see, Miss Gates," Russell said and signaled to the bobby at the door to usher all four of us women from the room. As we went to the morning room, the elder Lady Kaldaire called for tea.

"Gracious," Lady Linchester said. "It's so exciting in the city, Roberta. No wonder you prefer to live here."

"What will happen to my husband?" Cecily asked her sister-in-law while lowering herself gracefully into a chair.

"We have a very good solicitor. I'm sure he can put a word in the right ears. Laurence will have to testify, but I'm sure Denby will hang. He won't bother Laurence again."

"And will that nonsense about the DMLR railway have to come out?"

"Yes. But not officially. Only in rumors among our circle of friends." The elder Lady Kaldaire's tone was dry.

"Oh, dear heavens, no," Cecily cried out. "Please don't tell anyone. He'll be shunned for cheating our friends, and the children and I will suffer. I've only just come to London and already I'll be forced to return to the miserable countryside to avoid society's snubs. Please don't tell anyone."

"Oh, it'll be forgotten. In a generation or two," Lady Linchester said in a stern voice. "Think of the misery Lady Taylor went through for years, and her late husband had done nothing wrong."

"Except start an ill-fated investment," Lady Kaldaire said. "If anyone asks me, I'll say you two went back to the country for your health. But if anyone asks, I won't deny that Laurence cheated his friends. Now, you'd better instruct your maid to start packing."

Cecily gave each of us a wild-eyed look before dashing from the room.

"I do believe Laurence will pay for his foolishness for the rest of his life," Roberta, Lady Kaldaire, said. Then as the tea arrived, she began to pour with a smile on her face. "Denby will be hanged for two murders, Laurence will be persecuted by Cecily for eternity, and Horace has been avenged. I feel quite proud of us."

Lady Linchester began to list people she needed to write to about her adventures in town. No doubt she'd describe the current Lord Kaldaire selling stock to three different friends as well as his role in two deaths. Lady Kaldaire suggested a few more names.

I drank my tea in a hurry. As far as I was concerned, I'd carried out my mission for Lady Kaldaire. "If you don't need anything else, I should get back to my shop."

She smiled at me. "Thank you, Emily, for everything. You've been a great success. I shall tell all my friends about you."

That was the last thing I needed. "Only that I design wonderful hats." I hoped I never had to do any more detecting. Or put my cousins at risk again.

"Of course, Emily. What else could I possibly say?"

Lady Kaldaire spoke in such an innocent tone that I knew I was in trouble. I just had no idea where the danger was coming from, or when.

But as I returned to my shop, I realized we had no idea why Denby would have killed Pruitt if he knew Lord Wyatt hadn't agreed to pay for the murder. Did he have another motive? Or had Lord Wyatt agreed and both men were keeping quiet?

* * *

When I opened the shop the next morning, Inspector Russell was waiting for me. "Is your assistant here?"

"Not yet."

"Good. I'm worried about you, Emily."

"I worry for you, James. You're a policeman."

"Denby is a dangerous man. Crossing him has led to several deaths. He stabbed one constable and broke the arm of another when we went to arrest him yesterday. You shouldn't have confronted him on your own."

I focused on the one thing I thought was important. "He tried to escape?"

"Yes. Fortunately, he was unsuccessful."

"Are the policemen all right?" It could have been Inspector James Russell. I didn't want him injured. Ever.

"Yes. Both are recovering. Denby is now in chains awaiting trial. We finally have him for one murder as well as blackmail, thanks in part to you and Lord Kaldaire."

I had to smile at getting his acknowledgement. His was the only one that mattered.

"Before he learned about the murder charge, he fingered one of his henchmen for the attacks here. A local thug with a long scar on his left cheek." He grinned. "Fortunately, there's no honor among thieves. The thug is telling us everything he knows about Denby and how he was paid to attack you and the hat shop to warn you away from Kaldaire House."

"I feel safer now that the man with the scar is locked up, but what about the death of Mr. Pruitt? Will Mr. Denby be charged with that murder, too?"

"It's probable Denby did it, but without the note, we have no motive. We have no witnesses. Lord Wyatt was shocked when we spoke to him."

"Really?" I raised my eyebrows, not believing in Lord Wyatt's "shock." "Why would Mr. Denby kill Mr. Pruitt if not for money?"

"Wyatt admits he was blindingly angry because he thought Pruitt was going to elope with his daughter, or run off and ruin her. He was shouting in rage in the lobby of the club because a member had overheard his daughter and Pruitt planning a rendezvous and had chosen that moment to tell him. He doesn't remember Denby standing there. Once he cooled down, he went home and told his wife and they made plans to keep her inside and in their sight at the time of this arranged meeting."

"So he claims to have no reason to have Pruitt killed. Did Denby tell you why he thought Lord Wyatt would pay him?"

"Denby's telling us nothing." He smiled ruefully before his smile slipped off his face. "And you crossed Denby at Kaldaire House on your own, with no one protecting you. I don't know why he stabbed Kaldaire instead of you—"

"My family protected me." The truth just slid out, and I could have kicked myself as soon as it did. I saw the expression in Russell's eyes change.

Then he blinked. "What?"

I turned on him. "The Gates family, those criminals you're constantly trying to catch, saved my life. I don't expect you to stop chasing them, but they're not bad people."

All expression vanished from his face and from his lovely gray eyes. "Why were they there?"

"I asked them to come. Lady Kaldaire asked me to bring a hat for Cecily and then go into the study and open the window for a later entry."

"So your family could get in."

"No. Lady Kaldaire and me. We were going to search the study for clues. Find the note from Mr. Denby. Anything that would tell us who killed Lord Kaldaire. I asked my family to come because I wanted professional help with our search."

"And instead they came in and rescued you."

"Yes."

We stared into each other's eyes for ages as I watched James's darken and warm. He began to lean toward me when the shop bell rang.

"Mornin'. Ooops." Jane bit her lip to fight a smile and busied herself in a far corner.

"Lady Cramer has an appointment in five minutes. The last time she was here, she was dithering over a black and yellow deep crown with roses around the brim. Start there. I'll be back in a few minutes." I headed into the shop storeroom. "Inspector?"

He followed me in and shut the door. Leaning on it, he said, "How are you going to feel if I have to arrest your relatives? Or if they're taken in by one of a hundred other officers?"

"You, or they, would be doing your job. I won't help my family, but I won't help you either." I shook my head. "Not that they'd ever admit anything to me."

He studied the bare wooden floor. "I guess it doesn't matter. Not when a lord is courting you."

His words made me blink. "Who?"

"Lord George Whitaker. The man with the motor carriage. He gave you a ride home from Kaldaire House the other night."

"You were watching me?" I didn't know whether to be flattered or insulted.

"One of the lads was assigned to watch the house. He mentioned it."

"He and his mother gave me a ride. He's not courting me. I don't have the right pedigree."

He crossed his arms. "I know when a man is courting a girl. I heard about your friendship when I was sent to Rolling Badger to investigate another matter and ended up working the burglary at The Willows. Lord George Whitaker couldn't stop singing your praises. Everyone else said he was potty over you."

"They also would have noticed because I'm not suitable. Lord George is not my type. He hasn't a brain in his head. And I know when a man is being silly, James Russell." I heard the bell ring faintly over the shop door. "I have a customer and you must have work. If there's nothing else?"

He grinned and lowered his arms. "I was hoping for another invitation to dinner with you and Matthew. Now that we don't have to discuss police business."

I had to smile at his forwardness. "Tell me what night, and I'll tell Mrs. McCauley to make extra."

"I'm off Thursday evening."

"I'll expect you at seven."

"I look forward to it."

"So do I."

Then we stared into each other's eyes for a long

time, followed by a magical kiss that left me breathless. By the time he slipped out into the alley, promising to see me at seven on Thursday night, my face was quite heated and my lips felt swollen.

Thank goodness there was a mirror in the workshop. I straightened my hairdo and adjusted my clothes before I wiped the smile off my face and walked back into the shop. "Lady Cramer…"

If you would like to hear the latest news from Kate Parker, sign up for my email newsletter on http://www.KateParkerbooks.com

Author's Notes

I remember watching My Fair Lady as a child. I don't remember where I saw it, or much about the plot, but I remember the hats, the parasols, and the gowns. That show hooked me on Edwardian fashions. Combined with watching Mary Poppins, and I was in love with the simple innocence of the time.

The historian in me says wait! Not so fast. There was plenty about the era that was dirty, brutish, and cruel. But I choose in my books to try to capture the nostalgia and the essence of a gentler age. Just as murder, real murder, is horrifying, I choose to write cozy mysteries. I welcome the reader in to enjoy the era and the puzzle of the mystery. Step into my sleuth's fashionable shoes, don't trip on the long skirts, and come along for a ride in an antique car.

About the Author

Kate Parker grew up reading her mother's collection of mystery books and her father's library of history and biography books. Now she can't write a story that isn't set in the past with a few decent corpses littered about. It took her years to convince her husband she hadn't poisoned dinner; that funny taste is because she can't cook. Now she can read books on poisons and other lethal means at the dinner table and he doesn't blink.

Their children have grown up to be surprisingly normal, but two of them are developing their own love of literary mayhem, so the term "normal" may have to be revised.

Living in a nineteenth century town has further inspired Kate's love of history. But as much as she loves stately architecture and vintage clothing, she has also developed an appreciation of central heating and air conditioning. She's discovered life in coastal Carolina requires her to wear shorts and T-shirts while drinking hot tea and it takes a great deal of imagination to picture cool, misty weather when it's 90 degrees out and sunny.

Follow Kate and her deadly examination of history at www.KateParkerbooks.com
and www.Facebook.com/Author.Kate.Parker/

CPSIA information can be obtained
at www.ICGtesting.com
Printed in the USA
LVHW051205250119
605272LV00002B/25